Carol Birch is the author of ten other novels, and has won the David Higham Award for *Life in the Palace*, the Geoffrey Faber Memorial Prize for *The Fog Line* and was longlisted in 2003 for the Man Booker Prize with *Turn Again Home*. She lives in Lancashire.

Carol Birch

LIFE IN THE PALACE

virago

VIRAGO

Published by Virago Press 2000
This edition published by Virago Press in 2011

First published 1988 by Macmillan London Limited
Arena Edition first published 1989

Copyright © Carol Birch 1987

The moral right of the author has been asserted.

A CIP catalogue record for this book
is available from the British Library.

ISBN 978-1-84408-800-3

Printed and bound in Great Britain by
Clays Ltd, St Ives plc

Virago Press
An imprint of
Little, Brown Book Group
100 Victoria Embankment
London EC4Y 0DY

An Hachette UK Company
www.hachette.co.uk

www.virago.co.uk

To Len

Two years later, Judy Grey took a trip down south to London to see the place where she used to live. She sat in the same old café, at the same table, looking out at the street market. The fat Italian man, who was always saying something funny in a dry, faintly offensive way, stood behind the high counter and carried on loud conversations with his friends who sat here and there with plates of food and mugs of tea before them.

Watching the people go by in the warm jumble of the market, Judy returned to a past winter: she was sitting on the same chair looking at the same scratches on the red Formica, drinking coffee and eating soft, warm, underdone toast with Jimmy Raffo. Loretta walked past the window. Raff jumped up and gawked after her, tall and clumsy, bony-wristed. 'She looks bad,' he said, 'Loretta looks bad,' shaking his head a little.

A silver urn steamed and hissed. 'Looka this, looka this,' said the fat Italian man, who'd come out from behind the counter and was sitting at one of the tables reading the *Sun*, filling the small chair and flowing round it. 'They're putting holes in their heads now.' He slapped the newspaper with the back of his fingers. She looked at him for a moment, amazed. So much had gone, but he was still here. He'd served her coffee a thousand times, made some joke, squeezed her fingers a little too long as he gave her the change; now he didn't recognise her. Outside there was some commotion, kids being raucous, a man shouting: 'Not one! Not two! I give you three . . .' and something big trundled by in the middle of the road. Judy took out a little black pocket diary and laid it on the

1

table next to her coffee cup. After a while she picked it up and flicked through it slowly. In the front there was a map of central London with all the theatres and cinemas marked in red, then pages full of useful information like first aid and weights and measures and stuff like that, and then, on the personal reminders page (as if sometime she might forget), Loretta had written her identity. Further on she wrote: 'Council painted all our doors red.' 'Flood,' she wrote, 'Billy brushed water down the stairs.' And it splashed down over the balcony into the courtyard below. 'Saturday, Jumble sale, Cornwall Road,' she said. 'Man jumped out of window. Billy sick. Hurricanes.'

Judy put away the book and paid the bill, endured the hot fingers of the fat Italian man, went out into the noise and sunshine and walked along through the market, past the stalls and the hawkers and the open beer-smelling doorway of the pub where she used to drink, then slipped into the side-streets and took the familiar old route home again to Kinnaird Buildings, even though she knew they were no longer there. Kids roared in a schoolyard. Outside the shop where she used to buy her papers and milk on a Sunday, an old dog slept. Skyscrapers and mean streets, the same, all the same, but for the absence of those old crags crowned with black iron railings and washing lines, Kinnaird Buildings. All that was left was a huge barricaded area, walls of corrugated iron and padlocks and a sign saying that guard dogs patrolled. Beyond was rubble. An end of a building still stood in the dusty distance, a miraculous peak, layered and multicoloured, bearing the poor, abandoned, horribly suspended remains of people's living rooms, stains on weathered wallpaper, tragic gaping mouths of fireplaces. The corrugated iron was covered in boards bearing children's paintings. Judy walked up and down looking at them as if she were in an art gallery. Then she saw a hole in the fence the size of a big fist and leaned down to look

2

through, but a deranged dog hurled itself at the fence immediately and nearly took her face off.

Kinnaird Buildings was a square on the board that there was no way to bypass; she'd just picked a card from the Community Chest and it had said: Go to Kinnaird Buildings. So she just had to go. The first time she saw them she thought they looked romantic, in the doomed, decaying style, black and striking and covered in pigeons as they were. The pigeons had a ragged loser kind of look about them, moulting and skinny and awkward with pleasant, bashful faces. Some had one foot, some a foot and a half, some two. Kids yelled in the courtyards. A saggy armchair stood out by the bins. Cats sunbathed on cars. Music played somewhere. In the summer, she remembered, you could sunbathe on the roof amongst the chimneys. If you looked one way you saw the dome of St Paul's; another way, Big Ben. It was handy. If your clock stopped, you could nip up to the roof and check the time. In the night you'd hear it chime, deep-throated, and the hoot of a boat on the river, the skirling of a train shunting into a siding at Waterloo. The Underground ran beneath: you'd feel the vibration of the train like a minor earth tremor, and it was comforting, something alive in the earth. Oh, the romance, dirty old town!

Judy turned and walked away, up to the station. London was the same. It changed its accessories but it never changed its underwear. The graffiti told you the score. RIOT, it cried. DON'T PANIC, it said. She took the train to Clapham Junction and gazed out of the window at the snaky silver tracks merging and dividing in the sun. She'd get back to her friends' place and say, 'Guess where I went today?' and then they'd sit around burbling about the old days as if they were ninety, smiling like fond fools about things that were hell at the time. She closed her eyes for a while.

When she opened them again, people were getting in and out of the train. She watched the faces on the

platform all directed towards the exit sign, then closed her eyes and looked inside again and was looking down from a fourth-floor window into the crowded sunny courtyard at the front of her flat. A bunch of people were standing around the bonnet of a white van. Sunny was there and a few other kids, and Jimmy Raffo, and Loretta and Billy, and someone else – like a dream you couldn't quite say who – all just hanging around talking. Sunny was three or something. She pestered Raff all the time. He picked her up, sat her on his hip as if he were used to having a child sit there, walked aimlessly about in the glaring sunshine. He moved unpredictably always, passing between moments of grace and near-excruciating awkwardness. Everything about him was like that, extremes pranging him so that there was a sense of desperate inner movement even when he was sitting still. The extremes were in his eyes too, but he covered them up with humour at his own expense. This look he turned upwards as he walked easily with the child on his hip, saw Judy, and smiled.

Loretta had a tarty look about her. She had hair that was messy and assertive, sometimes brown, sometimes blonde, sometimes orange, and she liked to show flesh. She was a big-boned, big-breasted young woman with a heavy-cheeked, healthy face that blushed easily, and an accent that placed her from somewhere in the great sprawl east of London. Loretta could look like a dignified woman or a fat teenager or a rosy-faced country girl. She thought of herself as gross and ugly, an image with which she battled anew whenever she dressed and made up.

Her parents had gone for those old fancy actressy names; Rita, her sister was called. When they were children, Loretta was fat and Rita wasn't. Later she'd blame it all on her mother, who had stuffed them with chips and cake and Coca-Cola and custard, and on her father, who'd given her his build. Rita, two years older, had always made it known that she was the prettier and wiser. Rita was the voice of authority. 'You look like a pig,' she used to say. Loretta was one of those awful whingeing kids with snot on its face. In her earliest memories she was hurt and ugly and fat and blushing.

They lived on a semi-detached street with small gardens front and back and a playing field opposite where schools came to play hockey and football and rounders. Loretta went to the school at the end of the street till she was eleven. She didn't mind school. She was good at games and domestic science but the rest floated past her. Her father was the school caretaker, Mr Boston, a humourless man immune to children, who wore a boiler suit and walked with his toes turned out.

But when he came home he turned into her dad, an amiable stranger, lumbering out of the boiler suit before he had his tea and settled for the night in front of the TV with her mum, wreathed in cigarette smoke, each in a separate wing of the three-piece suite. All the kids at the school called him Fatpants. Loretta grew up ashamed of him. He was ugly, and it was a terrible, shameful thing to be ugly. Her best friend at school, a girl called Andrea, was slim and quite pretty and used make-up skilfully by the time she was thirteen. Both of them loved boys in a painful, slushy, hopeless kind of way, but Loretta was sure that no boy could ever love her because she was fat and bore the stamp of the school caretaker on her face.

When she was about fourteen she got into the habit of starving herself, until she was buxom rather than fat. Then she discovered that if she dyed her hair and teased it out, stuck black around her eyes and wore a very short skirt, she could look eighteen and glamorous from a distance. She and Andrea walked the streets looking for something to do. Sometimes they went to clubs and youth centres. One night she came home from a dance, bored and upset because she hadn't spoken to any boys, and found the house full of people and her father dead. Dropped dead of a heart attack. Her mother didn't seem surprised.

At first Loretta felt no emotion, just a feeling of unease that went right through her like nausea. When she went to bed, very early in the morning, she lay awake turning over memories of her father like stones, looking for one that might tell her how she was feeling. At last she found herself remembering last year's holiday in Dorset, she and Rita sitting in a seafront café looking out at the people walking up and down a gusty promenade. Her father walked by, eyes narrowed at the wind, face preoccupied. He wore an old black suit, too small in the jacket, too large in the trousers, so that a single ludicrous button held it over his big front and the bottoms of the

6

trousers folded over his shoes. He didn't have to look like that, she thought, nobody had to look like that. She ran out and caught his sleeve and asked him for some money to put in the juke-box in the café. The wind whistled in from the sea as he fished about in his pockets and gave her some change. 'Is Reet with you?' he asked. 'Good.' Then he said he had to go and buy some shoes, the sole was coming right off this one. She stood and watched him walk away, her hand full of warm coins. His baggy trousers flapped like sails, whap whap whap around his legs, feet turned out, one loose sole on a shiny brown shoe going flap flap flap.

She'd watched him walk away with an obscure sense of shame that so ridiculous a man should be her father. Now that he was dead she realised that another emotion had also been present, an affection so reserved and embarrassed that it had never voiced itself, not even to her.

Things changed. Auntie Bren came to live in the house. Auntie Bren was a lazy ham sitting in the bereaved chair in front of the TV, criticising everything. Rita and Loretta stayed in their rooms, growing closer. Their mum didn't seem much affected by the death. She had a small stern face and a quiet manner and was always bringing God into the conversation – God be praised, God send, God help, God love, God knows, God forbid, God will answer. She started putting together a collection of pills from the doctor, with the thoroughness of a child just getting into stamp collecting. She kept them in a locked cupboard beside her bed, gave a few now and then to Bren, who had her own more modest supply, and very occasionally one or two to Rita or Loretta if they had some ordeal to get through like a test at school. 'You take one *now*,' she'd say sternly, 'and the other one at dinner time. *Not before*, Understand? They'll just give you that little bit more confidence.'

'We'd be OK if we ever wanted to do ourselves in,'

Rita said drily. 'She keeps the key under that flowerpot on the chest of drawers.'

Rita had style from a very early age; she grew tall and languid and flamboyant, left home at seventeen to share a room in London with one of her friends. Loretta was just fifteen, still at school, alone in a house of old women. She stayed out as much as she could. Sometimes she'd go to Andrea's straight from school and Andrea's mum would give them something to eat, then they'd go upstairs and mess around for ages getting ready to go out. 'Two young lovelies,' Andrea's dad would say benignly if he was in when they finally came down. He was a chief superintendent, and always sat with the dog on his lap, a yappy little terrier. 'You both look very, very pretty.' And Loretta would blush because she thought he didn't really mean her.

They wandered about, got thrown out of pubs for being too young, went to the cinema, sometimes to a dance, sometimes to an awful youth centre full of ping-pong and old records. This was where she saw Billy Booth one night, playing ping-pong with his friend Eric. She recognised him at once. She used to see him years ago helping out on his uncle's fruit and veg stall on a Saturday, one of the Booths, a big noisy family well known for wheeler-dealers and troublesome kids. He'd have been eleven or twelve then but looked much younger because he was so small. She could remember how he stood in winter, collar up, hands in pockets, woolly scarf tucked inside his jacket and crossed over, a kind of open Balaclava on his head, his face tiny and white with a soft, pointed chin. Then his mouth would open wide and bawl something deafening and incoherent. A great market voice he had.

He was still small, still slight. Loretta thought he was the most beautiful boy she'd ever seen, darting about with his ping-pong bat, dark curls shaking, serious-faced. The bones of his face were delicate, eyebrows thick, mouth gentle with a very large and finely chiselled lower lip. His friend was tall and plain and fair. Loretta and Andrea sat with some other girls on hard wooden chairs by the record player. One of the girls said Billy Booth was gorgeous but stupid. Someone else said you had to watch that Eric, he was an arrogant little bastard. The two boys, fifteen, self-conscious and a little jaunty, finished their game and started fooling around in front of the girls, miming to the records and playing their ping-pong bats as if they were guitars. Loretta watched Billy like a mother watching a child perform, quite unable not to stare. The boys messed around a while longer with an air of being slightly above and beyond it all before becoming very obviously bored and strolling out into the deepening blue night. They seemed to her exciting and rakish, off somewhere more important than this stupid place that smelt like school, and she wished she were going with them.

She saw Billy everywhere after that; sometimes he was alone, sometimes with his arm around a girl, a different one each time. She listened whenever she heard his name. Everyone liked him, it seemed; even the people she didn't like liked him. Billy was some sort of neutral ground where everyone felt safe. She wrote BILLY BOOTH on her bedroom wall, hung around where she thought she might see him, cried sometimes as she lay in bed. She was tragic, desperate in some recess of her soul because Billy Booth never looked at her.

One night at the youth centre, a gentle squat boy with mongoloid features and white eyelashes came up to Loretta as she was getting her coat and spoke very politely to her. 'Please,' he said, 'may I walk you home?' Ollie was his name, a misfit who wore clothes his mother bought for him. She blushed and stammered, not want-ing to hurt his feelings, not wanting to walk home with him. 'It's only this once,' he added quickly, seeing her dilemma and understanding it. 'They said you wouldn't.' This made her feel worse. He smiled vaguely, embarrassed. A bunch of boys stood nearby and she felt that they watched, sniggering, and disliked herself for the revulsion she felt.

A lanky boy put his arm round Ollie's neck and pulled him away roughly and affectionately; another came close and said to her confidentially, 'Go on, Loretta, he just wants to tell his mum he walked home with a girl, and they all bet him you'd say yes.'

She didn't know what was going on. She hated all the stupid, sniggering bastards. 'They're setting you up,' Andrea said, 'don't take any notice of them. Come on, Loretta, let's go,' and hustled her to the door.

Ollie appeared in front of her again. 'You go down Briar Road, don't you?' he said.

'Yes,' she said, falling into step beside him as they went out and turned along the street. Andrea, uncertain, bobbed alongside. It was cold, her breath came out like steam and she watched it, wondering what to say. Four or five boys walked a little way behind, giggling and raucously pushing each other about. Ollie put a tense arm on her shoulder and she stiffened but said nothing because she didn't want to make him look a fool. Maybe she was making herself look a fool, she didn't know, she was totally confused. She thought he was very ugly and didn't want him to touch her, felt mean and stupid for thinking this, wondered about him, couldn't possibly imagine what it must be like to be him. She was sure he didn't even like her much, this was just some sort of challenge, his or theirs, she didn't know. She saw Andrea fall behind from the corner of her eye. Everyone treated Ollie differently in some way without admitting that they did so, as if he were on some subtly different plane, not of intelligence but of feeling. She saw this now. She also saw that he saw this. Yet he smiled all the time and you never heard him raise his voice.

'Will you have far to walk back to your place?' she asked him.

'Not far,' he said.

They crossed the road. The boys crossed the road. They're not going to follow us all the way, are they? she thought. What happens when we get to our house? Oh God, what if he tries to kiss me! And them all standing there watching . . . Ollie's arm, stiff and self-conscious, moved from her shoulder to her waist. The boys came closer. 'Don't take any notice of them,' Ollie said, 'they think they know everything.' She wanted to say, Take your arm away, that wasn't part of the dare, but somehow she didn't. His hand slid down a little more till it rested, much as a doctor's hand might rest, on the slope of her hip.

'Look where he's got his hand!' she heard one of the boys say, and suddenly she wanted to cry. For him, for her, she didn't know, she just felt awful.

They came to a row of darkened shops with one glowing door and window casting light across the pavement, the smell of fish and chips on the cold air. The chip-shop window was all steamed up and she could see a ghostly queue on the other side of it. As they passed, Billy and Eric came out carrying bags of chips that steamed in their hands.

'Hi, Ollie,' Billy said, offering the bag. 'Been down the Crescent?'

'Yeah.' Ollie took his arm away from Loretta. 'I'm just walking home with Loretta.' The boys caught up; Andrea was with them, looking sulky. People drifted in and out of the chip shop and everyone stood aimlessly around. She saw one of the boys laughing as he told Billy something, saw Billy look over at her and Ollie. He wasn't laughing. He glanced at Ollie and then looked her straight in the eye without smiling for about ten seconds. Then everyone broke up and drifted home and Ollie

11

walked her politely to her door, not touching her, said, 'See you around,' and walked on.

Loretta was walking home from the market with her mother's awful tartan shopping trolley a few days later when she saw Billy in a crimson tee-shirt and black jacket, walking towards her on the other side of the road. She saw him notice her. 'Oy!' he shouted and sprinted across between cars to walk beside her. 'Let's go through the park,' he said. They walked slowly through the park towards her home, hardly speaking. It was the wrong kind of day for a walk, the kind that made your nose run and your eyes water. She felt big beside him and his frailness enchanted her. They sat down on a bench by the duck pond and watched a small group of people feeding the ducks on the other side of the water. For a long time they sat without speaking but she didn't feel stupid about not speaking with Billy. The people had a little shaggy dog that sat biting itself somewhere, the arse or the foot, the way dogs do. One foot stuck up in the air like a pole.

'Must be good being a dog in some ways,' Billy said.

'Yeah,' she said, 'I suppose so.'

'You can get your leg right up in the air like that, see? Must be good being able to do that.'

Loretta looked sideways at him, watching him quite openly, with fascination. He was some weird, romantic alien, speaking magic words.

All their friends were drifting to London.

Loretta and Billy were going out two years before they went there too and started living together, always in shared places. They lived together peacefully, companionably, free from intrigues and emotional storms in the midst of others' chaos. Billy was a rock, a placid pool into which she looked and saw herself reflected, the only person in the world she didn't mind seeing her vomit without her make-up. The only people who didn't like him were her mum and Auntie Bren, who called him the booby prize because he couldn't read and write and didn't talk much. But their opinion counted for nothing with Loretta.

The times were careless. Jobs, rooms, friendships came and went. When she was twenty, Loretta became pregnant. They married in the same careless way that they lived, suddenly, in a registry office with Rita and a friend as witnesses, and afterwards had a meal in a restaurant and went home with a bottle of wine and a bottle of Asti Spumante, which had a champagne-type cork that popped and hit the ceiling. And that night, as they lay naked and drunk in bed, the door was kicked in with a great splintering of wood, the light went on, three big square men loomed in the room. Loretta's heart beat madly in fear. More men appeared, uniforms. They waved a piece of paper that they said was a warrant, made Billy get up and get dressed, made her get dressed under the bedclothes, all watching as she struggled to get into her clothes without showing herself to them. Damned if I give them a free show, she thought.

One of them laughed and said, 'The little lady's bashful.'

'Not so little,' another said, and they sniggered.

They were looking for drugs but found none and seemed disappointed. When they left, the place looked as if it had been burgled, the door hung broken, and Loretta felt shattered as the wood. Life was unsafe, home and bed no haven. They'd read her letters, handled her dirty underwear.

She never found out why.

She dangled her wedding ring on a piece of string over her belly and found the baby was a boy; she'd known it anyway. She was going to call him Ben. She bought a magazine with pictures of babies in wombs and stared at them all, the fingers and toes and veins, trying to transfer the images into her own body. Six weeks later, when she miscarried, she thought she must be crazy to care so much. It happened all the time. Billy cried and it was shocking, like an earthquake, even though he just put his head in his hands for a few minutes and made a series of small, deep, apologetic little sobs and then was through. Loretta didn't cry, but she sat and thought about what he would have been like, where he'd gone, what he'd known and what was the point of it – why come in the first place, only to slide out in a stream of blood? Changed his mind? He had little webbed toes, little webbed fingers. She'd seen them in the pictures. Her stupid great body had pushed him out. Then she thought that maybe it was the other way round, maybe the baby had rejected her, looking around with its all-seeing eyes at Loretta lying on the settee reading a book, a cushion at her back, twisting a strand of hair round two thick, long-nailed fingers. Quick, quick, let me out of here, not her, not her, for God's sake, not her! Round and round and round they went, the thoughts, and everyone said: 'It's not the end of the world.'

She always knew the sex of her babies, even before she dangled the wedding ring. Two girls followed, Sara and Rose. The red tide carried them away. The third came when they were living at Rita's place in Deptford. Rita had two rooms on the top floor of a big house. She'd made them cosy by draping the boring furniture with pretty fabrics, painting the walls, hanging posters. Loretta and Billy slept in the main room and never got the chance of a lie-in because Rita always got up at seven, not from duty but because she woke and was full of life at that time, buzzed about the place opening and closing doors, talking to herself, singing and putting the radio on, going up and down the stairs with her sandals flapping. Rita dressed like a genie and strode about like one. Wherever she was, on buses, in pubs, at home, she talked all the time to everyone in a fast steady voice, seldom smiling. She was so friendly she made people nervous. She worked sometimes but would only take something with an offbeat or glamorous edge, something in a theatre or circus or zoo or recording studio or cinema; most of the time she couldn't find anything like that and didn't want to compromise, life was too short and the final holocaust was coming, she said, why waste your last days on a checkout or in some stupid office? So she was home all day, rushing about sorting out mending and getting out the ironing board and making little buns in paper cases, laying out her books with bookmarks in relevant pages that she wanted to study, numerology, pyramidology, astrology, palmistry, tarot, hoovering the floor and dusting the fat Buddha that sat on the window-sill and fussing over pregnant Loretta.

Rita and Loretta began to drive each other mad. Rita liked a tidy place; Loretta did things like sticking her orange pips under the rug when she was sitting by the fire reading her book, some long romantic saga with a pretty cover and an air of seriousness that raised it above your average Mills and Boon. She left cruddy wet food in the waste-pipe of the sink, hair in the wash-basin in the bathroom. Loretta didn't care about any of this; she cleaned around but not under things.

Rita liked to speak about the coming end in an interested, detached kind of way, confidently quoting statistics to prove that doom was inevitable, that it would be soon, very soon, oh yes, definitely in your lifetime. She liked to speak of nuclear disaster, pollution, the next ice age, the breakdown of society, disease, starvation, the end, always the inescapable end. If you pointed out some possible chink through which the world might just slide and survive, she'd look at you steadily for a minute. You could see her using you as a thinking post. 'But no,' she'd say then patiently, as if you were really a bit dim. 'Don't you see that couldn't happen because . . .' and she'd tell you exactly why your doom was still certain, almost as if she were reassuring you. Then she'd go off and make the dinner, singing as she pottered about in the kitchen. The baby, Loretta thought, what about the baby? She couldn't understand why Rita wasn't chronically depressed.

Jane, the last girl baby, lasted five months. Loretta felt her move. And when she was gone, suddenly there was an awareness that the world had changed while she wasn't looking, that they were men and women, not boys and girls, that something must be done. Soon after, they moved into Kinnaird Buildings.

All the places they'd looked at were small and expensive and wanted huge deposits. Then Billy heard about a flat from Eric, who lived in Kinnaird Buildings with three other guys in a flat known as Littlejohn's. Kinnaird Buildings was the kind of place where the Council put its problems. Some of the flats had baths in the kitchen, usually under the sink, but these were pretty useless because there was no hot water anyway. There were always empty places in the Buildings; people squatted them and got evicted and moved into another empty flat while someone else squatted the one they'd just left. The Buildings were lively, humming with tension, through the nights as well as the days.

Billy and Eric broke into a top-floor place that had been empty for a year or so. The caretaker came up while they were fitting the new lock and they giggled as they hid behind the door, holding it closed against him. It was a game. When he went away, suspicious but washing his hands of the whole affair, they finished the job quickly and left it at that till tomorrow. The light was fading and

16

you couldn't see much inside. Billy went home and told Loretta he'd got them a place, two rooms, kitchen, toilet, cooker, nice neighbours. Their own front door.

And it was over, Rita and Deptford, and a new epoch began. It was as if she suddenly woke up and found everything happening very fast, like going on holiday as a child; she just went with it, not quite in control. A friend of Eric's came over in a white van to pick them up with all their gear, a carpet, a trunk and a mattress, and a very old record player. It was morning, clear and crisp, the sky white. She was sitting in the front of the van with this guy Willie, who spoke in a slow, heavy, disgusted Manchester accent. She thought there was something a bit repulsive about his heavy smooth red lips that sneered a little around his words. He was dark, sour-mouthed and fleshy-nosed, with a black tee-shirt and short muscular arms. As he drove he talked slowly, never taking his eyes from the road, addressing himself more to Billy in the back with the luggage and the carrier bags than to Loretta, who leaned back and watched the traffic, dazed into blankness by the necessity for upheaval. A great wall unfolded, endlessly. She thought it looked like a prison.

'They're sound,' Willie said in a vaguely aggressive tone. Loretta had no idea what he was talking about. The inside of the van was very clean and a St Christopher dangled from the dashboard. 'Sound people,' Willie said with sudden obvious sincerity. 'It's OK, y'know, you'll be OK there.' Loretta started to like him a little.

They stopped at a petrol station and Willie got out and worked the pump and went to the office to pay, walking across the forecourt with the conscious air of a Midwest trucker in an American film. When he got back in he looked at Loretta and smiled. 'Your glove's on the floor, love,' he said. She reached down and picked it up, scared all at once, full of a longing for settlement. She'd never even seen the Buildings. When she did, strangely, she felt relief. The van circled them along a route of small streets before cruising over a ramp and passing between the front of the Buildings and a big flagstoned area where young boys played with a football. The Buildings were dark and perpendicular and looked as if they had a history. A small, scruffy, fierce-looking man with a beard came out of one of the doorways and Willie raised his thumb and called out the window: 'Hey! Johnny!' The small man nodded and peered curiously at Loretta; then they turned a corner, scattering pigeons, and eased down to the far courtyard where a bunch of black kids came and watched while they unloaded their stuff and carted everything upstairs.

It was a jumble of impressions. Empty rooms. Green and purple wallpaper. An open fireplace still holding the remains of a year-old fire. Windows, voices somewhere, echoes, a figure on the opposite landing. Spotty cream paintwork on the doors and windows and skirting boards, rubble in the toilet, piles of crap under the sink, a rotten greasy area on the kitchen wall. Loretta and Billy walked from room to room grinning at each other, thinking what they could do with this place, ran up to the roof and looked at the view. The roof was wonderful, long and flat, covered in railings and gates and chimney stacks. 'What d'you think?' Billy kept saying. 'What d'you think? Think it's OK?' He was anxious to be told he'd done well. 'I think it's great,' she said, and she meant it. Billy ran on down the stairs in front of her. Billy always ran up and down stairs.

Eric had arrived. He and Willie had got a fire going in the grate and it was drawing well, a good omen, cheerfully blazing and spitting. They got curtains up and cleaned and scrubbed and laid the carpet, lit candles and borrowed a camping gas ring and found out where to go to get the gas and electricity turned on, made up the bed and put things on the mantelpiece, found a place for their clothes and a place for their records, and when it was all over went to the public baths down the road and got clean.

Later a woman called Dee who knew Eric and Willie came over the roof from the next staircase and invited them for tea, seeing as they didn't have no electricity or anything. 'Miserable,' she said, 'sitting around in the dark with a can of beans.' She was about thirty-five, with thick dark hair and big glasses and a hard-featured uncompromising face that didn't fit her gentle, very Cockney voice. She was one of those people who keep telling you how nice they are: 'Anything you want, just ask me. I'm like that. I won't see no one stuck. My house is your house. I never turn anyone away. I can't help it, soft I am.'

Dee's place was smoky and comfortable, gently lit, with a coal fire crackling and kids' books on the floor. Her husband, Eddy, was a big, broadening man with square knees and a wide neck and fat stomach, who sat in a chair like a throne, bare white feet on a stool, never taking his eyes off the wide colour-TV screen even when he ate his tea. His face could have been good-looking but there was too much of it. It had a soft faded look in the middle of all the long wavy hair that parted round it and flowed away down his back. Every now and then he shouted abuse at the people on the screen. Two little boys ran in and out, leaving the door open and letting in a draught from the hall. Their names were Colin and Tom. After tea they began to fight and yell how much they hated each other. Loretta watched them, feeling sorry for the younger one who was about four, plain and complaining, getting into the habit of feeling sorry for himself. Colin was a couple of years older, darker and very pretty, with great, clear, heavy-lidded eyes and a full red mouth. Eddy screamed at them now and then and they'd shut up for a while then start again.

Dee brought out a stack of photographs of their time in

19

India and showed them to Loretta and Billy. When Dee and Eddy spoke of India, they spoke of people they'd met there who were now living in Brixton or Plaistow or Kentish Town, of getting stoned and palm trees and insect bites and how some dirty bastard had shit in the well, and what a nuisance the beggars were. 'Baksheesh, baksheesh!' Eddy mimed, holding out his hand and pulling a miserable face.

'You have to get hard,' Dee said, 'You just can't think about them.' The pictures were all of white hippies naked on beaches, palm trees and blue sea, white sand, little beach houses. It was just like a Bounty hunters advert. You had to look closely to see any Indian people at all.

Later Dee asked Loretta if she'd mind reading the boys a bedtime story. 'I'm done for for tonight,' she said, rubbing the small of her back, yawning, showing gums and teeth that looked older than they should, browning in places with gaps at the sides.

'OK,' Loretta said, feigning brightness. She was very tired. Someone knocked at the door. Dee stood and went out into the hall and peered through the spy-hole, drew back two bolts and a chain and opened the door. 'Hello, Rob,' she said gently. 'Come in.'

Someone fat and hangdog came in, nodded shyly and aggressively and sat down on a stool at the side of the fire with his knees together, legs tensed as if ready to run. He was not welcome though everyone greeted him cheerfully enough. He had big miserable shoulders in a brown jumper and a flat-topped head with sparse fair hair slicked back from an unhealthy moon face.

'How's it, Rob?' said Eddy, not taking his eyes from the screen.

He didn't answer. He lifted his eyes, which were large and moist and alarmingly desperate, and examined Loretta with them for some seconds in a strange, open, pleading way. My God, she thought, cringing inwardly.

Then he looked at Dee and asked if there was any tea going.

'I'll put the kettle on,' Loretta said eagerly and ran out to the kitchen and took as long as she could, hanging around amongst the potted plants and gaily coloured canisters, listening to the kids getting themselves into bed in the back room. When she came back Rob was just finishing telling them about some terrible atrocity that had just occurred somewhere in the world, and everyone was looking unwillingly solemn. 'It could happen here,' he said in a tone of indifference, 'easy as pie.' Oh no, thought Loretta at the back of the sparse, pathetic head, not another bloody Rita, I can't stand it. Miserable fat sod. She went out to read a story to the kids, who were sitting up in bed in a room full of scattered toys.

'Right,' she said, picking up books from the floor, 'what do you want?' An ambulance passed, siren blaring. 'What about this one, *Three Billy Goats Gruff*?'

'Baby crap!' Colin said, disgusted. So she sat down between them and told them a story out of her head, some ridiculous tangled mess about a taxi that went up into outer space, and they leaned against her, absorbed, amazing her.

Johnny Brannigan hated uniforms, flags, titles, the police, doormen, teachers, inspectors on buses, traffic wardens, security guards, supervisors in shops, doctors, ticket men, the armed forces, people who talked posh and bastards in flash cars with dusky windows. All these were the enemy. GOD was tattoed on one hand, SATAN on the other. His face looked as if someone had put one hand on top of his bushy black hair and another under his bearded chin and given a swift sharp squeeze. A year ago his front teeth had been knocked out in a fight and he'd never bothered to get them replaced.

When Johnny was fourteen he stole his first car, a red VW Beetle that belonged to someone down the street. He headed out of Manchester towards the M6, thinking of London. His foster father had been teaching him to drive in the car park at the back of their house, and Johnny knew enough to get by though he wasn't much good at reversing. But the stupid car ran out of petrol at Altrincham and he had to hitch back in the freezing cold, and when he got there they'd called the police to report him missing and there was a huge row. He lasted another six months with them, and ran away twice during that time.

The next foster home owned a black Wolseley with fancy red upholstery. He drove it as far as Blackpool, ditched it and tried to get a job on the funfair; he fancied himself as one of those lads who jumped on the back of waltzer cars and whirled them round and made the girls scream. But the police picked him up and sent him back again. This time he got counselled and analysed and probationed, but he started drinking and whenever he got drunk he stole or ran away. So they put him in a detention centre. When he came out he got drunk again and stole another car and kicked the policeman who tried to arrest him, so they put him in prison because he was old enough now; and when he got out of there all his friends were either working or away or in prison or with some girl. Then he met Willie Pinder, who was leaving for London the day after tomorrow. He used to knock about with Willie, and with Jimmy Raffo, years back in school. Willie was OK, so he stuck with him and ended up in a truck roaring down the M6 with fifteen pounds in his pocket, arriving in Hammersmith at three in the morning and knocking up Raff's brother Dave, who played sax in a band.

Johnny went pretty straight in London, mainly because he didn't want to bring trouble on the people he was staying with. He only went back inside once, when he got drunk and tried to steal a coffee maker for Dave's girlfriend. He did three months and when he came out Willie had moved over to Kinnaird Buildings and was living with Littlejohn and Eric, so he went there. Littlejohn didn't mind. Rooms were for filling with people, so long as they didn't scream and shout and cry and get pissed and smash the place up all the time. Littlejohn was from Liverpool. He was five feet tall, lithe and spiky, with a faint smile that never faded and a look of hairless youth. He was calm and casual and his nose ran all the time. He'd started out alone in the flat, but it wasn't long before Eric moved in on him. Eric was no trouble, he came and went, not saying much but looking as if he knew a lot; when he did speak it was usually to make some pithy, cynical judgement on someone and it was usually spot on. Then Willie came, then Johnny. Sometimes other people came and went too. Everyone changed rooms all the time. The only one who was always there was Littlejohn.

The place was a hotch-potch of old furniture. Littlejohn and Willie were the ones who usually got round to deciding that it looked like a pigsty and giving it a clean-up; they were the ones who remembered to buy toilet rolls, washing-up liquid and food, and usually the ones to cook it. Littlejohn was vegetarian and made vegetable stews in a huge pot, crumbling in an Oxo or a packet of soup. Willie made things like beans on toast with runny eggs on top, sausages, macaroni cheese, beefburgers. Johnny was useless at all this kind of thing and they let him get away with it. People tended to make allowances for Johnny, somehow.

Littlejohn used junk now and then. Sometimes he got it in Stockwell, sometimes managed to prise a bit out of Dee and Eddy, who'd had a scrip for years. Sometimes he got a bit junksick, but he was very stoical and got some sort of satisfaction out of getting through it. Johnny tried it but it made him puke his guts up.

Johnny lived in the Buildings, on and off, for eighteen months or so, and at the end of that time he too was using a little. One day he woke up and believed suddenly in all the things you read about heroin. Sod this for a lark, I'll stick to the booze, he thought, and wondered all at once if he should go back to Manchester. He was getting edgy anyway. Lately the Buildings had been patrolled by big police vans that cruised quietly, any time of the day or night, giving him the creeps. One had reversed over someone's cat and left it dead and squashed with its mouth open in the middle of the court-yard. Johnny had a terrible feeling that he was running just ahead of the tide: something would happen, he knew it, one day, something, and bang, inside. Back inside.

One night there came an anonymous knock at the front door. Johnny was passing, leaned forward with clumsy stealth and squinted through the spy-hole. A uniformed policeman, dark and solid, was standing outside looking down at a piece of paper. Johnny tiptoed into the living room and made frantic silent gestures at Eric, the only other person in the flat, who was just leaning back indolently and lighting a spliff.

'Old Bill's outside!' Johnny whispered.

'Fuck,' said Eric, pinching out the spliff and burning his fingers; he jumped up and grabbed the dope and ran silently out of the room and sneaked past the front door in the direction of the toilet. The policeman knocked again, with impatience, and both of them relaxed, knowing at once from the tone of the knock that this was nothing serious. But Johnny's face was furious. They heard a shifting about on the landing, then boots walking away down the stairs.

'What the fuck's *he* want?' cried Johnny.

'God knows,' said Eric, going back into the living room and looking cautiously out of the window. It was a top-floor flat overlooking a big yard and a high brick wall at the back of the tube station. Nothing was happening below. 'So I wonder what all *that* was about,' he murmured to himself, relighting the spliff.

Johnny ran into the back room and came back immediately, cursing and bristling. 'I'll break his spine, the little cunt!' he yelled, hurling down into the centre of the room two used syringes with faint traces of blood inside. 'Just fucking sitting there for all the world to see! Talk about careless! Stupid bastard! Who'da got it in the fucking neck? Not him, the bastard, us! Us!'

'Not on, is it?' Eric said mildly, screwing up his pale face and coughing as the smoke caught the back of his throat, scratching himself through a hole in his pink tee-shirt.

Johnny circled the room in rage, spines of paranoia projecting from him, then muttered and ran out to the kitchen, came back with a paper bag and stuck the syringes in and ran downstairs to hurl it into one of the big metal bins. 'Little bastard, little bastard!' he muttered. God knows what else he'd left lying around the place. He was still shaking with rage when he got back to the flat, stalking madly about ranting at Eric: 'I'm not having those bastards breathing down *my* neck again, treating me like shit – yes sir, no sir, stick it up your arse, sir! Oh, he's a dirty little bastard leaving his shit lying around all over the place, going around with his poncy nicelittleboy face, I'm such a nice guy, oh yes, yes, turning everybody on . . .' He mimicked Littlejohn, eyes and upper lip stretched stupidly, beard waggling: 'Oh yes! Oh yes, I'm such a nice guy! Fancy a turn-on? You sure? Everybody likes me cos I'm so fucking nice I make people want to puke! Hah!' He made it sound as if Littlejohn had an Eton accent because that was the accent of the enemy.

A few days later the same policeman called again. This time, only Willie was in and the place was clean. Willie never panicked at the sight of the police. 'Scared, were you?' he'd say smugly. 'Got you in a lather, did they? I'm not scared. They don't frighten me.' So he opened the door and said, 'Yes?' The policeman wanted to know if Eric Scammell lived at this address, and Willie wondered what the hell Eric had been up to and said he didn't know anyone of that name, he certainly didn't live here. Eric thought hard when he told him and said he couldn't think what it was all about unless it was for maintenance or something, he had a wife and child he hadn't seen for a long time and he hadn't had enough to pay them for ages. He thought he'd better move out for a while, just sort of cover his traces a bit, so he moved into the flat Billy and Loretta had just left at the far end of the Buildings and inherited their decorating.

Johnny was nervous and he was bored. The place took on for him the feeling of a prison, the locks and chains and bolts and spy-holes on every door. He was sick of it all, sick of Littlejohn lolling about doing nothing every night, saying he was tired, he'd been working all day (Littlejohn was a plumber), and Willie pottering about

26

the place like some old biddy wittering on about how it was always him that did the washing up. No one ever wanted to go for a drink any more. One night he got so sick of both of their faces that he went round to Eddy and Dee's to watch a bit of TV, but it was even more boring, the kids in bed and Eddy and Dee just fading away in front of the set. Dee's new baby whimpered thinly in her arms and she rocked it like a mechanical toy, going, 'Ssh, ssh, ssh, ssh,' over and over again. Johnny made big kisses at the baby. The TV was boring too. He sank deep into his chair, his eyes closing. Eddy told him an agonisingly long and laborious story about how the Council was supposed to have put a gas fire in, they were putting fires and water heaters in all the flats but they'd missed theirs somehow, typical, and Dee had had to go to Citizen's Advice and blah, blah, blah ... so after a month ... said they'd sent an urgent memo ... so anyway, this geezer comes a couple of weeks later but of course he's brought the wrong ...

'Terrible,' mumbled Johnny. 'Terrible, terrible. That's the Council for you. Treat you like dirt. Bastards.' But he didn't care at all. When he could stand it no longer he borrowed a couple of quid and went for a drink. It was rock'n'roll night at the pub, all these people dressed up in fifties gear, men in Teddy-boy jackets with velvet collars, winklepickers, sideburns and greased-up hair, women with pony tails and wide plastic belts and big frothy skirts. 'Good Christ!' he murmured to himself, fighting his way to the bar, feeling that if an elbow accidentally got into his eye he'd flatten the bastard. A band of Teddy boys played old Elvis numbers and danced in formation. The whole place was pissed and roaring and jiving apart from Johnny. They had these nights once a week. Closing time you'd always get a few pissed rockers out looking for punks to beat up. Johnny couldn't stand it for more than a couple of drinks, he was on edge and there were one or two creeps standing about

27

whose looks he didn't like – he thought one of them had been giving him dirty looks when he first came in – so he left and walked home morosely. He had a headache and thought he might go to bed, but when he got there the first thing he saw was fat Rob sitting like a pale toad in his favourite armchair. Littlejohn was playing guitar, the same boring old bits he always did, and Willie was lying in a chair reading a book with his feet on the mantelpiece, a position that looked ridiculously uncomfortable. The radio was on, some singer who sounded like he'd got about half a ton of phlegm stuck in his throat.

'Guess what?' said Willie, not looking up from his book.

'What?'

'Rob's been put out of his place. He's staying here for a bit.'

Johnny said nothing. But inside: Oh shit! Oh no! Rob was one of the most miserable people in the world and he couldn't even be romantic about it because he looked all wrong with his slack moon cheeks and dishwater eyes and greasy colourless hair. He wasn't bad, he was just miserable. He was like a dishcloth left in dirty water overnight, and he was infectious. No one wanted to be with him. Sometimes, as he sat and sat, just staring and scratching his head occasionally, tears would fill his eyes. Johnny couldn't stand him, but the worst of it was that he felt sorry for the poor miserable bastard. Willie raised his eyes and gave Johnny a steady look: yeah, bloody drag, still, what can you do?

'Got home and there's a board over the door,' said Rob softly. 'My things are still inside.'

Johnny flopped down in a chair. 'Ah, they're bastards, man,' he said weakly. That did it. Dole day tomorrow. Get up early, down the dole, piss off up to Manchester, see some old mates. He imagined how it would be if he stayed: Rob just sitting, sitting, hands on fat knees, waiting for a day to pass; Willie getting irritated and surlying

28

about sneering at Rob and feeling bad for doing it; Littlejohn just there or not there.

Johnny fell asleep in the chair. When he woke up they'd all gone to bed except Rob who was still sitting there, hunched over and creepy in the darkness, clumsily poised like a spider in the corner of a web. So he hoisted himself up from the chair and staggered, drunk with sleep, away to bed, sure now of what to do, and in the morning got up early, collected his dole, came back to the flat where Willie and Rob were stuffing their faces with Scotch pies and cream soda, grabbed a few things and walked out again, down to the tube station to clatter down the spiral staircase full of old graffiti: Smoke wet cement and get really stoned, V D and the Necrophiliacs, Punks, fuck cunt shit. He sat on the platform, thinking with great nostalgia of Manchester, dear dirty old town, salt of the earth, friendly faces on buses and all that, took the tube to Euston and got on a train for Piccadilly.

When he stepped out at Piccadilly Station it was already late afternoon, and the wind whistled and tugged at him. He moved quickly, knowing exactly where to go, who to see, until by ten o'clock he had a place to stay for a few days with people who'd never refuse him even if they didn't rejoice at his arrival. The next day he just walked about the city feeling jaunty and sentimental, visiting sites of old memories, looking up friends he hadn't seen in years and finding them strangely unsatisfying. He left Raff till the middle of the afternoon, hearing things about him here and there, that he'd just done four months for kiting, that Patsy had gone off somewhere with the kids and he was staying at his mum's. Raff was a tie that had somehow endured for sixteen years, God knows why, because Johnny thought Raff was basically stupid, wide open. Raff would always be a big-featured, scrawny-necked, gormless kid sitting at the next desk to him by the wall.

Raff's mum lived in a block of flats a bus ride from the centre of town. There were lace curtains at the frosted-glass door and the bell had a soft two-noted chime. Johnny smiled when she opened the door. She gave a little shriek and cried: 'Oh, it's Johnny!', stood on tiptoe and gave him a big smacking kiss on the bit of his right cheek not covered by hair; his nose itched with a sudden sharp intake of acid perfume and a softer cosmetic smell. Then she stood back and looked at him and he saw how much older she was, face softer and more wrinkled, eyes more faded and yellowy than he remembered, but she was still refusing doggedly to let herself go. She'd always done herself up nicely, Raff's mum, nail varnish and make-up and stockings and all that, but she didn't plaster herself like an old tart. She had a round, smily face and very white, even, false teeth in a bright lipsticked mouth. When she turned and walked before him down the little hall to the living room she looked from the back like a much younger woman – trim, dressed in black, pale legs in pink carpet slippers, fair and grey hair that curled onto her shoulders.

She led the way into a small, neat room, very warm from a hissing gas fire, with green, rush-patterned walls and a lace-draped window with flowers. There was a soft red three-piece suite with a black and white cat cosily dozing on one of the chairs, a glass-fronted cabinet full of fancy plates, glass animals, paperweights, a shell-covered box, a Russian doll. A painting of the sea that Raff had done when he was sixteen hung over the mantelpiece, and the sideboard was covered in photographs of Raff's children and of Raff and Dave and Malky at different times of their lives: school badges, gappy teeth, ties, desperate smiles, the lot. It gave you a sinking school feeling to look at them and must be driving poor old Raff barmy.

He was out, she said. 'Shift that cat,' she said. 'Buster! Buster!' and settled him by the fire, made a cup of tea and fussed over him, cigarettes, cheese scones, Jaffa cakes of course. Raff had liked Jaffa cakes when he was a kid, so she'd feed him Jaffa cakes as often as she could and he'd go on eating them even if he grew to hate them because he wouldn't bring himself to refuse. She stood on the rug, one hand cocked by her head with a smoking cigarette between the fingers, talking to him while he ate, smiling often so that her face was forever crinkling and softening, getting loose around the neck now, he noted. Oh, she was fine, she said. Feeling the pinch a bit but who isn't these days? She wasn't doing so bad, working as a secretary still, keeping body and soul together anyway. She laughed. And Jimmy was fine, enjoying his freedom. 'I'm spoiling him a little bit, trying to make it up to him – well – you know he's been having some trouble with Pat, don't you?' She pulled a face that implied it was a bad scene but all under control really. 'It's not Pat, you know,' she said, 'it's the kids, he misses the kids.' Johnny nodded. She'd never liked Patsy. On the sideboard the kids looked out of a gilt frame, big-eyed, dark, the elder with an arm around the younger. That must be driving Raff barmy too. She asked if he'd seen anything of Dave. Johnny said he hadn't seen him for ages. 'Oh, we never see anything of Dave!' she said gaily. 'He's the big man down there, with his music and everything. Now and again he honours us with a visit!'

Later she asked if he fancied a little drink. 'Well, after all, I suppose you could call it an occasion, Johnny comes marching home again, ha ha!' She opened the sideboard and took out a bottle of whisky just under half full, and two little glasses with thin green stems, poured and handed him one, left the bottle open on top of the sideboard and sat down opposite him. 'Don't want ice, do you?' she said, sipping. The whisky looked as if it had been watered down and tasted slightly weaker than it

31

should. 'No,' he said, 'this is fine.' So they drank and talked and got merry. Johnny made her laugh with stories about Kinnaird Buildings, leaving out all reference to drugs or the fact that they were squatting, giving a kind of all-jolly-lads-together impression of the place. He got excited, talked loudly, laughed, gesticulated. Her laughter and movements got looser, and she lay back in her chair and stretched her legs in their pale, flesh-coloured stockings and pink slippers. Her ankles, one crossed over the other, were very long and thin, almost abnormally so. She was all right, Raff's mum, nice woman, you could have a laugh with her and she wasn't always looking down her nose. She never made stupid comments about his GOD and SATAN tattoos. She'd act like you weren't there sometimes, start singing or talking in a silly voice or messing with her face or washing her hair or something – probably because he'd been around the house so much when he and Raff were mates together. She'd always had a soft spot for Johnny – had this romantic image of the poor orphan boy, rough at the edges but good as gold inside; Johnny knew how to play on this, just the right word, the right look here and there. But the affection was genuine. He'd have knocked the head off anyone who bothered Raff's mum.

Raff walked in. He said, 'Hiya, Johnny,' as if he'd only seen him a couple of days ago.

'Hi,' said Johnny, raising a hand on the arm of the chair casually, 'it's good to see you.'

Raff was wet and cold. His face was pale but he was red runny-nosed from walking up the hill into the wind. He sniffed and wiped his nose with his hand, stood by the door for a moment, tall and willowy with high, crooked shoulders. His eyes had a look as if they were lying in harbour after some storm. His mum started talking at him, fussing, telling him he was soaked, pulling at his jacket; he shook her off with a mildly irritated movement, smiling faintly and answering with mechanical monosyllables, then took off the jacket and left it messing up the back of the settee for her to remove and hang up, sat down in the chair opposite Johnny and leaned back, crossing his legs and nestling with a hard-mouthed, petulant look against the green cushion and the cream-coloured lacy antimacassar with the embroidered milk-maids. His face was irregular, messy-browed. He rolled a cigarette and lit up, coughing, grinning and grimacing at the same time, then got up with the cigarette clamped between his hard lips and the smoke getting in his eyes, put the cap on the whisky bottle and stowed it away in the sideboard. 'It's really bloody awful out,' he said, sinking back into the chair, 'God, it's hot in here.' He started treading his shoes off his feet, mashing the backs of them. The cat sprang to his lap and stood getting its head stroked, butting with its blunt black nose and purring.

'You're staying for your tea, aren't you, Johnny?' Raff's mum said.

'Wouldn't mind,' Johnny said appreciatively, 'if it's no trouble.'

'No trouble at all, lovely,' she said and went into the kitchen where she banged about, singing some old torchy kind of song in a deep, throbbing, imperfect voice.

Raff leaned forward with his long fingers drumming on the brow of the cat. 'She loves it,' he said just above a whisper, grinning. 'Anything I want I can have, I'm not kidding, treats me like bloody royalty, I'm getting dead spotty an' all, you ought to see the stuff she feeds me, I'm going mad, Johnny, I've got to get out of here.' He spoke evenly and slowly and expressively.

'I can imagine,' Johnny said and they stifled laughter.

Raff leaned back sprawling, floppy head and arms, legs all over the rug, serious again. Johnny swirled whisky around his glass. Raff could've made the mourners at a mass funeral laugh when he was in the right mood, but none of it was in him just now. They talked, asked after people, compared prison notes, told a few stories. 'You heard about Patsy, of course?' said Raff. Johnny said he had but didn't know anything about it, what happened? He fancied another drink but sensed it wouldn't be right to ask. Raff smiled wryly and shrugged: that's how it goes. 'Oh, she went really funny, really . . . y'know, it was lots of things, been going on for ages. Right now I don't give a fuck.'

Johnny looked at Raff sweating in all this domesticity and remembered seeing him just after Luke was born, in a tiny little place with pails of nappies and a funny smell and Patsy sitting out on the one-person balcony and a pram blocking the hall; too much of all that, too much too soon. Johnny thought Raff was better off out of it and said so. 'Yeah,' said Raff neutrally, poking at the cat. He couldn't leave it alone, had to keep picking and prodding at it, teasing to just the right degree so that it didn't get vexed enough to jump down but couldn't settle properly either. Now and again it bit him gently or batted him with a paw.

Raff's mum went out after tea and Raff got his dope out and they had a smoke. 'Don't drink with her,' he said, 'I never drink with her. Jesus, it'd be terrible if I started drinking with her.' He kept sprawling back and leaning forward to speak, tensing and relaxing like a Jack-in-the-box, 'I wish she'd get a feller, I really do. Makes me feel bad how much she likes having me here. Feel like I'm about six again . . .' speaking seriously but with grim, self-mocking humour, 'I'm having a really weird time, Johnny, I mean . . . God, I've got to get out of here, you know what she's started doing? She cuts the crusts off the toast for me. I like the crusts . . .' Johnny laughed. 'It's terrible!' Raff cried, laughing too, jumping up and waving his arms about and speaking in a light tone of all the things that were driving him mad. He said he'd been for a job in a saw mill with some guy he'd met. He said he thought he might go abroad. Then he spoke about Patsy, saying that she was stupid and small-minded and selfish, didn't know what she wanted, unbe*liev*ably selfish . . . but she'd get hers one day, wait till her karma catches up with her, I'd laugh in her face, no one can do what she's done and get away with it, I don't know how she sleeps, I bet she doesn't . . . His tone was complex – defiant, unconvinced, flat.

Johnny didn't know what the hell he was talking about but nodded sympathetically, and then because Raff looked kind of fierce he spat for good measure: 'I'd give her this!' and raised his fist and shook it. Raff sat down then and leaned back, suddenly calm, regarding him in a slightly unnerving way, no particular expression on his face.

In the end they went out for a drink. Johnny had imagined him and Raff sitting yarning about old times in a nice boozy glow, getting out of order, having a laugh, going to call on some old friends and staying up all night, crashing out, waking wrecked, going back to Raff's mum's for a big breakfast in the afternoon. Instead Raff started on about himself again, the same things, his tongue running on in that light, aggravated tone – Patsy and the kids, Luke's birthday in a day or two, no right, no moral right to take a man's children away like that, all because of her own fucked-up head, and when he found out where she'd taken them he'd be there like lightning and get them and not a sinner on earth could stop him, they could kill him first, he'd have one of them anyway, any court in the land could see that he should get one of them. Johnny thought that was ridiculous. What would Raff do with a kid trailing round after him?

'It's permanent,' Raff said suddenly, setting down his pint and looking straight at Johnny. 'You know that, don't you? I'll never see them again.'

'What?' said Johnny.

'I think she's taken them out of the country.' He sat back and drank. Oh, Christ, thought Johnny, I should've

35

stayed in London. They sat silent for a while, feeling old, two young men of twenty-six. Johnny's dole money was nearly gone and he wondered if Raff could lend him any, wished he'd asked earlier. This didn't seem the right moment but he asked anyway and Raff lent him a fiver. They went to another pub, and another; Raff cheered up, said he thought he might go to London for a bit, stay with our Dave in Hammersmith, see how it goes. Johnny gave him Willie's address. 'I'm staying straight,' Raff said. 'No way am I going back inside again. I don't want to walk into any bad scenes down there.' Johnny said it was OK, more or less; bit of smack around. 'Fuck that,' said Raff.

The pub grew noisier and noisier so that they had to shout. Some old friends came in and everyone was laughing, buying drinks for Johnny, the wanderer returned, who told loud funny stories and shouted his exploits, and at some point lost track as the wheels speeded up and speeded up and there was too much hilarity and sound and light and too many shiny faces, then wet, dark, cold streets and the sound of himself running, shouting, roaring, out there and in his head, echoing on the inside, resounding, bouncing from the walls of his skull, and Raff saying to him from somewhere: No, no, come on, Johnny, let's go home, and the sound of breaking glass, a light in a window, Raff walking away down the street towards the big road where traffic passed, moving lights in the dark and the wet, breaking into a run, decking gracefully and drunkenly onto an all-night bus that soared away with him lurching up the bright-lit stairs: and Johnny alone on a dark pavement and a sound of wolfish howling that came from himself, the lonely werewolves of Manchester raising snouts to the clouds drifting over the silver Dayglo moon, a roaring and a thundering, many voices in the distance, waves crashing, hissing inside his ears and a sense of terrible loneliness, then nothing, nothing . . . till he regained consciousness, aching and nauseous, soiled with blood and piss. In a cell. Someone told him he'd nicked a car and robbed an off-licence and resisted arrest and assaulted a police officer. He groaned and closed his eyes, sinking down into the jagged teeth of a headache, and knew that he was, after all, going back inside.

Loretta and Billy moved three times in Kinnaird Buildings before coming permanently to rest. The first time
was about a year after they moved in, when Loretta was
working at the store and there were bombs in the West
End. She sold things like talcum powder, bubble baths,
soap-holders. She lost track of time in the store, away
from windows, and at first her feet hurt so badly it was
like wading in something hot all day, but when she got
used to it she was happy there. She liked the bustle of the
West End in her dinner hour, and seeing so many different kinds of people all day long. Some ways it was like
being back at school, though – the rules, the way the
supervisors and the managers treated you.

Billy found the eviction notice pinned to the front
door, like a declaration of plague or something, when he
got back from the café. He was between jobs and liked to
go down every morning to one of the cafés in the market
and sit with a newspaper and some tea and toast and talk
sometimes with the man behind the counter. If he missed
a few days, the man would shout at him when he came in
again: 'Why you no come for your breakfast no more!
You no like my toast? My toast is good!' The notice
pulled him up and ruined his day: he knew what it was
even though he couldn't read it. The worst thing was
telling Loretta. She got depressed about it for a while,
sentimental, the first place of their own, how they'd painted it, bought things for it. But of course it was expected.
Billy went to the Town Hall and waited for ages in a
room like a doctor's waiting room. He was good at waiting. He asked for a rent book but they wouldn't give him

one, so he put their names on the waiting list, went away and recruited Eric and borrowed a nail bar and pulled away the wood that barricaded the door of an empty flat in another block. Again upheaval, moving, so much more to move now, so many possessions; everyone helped, and afterwards they went into Littlejohn's and Willie made popcorn that pinged like hailstones all over the closed lid of the pan. Next day was a royal holiday and you couldn't get bread anywhere. A steel band played in the street and at night there were fireworks over the river, the most beautiful fireworks Loretta had ever seen. Everyone stood on the rooftops to watch.

The second flat was never home: why decorate, why put down roots, why bother? Dee got pregnant with Sunny while they lived in that flat. Loretta remembered feeling jealous when she found out, and then she too was pregnant again and it was awful and thrilling and forbidden, like standing on thin ice. Billy was working in the bakery, so she gave up her job at once and took things easy, never ran upstairs or down or lifted anything heavy, took all that the doctor gave her, all the homoeopathic things Rita gave her, didn't drink or smoke, and prayed from time to time. This one was a boy. She tried not to think of any of the others in case she transmitted something to him and made him feel like the next chicken in line waiting for the knife across the throat. 'Don't worry,' she said to him sometimes, 'it's OK, just don't worry about it.'

Dee gave birth to Sunny, who spent the first few days of life withdrawing from junk; and for all Loretta could say, the knife fell on the neck of the chicken. Her body voided the child, spat him out like a piece of bad meat. Loretta took to her bed and counted the silly pink flowers on the wall. Billy sat down beside her on the bed and held her hand; when she looked up he smiled timidly. 'I don't want you to go through this again, love,' he said.

'No,' she said. 'I won't. Not again.'

When she was better she went as a waitress in a plush, jazzy little bistro in town, with a young St Lucian girl called Nina who she'd met when she worked in the launderette. Nina lived in a tower block not far away, with her mother and sisters and her fat contented baby who loved to be held, to tuck his fragrant head under Loretta's chin and pull her hair and dampen her with charming milky dribble. Nina was very black with tight-stretched skin and a broad, hard, curvy body that she carried like a peacock carries its tail. She fussed over Loretta like a mother, even though she was only seventeen and Loretta twenty-nine: 'Button your coat up!' she'd snap on a cold day, grabbing Loretta by the throat and doing it for her.

The next move came. This flat was damp and looked out on a big iron gate and the scaffolded side of a tall building. Standing at an open window one night, she heard a bomb explode in the distance; it seemed also to explode inside herself, inward and cutting, an awful compassion. She began to have feelings that the city might eat her up. And time moved on. Billy, dogged and relentless, pestered the council; Rita moved to Balham and was living with Keith, a nice man with a flat face who talked as much as she did at the same time as she did, so that to visit them was to become the audience for two separate streams of consciousness, and somewhere in all their words, somewhere, always, there was doom.

And then they were given a rent book, something unimaginable, some string pulled, she never understood why. Maybe they just got sick of Billy's face. There was security, a legal key, time to make it nice – this flat on a new courtyard, the noisiest yet. You heard fights, cries in the night. Sometimes a madman mumbled and roared from his window. The tube trains ran beneath. And they had hot water and a gas fire and it was clean and dry and home now for longer than a little while.

*

Judy lived opposite. Before she got to know them, Judy used to peep through her spy-hole now and then and see Loretta and Billy and their visitors come and go. She'd got her flat on one of those first come, first served, queue-up-all-night Council deals that got announced every now and then, and she lived there in a solitude that was a dreamed-of holiday, a golden retirement. Judy had had so many different jobs she'd lost count, but mostly she'd been a French teacher in the north of England, and at present worked part time in a West End salad bar, doling out food and scooping twelve different varieties of ice cream. She spent hours writing poetry that she screwed up and threw away two or three weeks later. Judy had escaped, survived, come through years of entanglements with charming weak men who'd sucked her soul like a lollipop. She'd left them all but carried each one in a sack around her neck like some medieval punishment, knowing that one more might break the bone. When she'd found herself alone and decided to stay that way, suddenly, strangely, she was quite happy. My God, she thought, was it really that simple? And it seemed, looking back, that she'd gone from one island of need to another throughout her life and was now leaving all land behind. Forward into the sun, onward to the edge, courage my heart. She wrote poems about it and threw them away.

One night as she was trying to write a poem, a disturbance broke out in the courtyard below, three or four male voices back and forth, rising at each other like stags in pride. 'Oh, shut up,' she whispered, trying to concentrate. 'Please shut up.' They went on and on till it ended in a fight: thudding and shouting, then car doors and running feet and the sound of a police walkie-talkie. She couldn't think straight, so she stood up and looked at herself in the mirror for a moment, puzzled as if she'd just woken up. She had a vague, kind, dreamy look and smiled sympathetically, foolishly at herself. Someone hurtled upstairs, gulping loudly as he rounded the landing outside her door and dashed on up to the roof. He left the roof door open; it would bang irritatingly in the breeze till someone went up and wedged it with rope. These things happened from time to time. You heard things. You had to become like all the other eyeless, earless, mouthless human beings, turn up the volume to drown it out, look away, you were no saint. What could you do? A weeping and wailing at 3 a.m. was the soundtrack of a movie, a fine piece of acting. Believe in the heart scalding and cracking in the dead space between the backs of the Buildings and you'd crack with it: go mad, become a saint, keep your distance, reach for the volume knob, yes, folks, that was one more tale from the naked city.

Every third-rate poem she tried to write died in the lee of all this.

Someone tapped on the door. Judy ran to it, peeped through the spy-hole and saw Loretta. She opened the door. 'Did you see that?' said Loretta in an outraged tone.

'What?'

'Didn't you *hear*? The police were there and everything. Look!' She pointed to a spattering of fresh blood that trailed around the landing and on up the stairs, a dotted line of deep red stars that would be brown by morning.

'I heard something,' Judy said, 'but I didn't take any notice, you hear so many things . . .'

It was cold on the landing and Loretta shivered in a thin white dress from Brixton Market. 'There's been all sorts going on out there!' she said, still outraged.

'Well, don't freeze to death.' Judy stood back and held the door wide. 'Come in.' So she came in and stood uncertainly in the middle of Judy's red womblike room full of friendly dog-eared books, introduced herself and started to talk. All this trouble, she was sick of trouble, she looks out and she sees this boot go right in, and the police, the police are fucking useless, they take the wrong guy away, they don't care so long as they get someone. This place is really taking a dive. Lovely room — lovely rug, lovely colours. Don't you get scared on your own? Judy made coffee and sat listening, still, looking wise and feeling shy. 'You got a bath in this flat?' Loretta asked. Yeah, but no hot water. 'Typical,' she said. 'Huh! Typical!' She talked for a long time about her life and Billy, and then she invited Judy to come over for a meal tomorrow night, you're a vegetarian, oh, that's all right, I'll do a flan or something, you do eat cheese, don't you? Judy said she did.

Next evening she met Billy and Rita and Keith and got drunk with them. Someone called Willie came in, jolly and arrogant, and latched onto her as the spare. God, she thought, it's always the ones you wouldn't touch with a barge pole. He kept crowding his leg against hers, so she went to the toilet and looked at herself in the mirror with affection, drunk, pushing her fingers through her hair, you're OK, you're OK, not bad at all, oh, Vanity, Vanity, and went back and sat further away from him. And later there were more people, someone else's flat, much laughter, music.

Weeks and months passed, many changes, new people in the Buildings. Judy established her status. Loretta didn't take her seriously at all and was always trying to set her up with someone or other, or scolding her for being so vague, but she just laughed it off. She had her identity: Judy lived alone, Judy was a friend to all but kept her distance. Loretta started thieving little things from big shops and stores. When it happened she was always amazed. Something appeared by her hand, something ticked in her brain and it happened. And then it was too late, it was in her bag or pocket or whatever and she'd be tingling with a kind of inner blushing, a terrible excitement till she was free, out in the street, unpursued, the relief making her want to run and run the way she hadn't run since she was a kid. Wondering was it worth it for a can of peaches, an eye pencil, a purse. Oh, sod them, she'd think. They can afford to give me a little present now and then.

Some days terrified her. She went on the bus to Brixton one day with Nina and her baby Stephen, who sat smugly on Loretta's knee, warm and sweet and heavy, smelling of milk and some kind of spicy fragrance Nina rubbed into his hair. She nearly nicked a pair of peacock-blue tights that day, but somehow didn't, and afterwards saw a woman in the store watching her strangely, trailing them to the door. It made her sweat and feel sick, oh, God, what could have happened, the police, getting Nina involved, all the horror. Loretta was scared of the police. She knew enough of what they could do. She'd seen the way they hassled the black kids. Nina's friends were always getting pulled in. She had terrible visions of court and prison and her name in the paper.

She tried to stop, but then it was Christmas and everywhere was full of bright, wonderful things that wanted to be touched, wanted to be wanted, and somehow there was never enough money and it happened, it just happened again. Someone had a room full of Christmas trees that year, the smell of pine glorious whenever anyone opened the door into that room. Dee and Eddy had a party; everyone pulled Christmas crackers and a great spreading tree glittered like something out of Dickens. Colin came and stood in front of Loretta and made her feel old. He looked about nine and walked around like Marlon Brando, mouth full of sticky toffee, ear-ring in one ear, Sid Vicious tee-shirt. 'Lovely Loretta,' he said, 'Pull a cracker with me.' My God, she thought, look at him, he used to suck his thumb and poke me and giggle about titties and he had fluffy ducklings on his wallpaper. She pulled the cracker and won a green paper hat, a little charm and a bit of paper with an awful joke on.

Joe McKinley moved in with Littlejohn and Willie when Rob moved out. Joe didn't smoke or drink or take anything apart from dope, which he smoked regularly in a little pipe that fitted nicely in the palm of his hand, and he wouldn't let Littlejohn fix up in the living room any more. Willie fixed too now, but he was like a seagull with a bit of bread, always ran away with it. Joe hated smack.

Joe knew Dave Raffo through some people at Reading University where they'd both gone ten years apart. Joe had a degree in philosophy and scores of books that everyone kept euphemistically borrowing without telling him. He cleaned cars for a living. Joe was black and freckled, with close-cropped hair and a soft sardonic voice that made everything sound clever and dismissive and slightly complaining. His eyebrows were two thin raised arches that constantly furrowed his brow. He got upset over little things like dog-ends dropped down the toilet, the way they floated there for days slowly disintegrating, Eric trimming his stubble over the sink, particularly as he wasn't even living there any more and had his own sink to go and mess up, sauce bottles left with congealed tops and drips running down the side. Joe was a nag.

One day, as Joe sat playing chess by the window with Eric, someone knocked on the door. Willie was making sardine sandwiches in the kitchen and went out into the hall with a buttery knife in one hand, looked through the spy-hole. A girl or maybe a boy stood on the landing, looking away towards the stairhead. He opened the door.

It was a girl with a peculiar face and very short fair hair. 'Is Johnny here?' she asked aggressively.

'He's gone to Manchester,' said Willie, surprised at her air of challenge. 'He's in nick, actually.'

The girl gave a frantic, overdone little shriek and slumped against the wall. 'Oh, Jesus,' she said in a high, strident voice, 'oh no! Oh, Jesus! Oh, I don't believe this!' A fat laundry bag leaned against her leg.

Willie scratched his head. 'Oh dear, oh dear, oh dear,' he said in a brisk, kind-uncle voice, 'I didn't think he was *that* marvellous.' She looked at him as if he were stupid. 'Come in a minute,' he said, beckoning with his head, and she walked in immediately, scowling, hauling the bag up and over her shoulder. She sat down with the bag between her legs, ignoring Joe and Eric and their game of chess.

'So what's he done?' she said loudly.

'Nicked a car and some booze,' Willie said. 'Thumped a policeman.'

'*Johnny* did?' She looked amazed. 'You're joking! Johnny?'

Joe and Eric watched as if it were a play, wondering if they were supposed to know her. Willie shrugged. He asked if she'd like a cup of tea and she nodded wearily, suddenly hanging her head and sucking her thumb like a sulky child. 'I don't believe it,' she said again. She had a Liverpool accent that echoed Littlejohn's in every detail, and everyone realised at the same moment that they were talking about the wrong John. 'Oh, *Little*john,' Eric said. 'You mean Littlejohn. He's at work. Hang on, what's the time?'

'Four fifty-two,' said Joe.

'Oh well, he'll be back soon.'

'What's he do?'

'Plumbs,' said Willie. 'Toilets and things. We call him the lav man.'

She cheered up and became quite friendly when she

46

found that Littlejohn wasn't in jail, took off her jacket, pulling faces as if silently holding a conversation with herself, wandered about the room looking at everything as if she were in a shop or museum. She said her little girl was at a friend's, she didn't like to leave her too long, she'd known Littlejohn donkey's years, he was a brother to her, a great bloke; she'd been living with his brother, a right bastard, a right rotten, creepy bastard, you wouldn't believe the two of them came out the same hole. She was small and very young, with thin legs in thick woollen tights and a starving-child shape, and she didn't appear to be aware of her face at all – it did a job for her any old way, making expressions, chewing its lips, looking lovely or like hell depending on how you caught it. Her eyes were blue and bulgy and the lower part of her face shelved away from them steeply so that there was a slightly scary death's-head–bush-baby look about her.

When Littlejohn's key turned in the lock she sprang up and faced the door and was ready: 'He's gone!' she cried as soon as he came in. 'Oh, Johnny! At last the bastard's gone! What shall I do? I hate him, I hate him, I hate him, I hate him! I had to get out, he had a row with the landlord and the landlord hates me! He's gone, thank God, he's gone, thank God! What shall I do? What shall I do?' She burst into tears and stood with her face in her hands and her shoulders heaving.

Littlejohn, dazed, made her sit down and sat beside her, one arm across her shoulders. 'Jesus, Sharon,' he said helplessly, 'Jesus, Sharon.'

Willie came in with the tea and poured her a cup. 'Enough!' he said, thrusting it under her nose. 'Enough!'

Sharon moved into the back room with her daughter Mandy, a dark, plain, soft-eyed little girl of five, always clean and neatly dressed with matching buttons and pretty patches to camouflage the threadbare bits, so shy she was hardly there at all. Sharon filled the flat with potted plants and air fresheners and kept her door closed at all times whether in or out of it even for a few seconds. Only Littlejohn walked in and out with any freedom. At first everyone tended to regard Sharon and Littlejohn as a couple simply because they'd known each other for so many years that they took each other for granted, and because he sat on Mandy's bed in the evening telling her stories. But there was nothing between them. Littlejohn had no interest in women.

Littlejohn was a registered junkie and Sharon had a small, growing habit. She'd started snorting it when she was living with Ian; when she did, it didn't matter that he made her flesh creep, that she hated him, that she hadn't got any friends and didn't know where to go. She thought it was romantic, bruised innocence, blighted youth, needle of death, all that kind of stuff. But Sundays were terrible. Sundays they always ran out and it was a million miles to Monday. Willie would slope away somewhere for the weekend, Joe would go out because he couldn't stand the atmosphere, and Littlejohn and Sharon would suffer. Sometimes Joe took Mandy to the park because he felt sorry for her and because on Sundays Sharon always tried to palm her off on somebody. She tagged along after him as if he were a mother duck, walking when he walked, stopping when he stopped. Once he took her into a café and bought her a Fanta and a jam doughnut, and she rubbernecked all over the place as if it were the Ritz. Poor little bastard, he thought.

Back in the flat, Littlejohn and Sharon would shiver and rub their eyes and change their positions in the room about a million times, and sometimes one of them would go out and puke in the toilet. Being junksick was the utmost reach of boredom. And sometimes someone would turn up with some gear like the cavalry riding over the crest of the hill, and then everything would be normal again and Sharon would run down to the Greek shop and get something for supper and pick up Mandy and make some food while Littlejohn and Mandy fooled about and watched TV. And time passed and she thought, What am I doing here? What am I doing here?

Sharon couldn't stand the idea of being alone. That was the only reason she could think of for staying with such a bastard for so long. She never quite felt she had a right to go anywhere or do anything. She was only twenty-one and she weighed up every man she met automatically, disinterestedly, knowing she'd end up with one some time, God knows which. After a while she started to fancy Joe, more as a hobby than anything else.

He nagged her and showed off his knowledge. He thought it was nice the way she took care of the kid, kept her clean and sent her to school and everything, but she was weird-looking, and anyway she was a junkie and he was sick of all this, he was moving out soon. All junkies, he told her, were basically stupid, the ultimate ostriches, heads up arses. But he couldn't help posing a bit, honing his ego. In the end they slept together because he found her alone on Christmas Eve singing stupid songs with the radio when she thought no one was listening. She sang 'Little Donkey' and 'When A Child Is Born' and 'Shall I Play For You My Rupupumpum'.

Weeks passed till they were almost but not quite sharing a room, going around together, arguing a lot, making a point of being uncommitted and saying things like, Well, it's nothing to do with me, you do what you like, and the flat was too small and too full and she was always constipated and telling him about it and he didn't want to know about that. And still he took Mandy out on Sundays and she said things like, My daddy plays tunes on a piano. Till he met her coming out of the toilet one day, her mouth looked twisted, and he thought, My God, what am I getting into? She was just some awful-looking child, filling him with pity and guilt. He went out and stayed at Dave Raffo's place in Hammersmith, didn't return till next afternoon, Sunday, a time he knew would

49

be dreadful and conducive to argument. Willie was out. Littlejohn sat junksick by the fire, face stiff and miserable. Sharon was not to be seen, but he found her in his room, red-eyed and shivering, taking up all the space on his mattress. 'Thanks very much!' she snapped when he walked in, struggling into a sitting position and wiping her nose. 'Very, very considerate of you!'

'What have I done?' he asked, feeling detached from this whole scene but acting an air of righteous bewilderment.

She sprang to her feet and padded about barefoot, moist-eyed, sniffing. 'I wanted you to take Mandy –' sniff, 'you know what Sundays are like, she's been here all day –' sniff, 'Loretta's got her now, she's having her tea there –' sniff, 'I don't suppose it even crossed your mind you might be needed here, hm? Oh, no! Course not!'

Joe shook his head slowly, deeply wronged, whistled once or twice and laughed without humour. 'You talk to me of consideration?' he began quietly, impressively, aware of his effect. 'You say *I'm* inconsiderate?' with one hand pressed flat and tense upon his breast. 'Me? You don't think it's just a little bit inconsiderate of *you* to chuck the poor little bastard out every Sunday? Because you get into this ridiculous state? And then you want sympathy?' He let his voice rise just a little, but dangerously. 'You're not laying this one on me! She's not *my* kid.'

She stood rigid, then kicked the door so hard she must have hurt her foot. 'Don't go on at me!' she screamed. 'Don't go on at me! You know I can't take it today!' and flinched and shrank into a corner with a clumsy quivering movement.

'Oh, don't be stupid!' he said. 'I'm not going to hit you,' and went out again and walked about feeling dismal and mean and defiant. Driven out of his own room, for Christ's sake! He'd have to go.

50

But in the end it was Sharon who went. She just announced casually one day that she was doing a swop with Eric, made herself untouchable, started packing. Willie and Eric helped her move. She had a TV and an old washing machine and loads of bags and boxes. Joe skulked in his room; it was OK, she didn't care, he didn't care, no one cared, but still he skulked in his room. They made one trip and returned for the washing machine, an old tub which stood out on the landing. He sneaked to the spy-hole, saw Willie and Eric struggling with the machine, Sharon with a huge plastic sack held skilfully on one shoulder, Mandy just standing there watching. He felt like going out and saying something friendly, something to establish their continuing relationship, but couldn't think of anything so he bent his head and spoke through the letter-box in a stupid old-crone voice: 'My washing machine! Someone's stealing my washing machine!' She looked up, surprised for a second, then smiled sourly and stuck up two fingers at the door.

It didn't make much difference. She still came around, they still slept together from time to time, he still nagged and took Mandy out on Sundays. But he tried to guard his territory more closely. He was doomed to failure in this. People encroached. They turned up wanting places to stay, to kip down for a night, two nights, more. Sometimes he went to sleep alone and woke to find some stranger sleeping on his floor. Jimmy Raffo stayed a few times after missing the last tube back to Dave's. One night someone screamed hysterically out back in that great doomy space between the buildings; glass went smash – smash – smash – smash – smash methodically, even wearily. It went on for some time and ended in a long bitter male sobbing that chugged on and on for what seemed like an hour.

'Oh, God!' mumbled Joe, longing for sleep.

'Listen to that!' Jimmy kept saying nervously. 'Listen to that! Oh, the poor bugger, I wish he'd shut up!'

51

Jimmy was like a big kid. He was one of those people who talked while you were trying to get to sleep. The disturbance outside ended and he lay there on his back shooting at the ceiling. 'Kapow! Kapow!' he whispered. Silence came. Joe heard Jimmy laughing in a stifled way in the dark, the sound scarcely more than that of his lips drawing back to smile. Joe drifted towards sleep. 'Do you ever get a funny feeling in your head,' said Jimmy, 'like your brain's gone sort of, you know, like when you're on the dodgems and it goes out of control, when it sticks on one spot going round and round on the end of the pole, you ever done that?'

Joe brought his brain out of a half dream and tried to put it back into gear. 'What?' he said.

'Yeah, y'know, and then the man comes and gives the wheel this great big spin to get it going again, or whatever he does. So what d'you do? You sit there waiting for the cosmic dodgem attendant.' He laughed. 'That's a good image, ha ha, I like that, you could write a song about that – the dodgem cars of my mind, ha ha.' He was quiet again and after a time Joe fell to the edge of sleep. 'Did you ever have a gang when you was a kid?' Jimmy asked. 'We did. Me and Johnny Brannigan and a kid called Harry Keyes. We used to call him Pancake Keyes. We never beat people up or anything. Kings of the Wild Frontier. Hah! Kings of the Wild Frontier!' Then he sang softly: ' "Davy! Davy Crockett! King of the Wild Frontier!" '

Fifteen minutes later Joe came to and Jimmy was talking about Rembrandt as far as he could make out. 'Shut up, will you?' he said. 'I'm trying to get to sleep.'

'Oh,' said Jimmy, 'sorry. It's a throwback to childhood. I used to rap to my kid brother.'

Next morning Joe was awakened by the light and by Jimmy singing 'The Trail of the Lonesome Pine' softly on the other side of the room. He looked across and saw

Jimmy lying on his back with his eyes open, drawing on the wall with a Biro. Joe dozed and let the voice drift in and out of his head, it didn't matter, it was pleasant enough. After a while he heard him get up and go out. Jimmy messed about the place waking everybody up, making tea in the kitchen, throwing open the living-room window. He'd make himself at home wherever he was. Half an hour later he barged back into the room and thrust a steaming mug of tea in Joe's face. 'Reveille,' he said. 'Aren't you a lucky chap? Tea in bed.'

'What time is it?' asked Joe.

'Twenty to ten.' He went out and Joe heard him talking to Willie in the next room. They were old friends. Later when Joe got up, he saw that Jimmy had drawn a cartoon on the wall, Popeye the Sailorman eating a can of spinach. It was perfect.

Winter came, more changes. Rob went away altogether, travelling, he said mysteriously; Johnny came back. Joe had hardly met Johnny but he knew all about him. The world was full of Johnny clones. Where Johnny went, sooner or later trouble followed. Joe sensed a change in tone, a faint rise in tension, and noted with disgust habit after habit that grated his nerves like small splinters under nails – Johnny licked his cornflake bowl out with an aggressive red tongue, flicked his new front teeth in and out while he watched TV, spat in the fire, farted loudly while lifting his arse, left ash and dog-ends and hair and roaches and dirty socks and bootmarks all over the flat, complained constantly about some bastard or another. He played the record player at full volume and called you a miserable fucking bastard if you turned it down, leaned out of the window and gobbed phlegm onto the heads of passersby, giggling: Haw haw, they'll think it's a pigeon. Usually he missed.

Johnny came back in January. Joe stuck it out till the beginning of March then moved into a flat of his own in the front block, overlooking the yard where the kids played football. Peace, he thought. Peace at last. A few weeks later Jimmy Raffo came over from Hammersmith and moved into the side room. The afternoon of his arrival Joe's place was full of people sitting around talking about the riots. Willie was there, Littlejohn, Billy, Judy, Colin, who was now more with the adults than the children even though he was only eleven. The front door, which was on the latch, opened and closed and Jimmy came in. 'Wasn't expecting you till tomorrow,' Joe said.

He had all his things in a big old shopping bag stuffed under one arm. He looked quickly around to see who was there, fixed at once on Judy even though he'd never seen her before and gave her a big friendly smile, which she returned with faint surprise. He came in and dropped his bag, chivvied Joe into going out and making him a cup of tea, coffee wouldn't do, said he was wrecked, he'd just walked all the way from Hammersmith, collapsed his long body into the vacated chair and grinned. 'Oh, isn't it great to have servants!' he exclaimed.

'How come you walked?' Willie asked. 'No money?'

'Yeah,' he said, 'I just thought I'd walk, you know how it is, you go out and find yourself walking sometimes. Anyway, the buses kept coming between stops. I hate waiting at bus stops.' Then he told them the story of his walk over here, making them laugh, addressing himself mainly to Judy as if he knew her well. She was struck by the humour in his eyes. He had a big mobile mouth, a three o'clock shadow and eyebrows that met in the middle. Joe came in and handed him a mug of tea and he sprawled back complacently, drinking with closed eyes. 'Oh, this'll do me fine,' he said, 'Dave's place has been driving me barmy, I'm not kidding, it's bloody mad over there, he's got the whole band there, kids, dogs, bloody arguments – madness. Oh, yeah, this place is fine!' and laughed and took off his shoes.

*

Loretta called in at Judy's a few nights later and found her sitting with a tall lanky guy with dark hair and a friendly face and a pink towel round his neck. 'This is Jimmy,' she said, 'he's just moved in over at Joe's. He popped over for a bath.'

'A *bath*?'

'Yeah,' he said, 'I'm a right cheeky sod. She only gets the hot water on today and she's not even had one herself yet. And a very nice bath it was too.'

He grinned at Loretta from his chair by the fire and she smiled back. 'I live next door,' she said, 'I'm Loretta.'

'Loretta!' he said. 'The famous Loretta! I've heard about you. All good. I was going to come and see you because someone told me you'd got some nice old blues records.'

'I have!' she replied, sitting down and leaning towards him. 'I've got loads! They're pretty old and scratchy, though.'

'The only way for a blues record to be,' he said. 'There's a fantastic quote which I should pull out now and impress you both with, about scratchy blues records, but I can't for the life of me remember what it is – only it's great, you know, something some old blues man said that hits the nail on the head. What was it? Let me think.' 'Bout time she got herself a feller, Loretta thought. He's nice. Am I in the way? 'I give up,' he said, 'I'll think of it at three o'clock tomorrow morning and come running across and wake you up to tell you before I forget it again.' Loretta thought he was quite delightful and laughed so freely and infectiously that they both laughed with her.

Judy asked if they'd like a cup of coffee. 'No, no,' Loretta said, jumping up too quickly, 'I have to go.' In the way, she thought, I'm in the way . . . but Judy looked puzzled.

'Don't be silly,' she said, 'you've only just got here,

of course you're staying for a coffee. Sit down.'

Jimmy Raffo stood up too, packing his towel into a bag at his feet. 'Don't make me one, Jude,' he said, 'honestly, I'm going now,' said goodbye and was gone so quickly he left a fold in the atmosphere, a lingering pause that lay between them.

'Well,' Loretta said, feeling awkward and not knowing why, 'that was sudden. Did he leave because of me?'

'Course he didn't,' Judy said, going out to make the coffee, 'He'd been saying he was just leaving for ages.'

Loretta tagged along behind her and leaned against the fridge, animated, implying things. 'Nice, isn't he? Don't you think he's nice? How old you reckon he is? Twenty-seven? Something like that. Hear the way he called you Jude? Very familiar . . .'

'You missed your mark, Loretta,' Judy said. 'You should've been a matchmaker.' She smiled. 'Yes, he seems like a nice feller. The world's full of nice fellers.'

They had these conversations all the time.

'You know what you are?' said Loretta. 'You're a right bloody boring old cow, you are. A right bloody awful boring old cow.' Judy laughed again. 'No, I mean it, honestly.'

'I know,' said Judy, 'I know you mean it.'

56

It was a mystery how Jimmy Raffo's parents ever got together in the first place. The only thing they seemed to have in common was that they were both lapsed Catholics; his father had Italian blood, his mother was Irish. There existed photographs of them looking happy together in earlier days, but this was all over by the time Jimmy was old enough to notice things. His earliest memories were of a small house with a light and happy atmosphere, a baby, a loud pretty mother who sang and danced, performing to the mirror and the baby and him. She sang 'That Old Black Magic', 'I Talk To The Trees', 'As Time Goes By', gesturing with her arms and holding an imaginary microphone to her lips, or she took his hands and danced with him, swirling around the room with the baby in her arms, bright skirt whirling, talking in funny voices, bouncing him between her knees and pretending to drop him.

In the house her face was pale and her legs bare, but if they were going out she'd rub rouge on her cheeks and paint her mouth crimson, pull stockings briskly onto her legs and dab perfume behind her ears and down inside her blouse. She pushed him in the pram with Malky, the baby, or he walked beside, holding onto her coat. Sometimes they went into town on a bus. Always she talked to people, on buses, in shops, in queues. She had many friends: sometimes in the afternoons the house would be full of women who made a big fuss of him, talked and smoked and laughed and drank tea, filling the air with woman smells.

At tea time everything changed. First Dave came

home from school, then dad from work. Dave was nine years older than Jimmy, the child of his father's first marriage, big and quiet and surly with his stepmother, gentle with the children. He scowled and belched and shrugged and bolted his food while she hovered about trying to please. When his father came in, time became long and hushed. Jimmy's mother turned into Agnes, who didn't smile or sing or dance or talk in funny voices. His father was an inspector on the buses, a tall quiet man who drew very detailed pictures of wild flowers in a series of tiny sketch books, using a mapping pen and printing neatly underneath both Latin and common names. He grew pansies and snapdragons in a little yard at the back of the house. The boys grew up knowing all about stamens and sepals and photosynthesis. Jimmy's parents rarely spoke to one another, though sometimes his father complained in a low, serious voice about some mess in the house, the ash those women left all over the place, clutter in the hall. Dirty, he wrote with his fingertip in the dust on the landing windowsill.

Jimmy hated school. He was weak and wore glasses and his ears stuck out, and he was always running home down the long terrace to his house, paradise lost, where his mother and Malky sat together in the warm safe little room from which he was excluded. Agnes would cry sometimes as she led him back to the detested redbrick prison where nobody cared about him. But he hardened quickly. It was explained to him that there was no way out and he learned to make the best of it, to run about and yell in the schoolyard, to make people laugh, to mould clay and make pictures with bright powder paints, which he brought home to his mother. She told him they were marvellous and stuck them all over the kitchen walls. His father thought he had a talent and took him around art galleries at the weekends, or out into the country if the weather was fine, where they hiked about and looked at plants and drew pictures of them in

58

one of the eternal tiny sketch books his father's pockets always yielded up. Jimmy never knew how to talk to his father. It was like going out with a benevolent but formal teacher.

When he was seven or eight years old they went on a charabanc for a day in Blackpool. He and Malky sat in one seat, his parents in the seat in front, their two heads, the dark and the fair, aloof and unspeaking for the length of both journeys, there and back. Blackpool thronged with people, the sand was hot and dry, the air along the Golden Mile sticky with smells, the windows bright with pink rock, sugary whirlywheel lollipops, shiny souvenirs. Jimmy bought a shell-covered box for his mum, threw up on the waltzer, fought with Malky, got slapped, and ended up losing himself in the stifling crowd on the prom while the rest of his family were looking in a shop window. He ran up and down looking for them. A strange woman in sunglasses took him by the hand and stared into his face with eyes only faintly visible. He thought she might be going to take him away; although he believed dimly that men were more dangerous in this respect, but you never knew, so he pulled away from her and ran, looking for a policeman. That's what you did if you got lost. Then he saw his parents and Malky standing by a zebra crossing waiting for the traffic to stop. Malky held his father's hand and all three of them looked sulky. He ran up and re-attached himself to them gratefully, looking up about to speak, when he saw that his mother's eyes were full of tears and that her make-up was smudged in a dirty streak on one cheek. He thought for something less than a second that it was because he was lost but realised at once that they hadn't even noticed. The traffic stopped and they crossed the road with a great squawking crowd. Malky saw candy floss and asked for it. '*Shut up!*' his father said in a terrible voice and gave his arm a shake. Jimmy saw his mother close her eyes and frown, then open them again and wipe the tip of her nose quickly with her hankie. Her eyes terrified him. They were moist and hopeless and naked.

When the day was over and they'd piled back onto the chara and gone home and to bed, he'd lain awake for a long time in the dark listening to Malky sleep, and the voices of his parents low and endless and deadly serious through the wall, hour after hour. He couldn't sleep because of fear, even though he didn't know what it was he was afraid of.

A new phase evolved. She was less present. Some days when he came home from school the house was cold and empty, the back door on the latch, Malky at a neighbour's. Dave, a big bespectacled sixth-former, would arrive home soon after, chuck his schoolbag aside, run upstairs to change into old clothes then set about making the tea for his kid brothers while Jimmy went and fetched Malky. Other days she was there singing in the kitchen, the fire lit, food sizzling on the stove. In the gaps between school and tea time, Jimmy began hanging around with a gang of older boys from down the street, kicking about the alleys and ginnels acting tough and hard.

But he wasn't allowed out in the evenings because his dad said he was too young. This seemed ridiculous to Jimmy as all his friends were out till nine or ten o'clock, so he made a point of being as awkward as possible without actually provoking his father to violence. His father was not patient: he sat in the front room with his sketch books and his ink and mapping pens and the radio softly playing, and he hated to be disturbed. Dave was out most nights and so was Agnes. Jimmy watched TV or played Subbuteo and fought with Malky till it was time to go to bed. Late at night sometimes he'd hear his mother come home. Once he saw her standing under the harsh hall light crying, her face raw and bloated.

Another time he heard a commotion in the early hours, came out on the landing and looked down to see her lying on the hall floor crying and moaning and vomiting. His father knelt beside her and held her hair out of her face. She dribbled into a pool of fresh reddish sick and whined thinly. 'Agnes,' his father said sorrowfully, 'this is no good, this is no good, pull yourself together.' Then he looked up and saw Jimmy looking down through the bars of the stair rails. Jimmy went back to bed, feeling like a spy, and much later when everything was quiet his father came upstairs and beckoned him onto the landing and took him downstairs, past a new stain on the hall carpet, into the strange late living room, told him not to worry, his mother had eaten something nasty and it had made her sick but she was all right now, she'd gone to bed. And then, to his horror, his father, who had never in his life done such a thing before, pulled him onto his knee and held him very tightly against his chest. His face was close against a white shirt front that smelt starchy and a little sweaty. He started to cry. Not a word more was spoken. Looking up cautiously after a while, he saw that his father's jaw was clenching and grinding, that his deep liquid brown eyes were bright and massive, fixed somewhere over Jimmy's head. He grew cold and started to shiver and his father let him go. 'Run up to bed now,' he said. 'You can lie in tomorrow. Go on, you're a good boy.'

Dave left home to go to university. Now and then he'd come home, a big slick brother to be admired, all dressed in black with a silver saxophone that he played soulfully in his old room. Malky was eight, a good quiet boy, doing well at school. Jimmy still hated school. The other kids liked him but the teachers didn't because he was noisy and disruptive and had no respect for them.

When he was ten his mother took him to a house a couple of streets away to meet a kid who was being fostered there. 'He's your age,' she said, 'and he hasn't got any family so you've got to be nice to him. He'll be going to your school, so he can go with you on his first day, you can kind of keep an eye on him.' Jimmy was apprehensive: it was awful to be ordered to make friends with someone. But when he saw Johnny he was relieved.

His mother and the foster mother sat and talked and told them to go out and play. Johnny went and got his football and they went out and kicked it around in the alley for a bit then walked up to the park. Johnny was OK. He was the kind of kid you'd want to stay the right side of, but he took to Jimmy straight away. He was small but crazy, prone to violent rages and absolutely without fear, so that even much bigger kids left him alone. The idea of Jimmy looking after him was ridiculous. He stuck by Jimmy with a kind of rough protectiveness, insulted him fondly, told him he was stupid, taught him to smoke, ran in and out of his house as if it was his own. He never called him anything but Raff. Jimmy's mum adored him. With a boy called Harry Keyes and a few others they roamed the streets and the parks and got rowdy and silly and were told to clear off if they stayed anywhere for too long.

When they were eleven they left junior school and went to a boys' secondary modern with a uniform and games field and science labs. Raff was in the B stream, Johnny in the D.

Raff broke his glasses on the morning of the second day, such a trivial thing to cast a pall somehow over all his future schooldays. His blurred vision drained his confidence as if a plug had been pulled. He didn't want to go. 'Oh, come on,' his mother said, pushing him towards the door, 'you can't start having time off so soon. Tell them when you get there you've broken your glasses and you've got to sit at the front.' His face felt funny and bare. He dallied about for so long that when he called for Johnny his foster mother said he'd already gone. 'He thought you weren't coming,' she said.

Raff walked down to the bus stop and waited. He couldn't see the numbers on the bus when it came and had to ask the conductor where it was going. 'Can't you read?' the conductor said nastily.

He was late. The school was an old churchlike building with a long gravel path leading to a thick wooden door, a high wall all along one side, and a surrounding miasma of school dinners which never seemed to fade. Unable to see, he bumbled inside. It was dark. There was a door to the toilets and inside, a row of cubicles, a urinal, coats hanging, all blurry as if his eyes were filmed with tears that never went away no matter how often he blinked. He bumbled out again and went to the hall. He'd missed assembly, but the hall was still full of boys sitting on the floor against the walls. He was confused and didn't know where he was supposed to go, couldn't tell one face from another. So he sat down alone by the door. Everyone ignored him. Finally a teacher, an indistinct thing, spoke loudly to him. The teacher had had to speak to him five times already because Jimmy couldn't see the man's face and didn't know he was being addressed. 'You! You!' the teacher said. 'What's your name? What? What? Whose class are you in? Well, what are you doing here? You should be in class!' He got up, walked blindly out and stood in the corridor realising he'd forgotten the way to his classroom; it was a big school and all the classrooms looked the same, particularly when you were half blind. By the time he found it the first lesson was over.

All of this gave him a reputation for being thick, which lasted longer than it should have. It was a lousy way to start a new school. He got new glasses in due course and reasserted himself, but he always hated the place. They called him the dago. The only subject he liked was art and that was considered soppy. There was a maths teacher who would get hold of him by the short hairs in front of his ear, drag him slowly from his seat and dangle him on ridiculous display, slowly twisting the hairs till tears smarted in his eyes, then drag him slowly down again, finishing with a sadistic little flick of a knuckle against the sensitive bone in front of his ear.

Oh, not a year of this, he thought, please, not a year of this, and determined to get himself put down into Johnny's class. So he gave up, fooled about in class, cheeked the teachers, played truant, took pride in the awful state of his uniform and got into trouble constantly for drawing Biro pictures all over his exercise books. He drew people that moved and pulled faces. He'd just casually scrawl two or three lines that looked like nothing at all, then add a smudge or a dot or something and there'd be a man jumping over a gate. At home they thought he was doing fine.

His father slept alone in Dave's old room now and went to bed early most nights. Two or three times a week his mother went out and came home late, drunk and emotional. He'd hear her come in. He'd get out of bed and go downstairs to help her, put out her cigarette, lead her to the settee if she was too far gone to make it upstairs, put her on her side so she wouldn't choke if she was sick in her sleep. Years later the lessons he learned from her helped him. Some deep sense of self-preservation always got him onto his side even if he was nine-tenths unconscious.

His final report from first year was a joke. 'I don't know what's wrong with you,' his mother said. 'You can do better than this. I daren't show your dad this, it's terrible.'

'I don't care,' he said.

'Well, I do. I want you to make something of yourself.'

'Like you?' he said.

She called him a cheeky little bastard and slapped him hard across the face, bringing tears into his eyes, then threw her arms around him and apologised. He pulled away and swore at her and went out to call for Johnny.

Next year they put him down into Johnny's class and the two of them went on a truant marathon. They hung about the centre of town, caught buses to anywhere, dared each other to go into shops and nick things, whatever they could reach, which was usually sweets or shoelaces or packets of Victory Vs. Then they started on the stores. They were chased a few times but never caught. They learned how to rob telephone boxes, cigarette machines, chocolate machines. The truant officer caught up with them in the end; Jimmy was thrashed by his father while his mother wept. He cried and swore at his parents. His father lectured him seriously about the trouble he could bring on the family, how he could be taken away and locked up, how his parents could be prosecuted. There was no escape. He had to go back to school.

For a long time he thought he sensed talk behind his back. He grew wary. It was nothing you could put your finger on, just a feeling. Then one day, coming in from the games field all sweaty and snotty, a big brutal boy called Collier breathed heavily at his shoulder and said loudly: 'Is it true your ma's a whore, Raffo?' Someone sniggered. Raff turned and hit Collier in the face and the boy slammed an arm into his throat, kneed him in the stomach, and the two of them went down thumping and grappling and rolling and gouging. Raff was a mediocre fighter. His nose bled and his eyes stung and his breath seared his chest. A circle formed around them. Out of it Johnny exploded, grabbed Collier, who was about eight inches taller and much heavier than himself, by the back of the neck and yanked him up from where he straddled and pummelled Raff. Johnny smashed Collier down into the concrete path and kicked him bloody until two teachers came and pulled him off.

She was going with a man thirteen years younger than herself, a mechanic called Terry. Everyone knew. Jimmy's dad knew and Malky and Johnny and everyone at school knew. She didn't try to hide it. Anyone could see them walking down the street together, waiting in the bus shelter arm in arm, sitting in the pub laughing and drinking. It was never mentioned at home. Things went on as they always had, except that she no longer had any authority over anyone and didn't seem to care. If she told Jimmy to shift his shoes and socks from the middle of the living-room floor or clean up his room, he'd say, 'Fuck off, you stupid old bag,' and walk out of the room. He was coming up to thirteen, a spotty gawk with bony joints. 'Jesus,' he'd say as he watched her put her make-up on, 'you're really getting wrinkly, aren't you? Old women look pathetic when they plaster themselves with make-up.'

'Oh, clever-clever,' she'd sneer. 'Think you sound really *old*, don't you? Big man! You don't know a thing, *child*.' Her lips would stiffen and she'd apply her perfume and hairspray like a soldier saluting, staring coldly into the mirror at her own eyes.

And still, as always, on certain nights he'd hear her stumbling about downstairs, hear her voice as she talked to herself, and he'd get out of bed and go down to lift her from the floor, steer her to the settee, make sure she didn't set the house on fire or knock herself out or choke. Unconscious, full of alcoholic strength and purpose, she would cling to his neck and sob and ask him to forgive her, embrace him with smothering amorousness, kiss him with lingering booze kisses on the mouth that moved and disturbed him. When she was settled, he'd turn the light out and close the door softly on her high, weak, ridiculous voice, slurring tearfully that no one had such a good son as hers, no one, didn't deserve such a good son, oh God, oh God, oh God . . .

She left. It shouldn't have been a surprise, but it was. Everything pointed to it. First came the long, sober, muffled late-night conversations downstairs between his mother and father, night after night, droning on and on and denying sleep to the household. Jimmy and Malky listened together once or twice on the landing, but couldn't make out much, apart from several times when it seemed that she wept and once when their father's voice cried aloud: 'But I love you!' They didn't look at each other, didn't comment, slunk back to their beds obscurely embarrassed. Then one day Jimmy came home from school and she was gone. Everything was the same except that her coats were gone from the pegs in the hall, and some things were missing – photographs, the shell-covered box he'd bought in Blackpool, all her stupid little ornaments, the high-heeled shoes under the sideboard. His father sat down with him and Malky and told them with great formality that their mother had left home because she was very unhappy, and maybe it was all for the best, they mustn't blame her or think it was anything they'd done or that she didn't care about them. 'We must all help each other now,' he said.

'Ah, she'll be back,' Johnny said. But she never did come back to that house, which was quiet and boring and full of her absence. Raff mourned silently and inwardly, a condition like a slow-bleeding wound somewhere in his chest, that became so much a part of him that he could carry on and go to school and fool around and laugh and hang about the streets with his mates, while it seeped. He got used to it. He began to study again because it took his mind off things, and was moved up into the next class where he met Willie Pinder. His father bought him some paints for Christmas and he painted tortured self-portraits on pieces of hardboard.

Johnny started raiding his foster parents' whisky supply, stole a car and ran away, returned again, ran away, returned. He said he was sick of Manchester. Raff told him he was a fool to drink, but he just made a disgusted sound with his teeth against his lower lip, an irritating habit he'd got into and did all the time. He went on doggedly running away and drinking and stealing cars till they took him away and put him in a detention centre.

Six months later Raff was caught stealing buns from the back of a bread van. It was so stupid, so pathetic, so lacking in style. The police were called. 'I was hungry,' he said. He got a caution and they told his father and the headmaster.

His father didn't thrash him now he was older, he just turned thunderous for days, seemed embarrassed and sullen whenever he encountered him and told him once in a deadly serious voice that he hoped he felt free to come and talk if he had any problems. 'Have you thought about what you're going to do when you leave school?' he asked.

Raff thought. 'I wouldn't mind going to art school,' he said.

His father told him that was a good hobby but there were no jobs for people coming out of art school. 'I'm talking about a *career*,' he said. 'You can always draw in your spare time.'

Raff was more careful in future. He stole cigarettes. He stole a battery. He stole milk from the back of a milk float. He stole a book about Indians of the Plains. His fifteenth birthday came and his father gave him some money; he bought woodcarving tools and carved Indians out of his bedposts. At school he messed about at the back of the classroom with Willie, mimicking the teachers and causing disturbances and getting sent out, making pictures on the desk lid out of ink and blotting paper and finely ruled Biro lines. At home he lay on his bed listening to loud rock music played on a Dansette record player, gazed at the ceiling and sang and wanked and wondered what the fuck he was going to do with his life.

One day he came out of the back gate of the school with Willie and saw this smart blonde woman with crinkly eyes, nice legs, a blue polka dot scarf tied like a cravat at the throat. He felt a jolt inside. Willie was talking. She stood by a parking meter watching all the

68

boys go by, her eyes roaming anxiously till they lit on him, then she smiled nervously. 'There's my mam,' Jimmy said wonderingly. Willie shut up at once. She moved towards them along the edge of the pavement, smiling faintly and glancing away from him and then back several times with an uncertainty that touched him. He stepped out of the crowd to meet her and stopped a couple of feet away, towering over her as he never had before, feeling huge and awkward and freakish, aware of Willie watching curiously as he drifted away with the crowd.

'Hello, lovely,' she said, 'I bet you didn't expect to see me.'

'No, I didn't,' he said.

'My God, you've grown.'

She looked just the same. He felt eyes, everyone watching them: Oh look, that must be his mum, the one that . . . 'Come on,' he said, 'let's get away from here,' and turned and walked quickly, looking at the ground and taking big strides. She click-clacked neatly beside him till they reached the back end of the park, where she stopped him by catching his elbow, stood on tiptoe to put her arms round his shoulders, drew his face down and kissed his cheek and hugged him tightly. 'There,' she said, letting him go, 'I knew you wouldn't want me to do that in front of your mates.'

'What you doing?' he cried, standing back and rubbing her perfume from the end of his nose, shaky with nerves. 'I don't understand you. What d'you just turn up like this for? Some sort of dramatic effect?'

'To see you!' she said, and her eyes filled up. 'Don't shout at me, please don't shout at me. You don't know how many times I've wanted to come and set off and turned back because I couldn't find the courage . . .'

'That's a load of rubbish!' he said. 'You could've come any time. I've always been here.' He didn't know what to

69

say, what to do with his face. He stood with his schoolbag hanging from one shoulder, greasy hair, a big spot on his chin. She made a big show of controlling her emotions, took out a pink tissue and dabbed at the skin under her eyes. 'Will you let me buy you a coffee or something?' she asked. 'We can have a little talk.'

'All right,' he said sulkily, and trailed along with her through the park to the big road full of early rush-hour traffic. They went into a coffee bar where a strip light flickered and canned music played, faced one another in a green plastic booth across salt and pepper and a red plastic tomato. Jimmy began to feel unsure of his throat and scowled.

She went to the counter and bought coffee and cakes and urged him to eat. He picked at the pink icing on a bun. She smiled at him. 'You don't know how smashing it is to see you. I can't get over how *tall* you are. You're a young man now.'

'Yeah,' he said drily, 'people do tend to grow a lot at my age.'

'Don't be clever, Jimmy,' she said very seriously. 'I want to talk to you and I can't talk to you if you keep trying to be clever. Do you want to hear what I've got to say? Do you?'

He shrugged and lounged in his corner, studying the cake and picking at the icing with his dirty nails. She didn't speak then for a while and he listened to the traffic hissing in the street outside. 'I'm terrible with words,' she said, 'I don't know how to put things. I'm very sorry about the way things turned out, love. I was ill, you know. I was ill for ages before I decided to go, you know, you're old enough to understand about these things, the drink, you know, and none of you were really a great help. Your dad, you know, I don't want to knock him but he was never a great help. You were more help than he was. You're not a kid now so I should be able to talk to you about these things. I didn't want you and Malc

70

involved in all that – all that – oh, all that horrible stuff, oh, you know what I mean!' She got tearful. 'You know more than a kid your age should. You're a real good son, you are, the things you put up with. I didn't want to put you through it any more . . .'

'You could have left word,' he said. 'You could've written or something, you could've—'

'I'm not proud of it, you know, Jimmy,' she said, suddenly stern. 'But I won't spend the rest of my life apologising. You can't understand. You can't. Don't ever expect me to explain myself because I can't. You've just got to accept that that's how it was.'

'Two years,' he said. 'You don't leave one word in two years and then . . .'

She ducked her head down into her hand suddenly and cried very fiercely and quietly, eyes clenched.

'Stop it!' he told her. 'Stop it! Stop it!'

She stopped as suddenly as she'd started and wiped her eyes carefully. Crying made her eyes look much older. 'Anyway,' she said in a weak voice, 'you weren't very nice to me. You too. Remember how you used to talk to me.' She scrabbled in her handbag for a cigarette and gazed out of the window. Jimmy drank the dregs of his coffee, counting the loose stitches on the seam of his schoolbag.

'I'm all right now,' she said. 'Remember Terry? He's a nice man, Terry. He's been very good to me, very, very good. He's put up with things my own family wouldn't. I'd love it if you could make friends with him . . .' She lit the cigarette and drew on it. Jimmy looked at her tilting back her head, dilating her nostrils, filling the booth with smoke. Her eyes were still moist. 'Actually I've seen you,' she said, 'I've seen you a few times. I've been past on the bus. You don't think I'd let you grow up without seeing you, do you? Malky too. I'm not as bad as you think.' He didn't believe her. He didn't believe her, or he did but it made things worse, he couldn't tell. She smiled

71

at him, sniffed and closed her eyes and looked away, then looked back and said brightly, 'Want another coffee?'

'No, thanks.'

'You,' she said. 'What've you been doing? How you getting on at school?'

'Average.'

'Oh, you've got a good brain. You've got a great brain. I've always had faith in you.'

He looked out of the window at the buses caught in their jams, full of expressionless faces, the sky turning dark, the lights, the long bus queues.

'Will I ever get a smile out of you?' she said. Then he looked at her and tried hard not to smile, but he couldn't help feeling proud in a way thinking of how other people's mothers looked, smiled faintly, and she said he had a lovely smile, leaned across the table and sang to him: '"I'd walk a million miles for one of your smiles . . ."' and laughed and said his face was mucky, got out her hankie and wet it with spit and made as if to wipe his face with it.

'Gerroff, Mam!' he growled, shoving her hand away.

She laughed. 'I know!' she said, 'I was only joking. I've got to stick a pin in your mood somehow.' She went to the counter and got two more coffees. They talked till the night was well fallen outside the misty windows. He told her about school, Malky, Dave, Johnny, getting nicked for the buns. She gave him her address and said she hoped he'd come and see her, Malky too. And Dave. P'raps best not say anything to your dad. Then she reached across the table and took his hand and squeezed it. 'You were the best,' she said, 'you were always the best. I know you shouldn't have favourites, but you were always mine.'

She was a secretary. She lived in a small flat with Terry,

who she drank with, fought with, mooned about with like a teenager. She kept the drinking under control with effort and pride. Malky and Dave hardly saw her but Jimmy visited often and took her presents for Mother's Day, Christmas and birthdays. She treated him as a child and a man – confided in him, scolded him, harangued him, sulked at him, smothered him, babied him. He didn't know what he was.

He left school. He worked in a laundry, in the Post Office, in a factory, went on the dole, got nicked for petty thieving. He was terrified that they'd put him away, struck numb by the magistrates' bench and the crowded court, but he was put under a supervision order instead and a social worker asked him lots of questions about his mother and his schooldays. In the evenings he went to the pub with Willie but he never drank. He grew. His spots cleared up. His mother bought him contact lenses and gave him money to buy clothes and asked when he was going to bring a nice girl to see her. But there was hardly anything doing in that line; he knew a few girls but he was nervous and always acted loud and clever around them. He didn't know if he was the type they went for really, he looked OK but there was something stupid and vulnerable about his eyes, something he couldn't get rid of. He liked girls. He fell in love constantly, fleetingly, never showing his emotions. He dreamed about someone falling in love with him. Once on the fair with Willie, obliquely eyeing up two girls on the steps of the dodgems, he saw one look at him and say something to her friend. Then they both looked and looked away and laughed in a smothered insulting way. He went cold with embarrassment.

One day he went into a record shop and noticed that the record players in the booths weren't fastened down to anything. He thought about it for a while, dismissed it, returned a few days later with a sack, went into a booth with a record to listen to and put the record player into the sack. He came out with it·on his back, pulling him down on one side, handed the record back to the girl behind the counter with a smile and walked out. He got to the end of the road, turned the corner, decked onto a crowded bus and stood in the aisle grinning to himself with the heavy weight pulling at his shoulder. He started to whistle and a woman smiled at him, his mood was so infectious. He winked at her.

It was so easy. Next he stole a watch. Then a cassette player. Then an atomiser of expensive perfume for his mum's birthday. It was being in the right place at the right time, guts, sure movements, timing, faith. He stole coloured spotlights and installed them in his room, expensive art books, a penknife, a slide projector. His spree lasted four months till he was caught walking out of a camera shop with a zoom lens. The police came and searched his room, found dope, found all the bent gear. Jimmy felt sick. His father was furious, white-faced, the neighbours gawping, the police car outside. He was sent to Borstal, some nightmare he'd fallen into, something that couldn't be happening to him. There were rules, masses of them, and he never seemed to know what they were and no one else ever seemed to know, you just heard things, and you couldn't ask or they'd think you were being awkward. A couple of times he broke some stupid rule and they took money off him. Some of the boys were crazy bastards. Some were O K, some were scared shit-less. Some of the screws were right bastards who treated you like shit. Sometimes they'd nick you for laughing, sometimes they'd laugh with you. You never knew. Once he got kicked in the back by a screw for singing. Some boy tried to hang himself while Jimmy was there, some boy cut his arms with a knife, some boy got his face cut open by another boy. Jimmy didn't think he deserved this place; he didn't think he was that bad. Sometimes he cried secretly in the dark. In the end he just put his head down and got through it, nine months, as low as possible, saying nothing out loud in case it brought him trouble.

He felt frightened when he came out. He went to live at his mum's for a while and later found himself a tiny room over a shop not far from Willie's place. He was eighteen. He looked up all his old friends and some new ones he'd made in Borstal, eased into freedom, celebrated, was plied with drink and gave in, finding it good, bestowing magical fluency on his tongue, confidence on his soul. He got a job on the parks and had money to spend and a suntan. His room became a messy heap where he made sculptures out of old bits of polystyrene and hung them from the ceiling. Good times. Freedom.

Willie's mum had gone to visit his sister in Canada and left him in charge of her council house, and the back door was always open so that his friends could come in and out and hang around in the kitchen. Jimmy called in one late summer day, slightly tipsy, carrying a plastic bag containing nothing much but a can of tomatoes. Willie and his girlfriend Joan were sitting in the kitchen and a small brown girl was putting a plaster on one of her toes, shoe off, foot in the air. 'I've got a high instep,' the girl was saying, 'can't get shoes that fit.' He sat on the only available chair a little behind and to the right of her, leaned forward grinning, half shy and half bold, looking at her foot as if it were something on show. It was a very slim, brown, delicate foot. She looked round at him, smiling too, her face suddenly so close he could see the pores between her eyebrows. At the same moment the can of tomatoes fell from the bag and rolled across the floor. 'That's my supper,' he said, retrieving it.

'What will you do with that, then?' she asked.

'With this?' he said. 'Ah, you wouldn't believe what I can do with a can of tomatoes,' and rambled off into some spiel, coming on like a gourmet chef or an advertising blurb. The girl laughed at him.

'He's a dago,' said Willie. 'What do you expect?'

The girl smiled kindly at him. She had slim limbs, long brown hair and a round snub face with brows that darted steeply in towards her nose. He thought she was very pretty. Her face had a magnetism that kept drawing his eyes and he felt frightened because he felt sorry for her, this total stranger, and didn't know why. She stayed about ten minutes and then left with Joan, looking back to smile at him as she went out the door. He kept thinking about her, like there was some ray he couldn't deflect.

Willie, it turned out, knew her quite well. Her name was Pat and she lived with two other girls, friends of Joan's. He left it for a few days, got her address from Joan, cleaned up his place in case he got lucky, had a drink for courage and went up and knocked on her door. Another girl answered and called back into the depths of a noisy flat: 'Patsy! Patsy! Someone for you!' and she came barefoot, surprised, asked him to wait a minute, it was chaos inside, oh, my gosh, I wasn't expecting anyone, vanished and reappeared in a couple of minutes.

They went for a drink, but the woman behind the bar wouldn't believe that she was eighteen so they ended up just walking about. 'I am eighteen,' she said to him, 'honest I am, I was eighteen in May. You believe me, don't you?' 'Yeah,' he said. He didn't care. She took his arm as they walked along. They went into an off-licence and bought some wine, went back to his place and talked. She sat on the bed, he on a chair by the window. She told him her parents had died when she was little and she had no brothers or sisters; she'd been brought up by her granny but her granny died last year; she was a waitress; she used to go to school with Joan; she'd split up with her boyfriend three months ago. He told her about his life, about Borstal and working on the parks, said he'd been stupid but he wasn't stupid any more, he had better things to do now, all that was over. The wine ran out and he went out for more. He was full of high spirits and talked and joked with the people in the off-licence.

'Look at him,' the old woman at the till said, laughing, 'look at the twinkle in his eye. He must be in love.'

When he got back she'd taken off her shoes and curled her legs beneath her on his bed and was leaning back to admire the sculptures on the ceiling. 'You're an artist,' she said. He couldn't believe how easy it was to talk to her. Hours passed. Suddenly the night was fading and the sky at the window was turning blue, and they were both surprised.

'God!' he said. 'Look at all them clouds up there!' Big heavy things appearing like tight fists against the deep blue. Then there was a deep silence in the room, a massive sound of nothing, a waiting. 'You know something,' he said, looking out of the window, 'I'm going to tell you something really funny now. You'll laugh at this.'

'What?' she asked.

He hesitated for a moment then said: 'I've never gone to bed with anyone.' There was another small silence, then she got up and came over to him and sat on his knee, slid her arms around his neck and gently kissed his mouth. She weighed nothing. He put his arms round her and hugged her so hard she gasped, and he apologised, scared of his strength, but she laughed and kissed him again, and after a while they closed the curtains, undressed each other in the dark and went to bed and made love slowly. She was far more experienced than him. He cradled her against his breast, this strange naked creature, then they changed over and she cradled him against hers. He wanted to cry. They slept. It was light in the room when he awoke and he stared with amazement at her face and shoulders and breasts, sniffed at her curiously like an animal inspecting another animal. She smelt very clean. She had a brown mole near the hairline and another on her neck. She woke up and smiled and cuddled against him, kissing him and rearranging the pillow under his head for his comfort in a way that made him laugh with sheer pleasure. And when they had made love again they lay quietly looking up at the polystyrene sculptures that dangled above, turning gently in a faint air current from the window.

'You're like a little brown spider,' he said.

'That doesn't sound very nice,' she said, stroking him.

'Oh, but it is,' he said, 'I mean it to be.'

'What does that make you?' she asked. 'The fly?'

'I'm a Venus's fly-trap,' he said. 'I live on a diet of little brown spiders.'

A week later she came to live with him. His life changed. They were obsessed with each other. The place was cramped and warm and womblike, full of fraught emotion and discovery. They spent most of their time in bed, talked about their lives, laid bare their weaknesses, cried, comforted, promised each other salvation. He found in himself a deep, painful maternal instinct. She could cry very deeply like a child. She had no one, she said, and now he was everything to her. She'd curl around his body, arms round his neck, legs round his waist like an infant monkey with its mother, and he'd carry her like this around the place. Oh, I love you, she'd say, I love you, I love you, I love you. She kept kissing him as if he was wonderful, the best thing she'd ever seen. He couldn't believe it. When she got sick on her periods she'd lie face down on the bed in pain, clenching her teeth and drawing in breath at particularly bad cramps, while he rubbed her back and hips and brought her cups of tea and stroked her hair. You're so good, she'd say. What did I do to deserve someone as good as you? He'd catch sight of his face in the mirror sometimes, same old face, wonder how it had come to mean so much to her, wake in the early morning and feel her sleeping against his back, one arm around him, and be overwhelmed with content and a sense of relief. This, he thought, justified all his suffering.

Months passed. He pushed and pushed Patsy to commit herself. He wanted to be married to her, to have a child, to build up something around him that would circle him with security, erase his youth. She said she wanted to wait a while. She was divided and never comfortable with the split. One side of her was passionate and sentimental, charmed by his waywardness, moved into his life recklessly; the other was the girl her granny would have known, sensible, straitlaced, nervous with the rougher element among his friends, disapproved of dope except now and then at weekends or at a party, didn't like to hear him swear, worried in case he broke the law again. She made him promise that he would never under any circumstances steal anything again, even if they were broke, even if the situation was perfect, even if something jumped into his hand and begged to be taken: she couldn't bear it if they took him away from her. 'Neither could I,' he said. 'I've got no reason to fuck around like that any more.'

'Don't swear,' she said gently, smiling and taking his hand and kissing it.

He took her to see his mum. Agnes had had a row with Terry and was drunk and tearful, hugged and kissed Patsy and said what a lovely girl she was, what a pretty little thing, seized Jimmy in a gross embrace full of desperation, cried and called him her little son and launched into some excruciating story about his first day at school. 'Oh, for Christ's sake, Mam,' he said, pushing her away. 'I'm going if you're gonna be like this. You're embarrassing Patsy.' Patsy said it was all right, she liked to hear about his childhood, and listened in fascination as Agnes sang his praises and dredged up all her old memories.

'Do you remember, lovely?' she said. 'Do you remember?'

'No,' he said.

'Yes, you do! You do remember! You do!'

A week before Patsy's nineteenth birthday they were married. They'd known each other a little over nine months. His dad gave them two hundred pounds and they moved into a little flat with its own small kitchen and a little balcony just big enough for one person to sit out on a kitchen chair. He was going through job after job, unable to stand any of them for more than a few weeks, trying to put money by. Patsy wanted him to go to night school and he went down and got some leaflets about it, but he was tired in the evenings and something balked in his brain whenever he looked at the forms. It was too much like school.

He worked in a marshmallow factory. He worked in a glue factory. 'You could go far here,' the man said. My God, he thought, and left.

He worked in a car-breaker's yard. He cleaned out the men's toilets in some club. The man called him back as he was going for his tea break and pointed and said: 'Look, you missed a pubic hair.' He walked out and went home. He worked as a watchman on a night shift with a bunch of old age pensioners. He worked as a storeman, lift operator, petrol pump attendant, removal man, messenger. He had a hundred funny stories about jobs he'd done, and could give a room full of people stomach ache from laughing too much.

When Patsy got pregnant he was overjoyed. Soon after, Agnes left Terry and came to stay with them while she looked around for a place of her own. She said it would be a bit of extra help around the flat, handy. She slept on the settee in the living room, sang loudly in the kitchen, took over most of the cooking and put them on a diet of food that Jimmy had liked when he was little. Patsy complained to him in a whisper in bed at night. 'It's all right,' he said. 'It won't be for long.'

Two months passed. She woke them up one night

singing 'Up, Up And Away' with some drunken man in the kitchen. The next day Patsy was sick and couldn't eat anything and kept going away into the bedroom to lie down; he found her crying quietly into the pillow, a bowl beside the bed. 'It's not my home any more,' she said, and he lay down with her and rocked her gently and promised he'd make everything O K again. Her forehead was sweaty and hot. 'I don't like you when she's here,' she said. 'You change. You go all lazy and horrible and just leave me and her to do everything, and I'm not well, I feel sick all the time, and it's not fair.'

'Ssh,' he said, 'ssh. It'll be all right.'

'Oh, don't keep *saying* that!' she said, pushing him away and rolling onto her side. 'You're just like a fucking parrot, it doesn't mean anything.'

He was shocked to hear her swear. 'But I'm at work all day,' he said, wounded and indignant, 'and by the time I get home she's done everything. What do you expect me to do?'

'Oh, go away!' Her voice was muffled by the pillow and her breathing laboured. He sat on for a while longer waiting for her to relent and turn towards him again, but she didn't, so he went into the living room and flopped down sideways in an armchair with his legs hanging over the arm.

His mum breezed in from the kitchen, fresh and well groomed. 'Move your little tootsies,' she said brightly, tapping the sole of his foot briskly as she passed. He winced.

'Mum,' he said, 'please don't talk to me like that.'

She laughed. Patsy came running out of the bedroom with a tear-streaked face and screamed: 'He's twenty years old! For Christ's sake! Why don't you stick him in a pram and wheel him away somewhere and just *leave me alone!*'

Jimmy jumped up and tried to put his arms round her but she jerked away from him, trembling, and Agnes stood outraged, saying, 'Well! All I do is say something in fun! Well! I know you're not feeling well, Pat, but . . .'

'Shurrup, Mum,' Jimmy said. Agnes tightened her mouth and stalked back into the kitchen, stalked out again, put on her coat ostentatiously, got her bag and slammed out.

Her absence was like the relief when a burglar alarm stops. Patsy sat down and covered her eyes. 'Oh, I'm sorry,' she said, 'I take it out on you but it's not you. Oh, I'm really sorry, love, I just feel sick all the time and I can't—'

'She's going,' he said, kneeling by the chair. 'She's going, don't worry. She's a pain in the arse and she's driving me mad.' He got into the chair with her and lifted her onto his knee.

'But where will she go?' Patsy asked.

'That's her problem,' he said bluntly.

Agnes moved out two weeks later. She went to live with a smarmy man who was something to do with nightclubs. From time to time she visited them and brought them little things for the baby. Patsy grew bigger and bigger. They spent all their savings on a cot and a pram. At nights the baby kicked under Jimmy's hand and she grumbled that she couldn't get to sleep because of it. She went into labour three weeks early, just as he was leaving for his job on the car-wash. For weeks he'd been building himself up for the birth; he was terribly squeamish and could never watch if they showed an operation on TV or if someone got their head cut off in a horror film. Once they'd shown, of all things, some poor bastard having his testicles removed or something, and he'd had to go right out of the room, couldn't even listen to the narration. But he was determined to go through with this, and he did till they started cutting, and then he went hot and his head swam and he had to go out. Will you go if I tell you to? she'd kept asking beforehand, but when the time came she didn't want him to go, he saw her eyes follow him to the door and felt that he was failing her. He waited outside till he felt better and by then the baby was born, a boy with sharp nails and a head of black downy hair. He cried because the feeling it called up in him was less like pleasure than pain, laughed when they placed the baby in his arms. 'Good God, look at it!' he said. 'What a funny little thing!'

They called the baby Luke. He was small-boned like Patsy, very dark with fine sky-blue veins between the eyes. When he cried, the only things that would shut him up were Patsy's breasts or Jimmy's arms. Sometimes Patsy could walk up and down with him for an hour to no avail, then hand him to Jimmy who'd chuck him up onto his shoulder and say, 'Come on, less of that, you little swine,' and he'd subside into faint hiccups immediately and fall asleep there. Jimmy was incredibly proud of his skills as a father and was always boasting. 'I'm the only one that can get him quiet,' he'd say. He took photographs of Patsy breastfeeding, madonna and child, sat in front of the TV with the baby in his arms and his finger stuck in its fist, bathed him, nursed him, took him round to show off to all his friends. He couldn't take the shitty nappies, though. He only changed Luke once and heaved all the time he was doing it.

The cot was by the bed. Sometimes he'd wake in the night and see Patsy feeding the baby, more asleep than awake, head hanging. In the mornings he'd get up for work and bring her a cup of tea and she'd have brought the baby into bed with her and they'd be lying in a warm nest, drowsing, her heavy eyes looking up at him. Luke was a good, contented baby. After the first few months he began to sleep through the nights, and in the mornings he'd wake and just lie chuckling and gurgling to himself and his toys. Patsy said she wanted another. She held his hand through the bars of his cot as she lay in bed, smiled and laughed to herself and made mouths at him, walked his fluffy yellow duck along the edge of the cot. His face became a strange mirror through which they saw themselves flicker like dream images.

Agnes came to visit. 'Oh, there's my little *bambino*!' she cried, ignoring Patsy, taking Luke greedily into her arms and smiling her fume-laden breath all over him. 'Come to Nana! Mmm – mmm-mmm!' pretending to eat his fingers. She tottered on her stiletto heels, loose and unsteady. Patsy hovered, terrified that she'd drop him. Luke started to cry. He had a bit of a cold and had been grizzling all day. 'Pat,' Agnes said reprovingly, 'this jumper's too tight. The poor little love can't breathe.'

'Oh, he's all right, Agnes. He's got plenty of room. Look.'

She never quite looked at Patsy. Jimmy kept out of the way, hung about in the kitchen making tea, said nothing much, took Luke gently away from his mother when he sensed Patsy's mood growing dangerous. Agnes smiled frantically and fussed and implied things: Jimmy's looking very peaky; don't you think Baby's face looks a bit flushed? Ah, he's not well, poor lovely, it's very cold these nights, that cot blanket's a bit thin, isn't it? You don't put a hot water bottle in? Oh, poor little love, are his poor little tootsies cold when he goes bye-byes? Her voice was so loud it seemed to bounce off all the walls. As soon as she left they quarrelled.

'Well, after all,' he said, 'she's the only grandma he's got.'

'Well, that's not my fault!' she snapped.

'I didn't say it was.'

'Oh, you!' she said. 'You always take her side.'

'Oh, Patsy!' he said, dumping Luke down on the settee and wedging him in with cushions and a teddy bear. 'Don't start, for Christ's sake! My head's spinning. Why do you always start as soon as she goes?'

'I didn't start,' she said, 'you did.'

'Oh, of course, it's always me!'

Luke wailed. Patsy picked him up and put him on her

84

shoulder and he threw up all down her back. 'Oh, God!' she groaned. He cried in a thin, miserable, enduring way, and she walked up and down, patting him and crooning.

'I'm not surprised he's sick,' Jimmy said, 'I would be too, the pair of you hanging over him like a couple of witches.'

'Shut up, Jimmy,' she said scornfully. Luke whinged on relentlessly. There were tears forming in Patsy's eyes.

'Give him to me,' said Jimmy. 'You know I can get him quiet.'

'Oh, of course!' she cried. 'You smug bastard!' She thrust the baby into his arms and went into the bedroom, her back stiff and furious, a great milky stain covering one shoulder blade.

He sighed and sat down and leaned back, holding the baby against his chest. 'Shut up, you miserable little bastard,' he said. Luke shoved his fist in the air and pulled Jimmy's hair so hard that tears came into his eyes. 'Ow!' said Jimmy, unbending the small fingers and rocking wearily till the crying stopped and Luke fell asleep with his thumb in his mouth and his hand curled about his nose, wheezing against Jimmy's chest, a faint smell of puke rising from him. For a second a surge of love passed through Jimmy, terrible and aching, like a premonition of loss. He felt at that moment that he could kill anyone who even dreamed of harming a hair on this child's head.

Johnny appeared. Raff went out boozing with him one night and came stumbling home at half past one, redfaced and stupid and grinning, woke Luke up and hauled him screaming from his cot to comfort him. 'What you fussing about?' he said, loud and irritable, to Patsy who was sitting up in bed and asking for the baby. 'He's OK. Aren't you, pug-face, aren't you, eh? You're OK, aren't you, hah! Come on with me.' He banged his head on the open door as he went into the living room, yelled and swore and mumbled. Patsy got out of bed, threw on her dressing gown and ran after him, grabbed the baby from him and said harshly that she'd leave him if he ever got like his mum. He laughed. 'You wouldn't leave me,' he said, 'you love me,' trying to pull them both into a crushing embrace. She pushed him, catching him off balance so that he fell down in the fireplace and lay there calling her a miserable bitch.

'It's well for you,' she said, raising her voice over Luke's screams. '*I* never get to go out.'

'Well, who's stopping you?' he shouted. 'You go out if you want to.'

'Where would I go?' she asked, leaving him struggling to rise and walking back into the bedroom. 'I've lost touch with everyone. I only know your friends now, and they're just a bunch of layabouts.'

'Don't you call my friends layabouts,' he said. 'You've got Joan. You see Joan, don't you?'

'Big deal!'

'Anyway –' he found his feet, followed her and stood swaying in the doorway as she shushed the baby, 'they're *our* friends, *our* friends, they're your friends too if you'd stop being so fucking stuck up. Who d'you think you are? You think you're better than everyone else, don't you?'

She started to cry with her face pressed into the baby, the baby's arms round her head as if he was trying to comfort her. The two heads rocked together sorrowfully. 'I'm so tired,' she said, 'I'm so tired. I'm so tired and you don't care.'

She wouldn't let him touch her. He slept on the settee and woke in the early hours to rush to the toilet and vomit, head pounding. At eight she came out of the bedroom and put Luke down to crawl about on the rug. Jimmy lay on his back watching her. 'I can't go to work today,' he said, 'I'm sick, I feel awful.' She came and squatted by his head and stroked his hair and kissed his face and asked him if he wanted anything. 'Aspirin,' he said. 'My head's killing me,' and she went away and came back with a glass of water, smiling faintly, shaking two aspirins into her palm.

'That'll teach you,' she said fondly.

After a while he sat up and began debasing himself. He said he was a fool, useless to everyone, he didn't deserve such a beautiful wife and child, why had she got herself lumbered with an idiot like him? 'I don't know,' she said, 'I suppose I must be stupid too,' but she was laughing and sat down beside him and hugged him and said it was nice to have him at home. She gave him Luke to play with and went out to make tea.

Jimmy leaned back, groggy and dizzy, took the baby's hands and pulled him up and down on his knees, feeling how strong the funny bow legs were getting. 'Hey, Patsy!' he called. 'This kid's gonna be running about soon!'

She came and stood in the kitchen doorway. 'You know what we need?' she said. 'A holiday. Wouldn't it be nice? We've never had a holiday together. I've always wanted to go to Ireland. Wouldn't you like to go to Ireland? It's only a hop on the ferry. It's lovely there.'

He thought. 'We've got no money,' he said forlornly. 'I can't even make enough money to take my wife and child on holiday.'

'You shut up,' she said. 'We can save up. Maybe next . . . no, not summer, p'raps . . . early autumn when the fares go down . . . yeah?'

'If that's what you want, my love,' he said, 'that's what we'll do.'

But then Patsy was pregnant again. The bit they'd saved dissipated in the move to a bigger flat on the top floor of an old house, and she suffered from almost constant nausea throughout what should have been their holiday autumn. The new flat seemed spacious compared to the old. It had the luxury of a big kitchen with wood panelling on one wall that Jimmy painted sporadically with weird people. He still had a few paints. He painted Patsy nude and pregnant, the best thing he ever did. He tried to paint Luke but it was much too difficult and he gave up.

The baby came in spring, a sturdy, strident, dark-haired boy they named Jesse. Luke was going on two. Somehow it developed that Jesse became Patsy's, Luke Jimmy's. Jimmy was between jobs and took Luke about with him whenever he could. Luke babbled all the time and dashed around inspecting everything within reach, was bright and fearless and clever and ran up and down Jimmy like a monkey, hanging on by an arm and a leg, grabbing his throat, poking his fingers in and out of his ears and mouth and eyes and laughing at him. Jimmy had to stop taking him into shops because he was a natural-born shoplifter, just grabbed whatever he fancied. In the evenings Jimmy drew pictures for him, which he scribbled all over. Your shadow, Patsy called him, your familiar.

The times were patchy. The highs were beautiful, the lows desperate. Malky came over and babysat sometimes so that they could go out together. They were changing, Patsy becoming less girlish, Jimmy less awkward. They lay together on the settee at nights while the kids slept, kissed and talked and reminisced, got sentimental and said how marvellous it was that they still loved each other after all these years (four and a half) when all their friends were forever breaking up. They decided to have another child in about five years' time when the other two were at school and sending for themselves. A girl next time, maybe.

Jimmy still thieved now and then, food mainly. Patsy didn't know. And they had rows, awful, screaming, heartbreaking rows, full of insults and threats and curses. They rowed mostly about his mum. They rowed about him not helping out enough around the flat now that he was out of work. They rowed about dope and booze. He was drinking more these days, came in like Santa Claus and ended up in rage or melancholia. They rowed about rowing in front of the children. They rowed about money. They rowed about Jimmy's way of taking care of Luke. Once he'd taken him out and had what he thought was a good day, but she went mad when she found out they'd been round Harry's place where everyone was smoking dope. Luke had left his cap there and caught an earache on the way home and puked all night because of all the crap he'd eaten. She said she wasn't going to have her kids around dope. She wasn't going to have his mum poisoning their systems and ruining their teeth with foul sugary slop, all that horrible pink stuff she brings . . . He turned and yelled in her face: 'What the fuck are you bringing *her* into it for?' And so it went.

The children grew. Luke talked and Jesse tottered.

On Patsy's twenty-third birthday Jimmy was caught stealing a Black Forest gâteau, taken down to the police station and charged. He was inclined to laugh about it, he knew nothing much would happen, he'd been out of trouble so long, but Patsy was horrified. 'Well, that's a fine birthday present!' she cried, flinging herself down on the settee in a tragic pose with her hands on either side of her face. 'Oh God! Oh God! Where will it end? You promised, you promised, you promised me! Oh God, I don't want you to go to prison!'

'Come on, Patsy,' he said feebly, sitting beside her, 'don't overreact. It's only a cake,' and started to laugh.

'It's not funny!' she said. 'You fool! If you think this is funny, you're a fool.' Luke was watching from where he played on the floor with a heap of torn paper and crayons. 'Go and play in the bedroom,' she said. 'Go on! Daddy and me are talking. And don't wake Jesse.'

'If you knew what you sounded like . . .' whispered Jimmy.

Luke left obediently, recognising the onset of a scene. The kids would stay quiet till it was over.

'Don't have a go at me, Pat,' groaned Jimmy, 'I've been in that fucking police station all afternoon and I've had it up to here. I'm sorry. What do you want me to do, crawl about on my hands and knees?'

'Do you realise what you're doing?' she said. 'You're not a child any more. Where does it end, Jimmy? Where does it end? Just a cake! How many other things? You just got found out! How many other times were there? How long have you been getting away with it, and me thinking all this time you were straight, stupid Patsy, dead thick, doesn't know what's going on—'

'I haven't!' he shouted. 'I haven't nicked anything else! This is the first time I've nicked anything since before I met you—'

'You lying bastard!'

He jumped up and strode about the room, swearing his innocence, lying badly, retreating, saying, well, one or two little things but he was never going to do anything like that again, and anyway it was for her, a nice surprise on her birthday— 'I don't want you to steal for me,' she said, jumping up, 'I never wanted you to steal for me. *Please*. Think. It goes further than just you, it goes on and on and on and on, and the next step is prison, and the next step – think about the kids, Jimmy.' She pointed to the bedroom door. 'I don't want my kids growing up with a father that's in and out of prison. And kids imitate. They're not daft. Luke really worships you, do you want him to turn out like you? You want him to go through all that? Because that's what—'

'No!' he cried, smashing out with his fist and sending a teapot half full of tepid tea flying from the table to spatter all over the wall. Patsy jumped. 'It stops here! You're right, you're right, you're right, you're always fucking right!' He sat down with his head dramatically sunk into his hands for a moment, then sighed and pulled off his shoes and lay back with an expression of suffering, kicking the shoes away into the middle of the room.

'Oh, put them away, Jimmy,' she said. 'For God's sake, please put them away.'

'*Christ!*' he roared, leaping up and hurling the shoes under the table.

'Don't shout!' She raised both arms with clenched fists in front of her, trembling. 'I'm sick of you! You bring all this trouble in to me and then expect me to run around after you picking up—'

'I've put the fucking shoes away! They're under the fucking table! You don't want me to mess the place up! You don't want me to nick things! You don't want me to smoke dope! You don't want me to drink! You don't want *me*! You want some other fucking feller, it isn't *me* you want at all!'

Patsy went away and stood at the window with shoulders hunched and head bowed and he knew she was crying. He sighed and moved about the room restlessly, muttering to himself. 'I *do* help,' he said defensively after a while. And it began again, that old argument about the division of labour, the one they had all the time, the one that never got resolved, boring, boring. She pointed out that there was a pile of washing up in the sink that had been waiting there since this morning and that he'd said he'd do it, and that the kitchen was full of paints.

'I'm painting the panels!' he cried. 'It's decoration! You want the place to look nice, don't you?'

'I want the fucking pots washed!' she yelled. 'That's what I want!'

'All right!' He stamped into the kitchen and started washing up, his face tight and furious, flinging everything about so roughly that it sounded like a works canteen at dinner time. He felt guilt and knew he was in the wrong. He also knew somewhere inside that he would continue to get out of all that housework crap for as long as he could and leave as much of it as possible to her.

'It's no good when you do it like that!' she screamed at him through the door, and he turned and dashed the frying pan that he was scraping away at with a bent knife against the window, which did not break but shattered in a complex radiating pattern. Patsy screamed. Luke opened the bedroom door and ran to her.

'There!' yelled Jimmy. 'Are you satisfied now?' He grabbed his shoes and jacket and ran out. He was going to get blind drunk, but when he realised he'd brought out the wrong jacket, the one without any money in the pockets, he just walked about feeling sorry for himself, sorry for Patsy, sorry for the poor little kids, sorry for everyone, until it was dark and getting chilly and he thought he might be able to get round her now.

The flat was quiet. The children were in bed. Patsy was sitting curled up in the chair by the fire, the radio playing very softly beside her. Her face was unsure. He sat down opposite her and they didn't speak for a while. 'I thought you'd stay out and get drunk,' she said quietly.

'Oh, shit,' he said softly, 'I do try sometimes, you know.' She looked at him with a strange expression, very sad, almost pitying. 'I'm sorry,' he said. 'What can I say?' She smiled. He stood and bent over her and kissed her cheek. 'Tell you what,' he said, 'I'll make you a nice cup of coffee, shall I?'

'Yes, please,' she said and started to cry.

'Pat?' he said. 'What is it? Please tell me. What is it now?' Something about her disturbed him gravely, but she stopped herself crying immediately and smiled again.

'Nothing,' she said. 'Honest, I'm OK now, go on. It's nothing.'

He straightened, went into the kitchen and put the kettle on, then noticed the shattered window with the light from the street-lamp outside illuminating the pattern. The fridge began to hum peacefully. Patsy had finished the washing up and tidied the kitchen, leaving his painting gear on the scrubbed top of the cupboard. He took a brush, dipped it in red and painted along a line in the pattern on the shattered window. He painted another line yellow. Blue, Orange. Then he got excited: you could really make something out of this, really get into it. He painted on. Purple. Green. Vermilion. Magenta.

'That's lovely,' Patsy said behind him, 'really lovely.' She put her arms round him, and when he turned, leaned against him and started to cry.

'Don't,' he said, 'please don't, Pat, I feel so bad, I don't want you upset any more. I hate myself sometimes for the things I do. Please, please, Pat.' But she went on crying, holding on to him and saying how much she loved him, she really did, no matter how it seemed. He was frightened by her intensity.

After a while she calmed down. They went to bed and made love and later, trying to fall asleep through his spinning thoughts, he felt, though there was no sound and no movement, that she was crying again. He touched her but there was no response. 'What's wrong?' he asked desperately. She lay on her back with her arms crossed upon her breast like an effigy on a tomb, and cried and wouldn't speak or come into his arms, until finally she said she couldn't tell him. Oh, Jesus, he thought, she's got cancer or something. He got up onto one elbow and leaned over her, unable to see anything in the dark. 'You've got to tell me,' he said, 'you can't do this.' Fear rushed through him, someone's doom, and he groaned and covered his face with his hand.

She said she didn't feel the same about him. She loved him but it wasn't the same, oh, God, you made me tell you, you made me tell you.

'What?' he said.

Her voice vibrated, shrill. 'It's me,' she said. 'It's not you, it's not you, it's me, I don't know anything any more, I don't know what's happening, I'm frightened all the time, I don't feel the same about you, what can I do?'

Jimmy lay slowly down again and covered his face with both hands. For a long time they lay stiff and straight, side by side. Sometimes he heard her catch her breath. 'Oh, Christ,' he said softly, 'it's one thing after another.'

They lay for so long each wondered if the other had fallen asleep. 'Why didn't you say anything before?' he asked.

'I couldn't.'

'How long?' he said, 'How long . . .' He swallowed. His spit tasted bitter.

'A long time,' she said. 'What could I do? I could never tell you. You were never really interested in what was really going on inside me, only when it fitted with what you wanted, you never cared, not about what was really—'

'Get out!' he said in a terrible, quiet voice. 'Pat, get out of this room now! I feel like I want to kill you.'

She jumped out of bed, he heard her stumble naked through the room to the door and pull it open and dash out into the room beyond. He felt strained and stretched and there was a singing in his ears. He lay for ages just letting time pass, staring open-eyed into the darkness. At first he heard her moving in the next room, sucking in her breath in gasps, turning on the fire; light appeared under the door. Then it was quiet. Later he heard a clock somewhere strike three. He rose very quietly, groped for his jeans and put them on and went into the next room, desperately tired. She was sitting in an old dressing gown by the fire, hands between her knees, staring at the rug. He stood in front of her.

'Whatever else you say,' he said, 'don't ever tell me I never cared.'

'It's not you,' she whispered, still staring at the rug. 'I don't know what it is. I don't know anything.'

He sat down opposite her and started to cry. She came over and tried to put her arms round him but he pushed her away. Some time later he looked up and saw that she was kneeling on the rug beside him, watching him with heavy eyes.

'What are we going to do?' he asked. She shook her head. 'You should've told me,' he said.

'Sorry,' she said, 'I'm sorry.'

He laughed and wiped his face, shook his head, cried. Patsy put her arms round him and they buried their faces in each other's necks and sagged there wearily till the light came through the window. They'd slept and woken and dozed and slept, and both were stiff and sore and there were sounds, the children stirring.

'We'll work something out,' she said, pushing him away from her gently. 'Don't worry, we'll work something out.' She got up and went away to wash her face and get dressed and see to the kids, aching with weariness. Jimmy went back to bed and lay staring at the ceiling till it was time to get up and drag himself down to the court and wait around for ages to get remanded, then came home and fell asleep on the settee with the kids playing around him. Patsy woke him up and gave him a plate of food and he started to cry while he was eating it.

Luke came and stood with his hands on Jimmy's knees, looking anxiously into his face. 'It's all right, Dad,' he said.

Jimmy was in purgatory, he'd done something wrong some time, he was being punished. He hated the pity he saw in Patsy's eyes, he ground his teeth, his head ached.

'Please,' she whispered to him, leaning over the back of the settee, 'try not to cry in front of them. You never know what effect it might have on them to see their father cry.'

A terrible time had begun. For weeks they argued, discussed, rowed, came together and fell apart. He went back to court and got lectured by the magistrate, a miserable, bolshie old bastard who gave him a three-month sentence, suspended, and told him he would go to prison the next time he broke the law. They stopped making love. She kept wanting to talk, talk, even tried to get him to a marriage guidance counsellor, but he was fucked if he'd have any of that – some patronising bastard telling him what to do, what was wrong with him, peering sympathetically at him over a sensible desk. Fuck them. He felt ugly. He felt in himself the re-emergence of the spotty, gawky schoolboy he'd bidden good riddance to years ago. The pathetic bastard had been there all the time, lying low, awaiting his moment. Maybe that was all he'd ever been.

He went out drinking whenever he could afford it, got terrible hangovers and swore and kicked things and went out for the hair of the dog. Patsy hated him when he was drunk. One night he came home full of whisky and beer, frayed and nervous, full of high emotion. His hands trembled as he let himself in. He reeled about the room. Patsy, kneeling by a chest of drawers as she folded away some clothes for the children, turned her head and watched him. 'Come here, little wife!' he said maliciously. 'Come and give me a big sloppy kiss,' grabbed her in a tight, cruel embrace that frightened and hurt and winded her.

'Get away from me!' she cried. 'I can't stand it when you're drunk! You're trying to break us up, that's what you're doing!'

He laughed, roaring stupidly as he whirled about the room. 'All I want to do is kiss my wife!' he yelled at the top of his voice. 'All I want to do is get my end away!' He took a flying kick at the bedroom door and it burst open and he cheered and ran to the window and flung it open, bellowed into the street: 'All I wanna do is fuck my wife! All I wanna do is fuck my stupid little wife! All you fucking bastards out there! Can you hear me! All I wanna do—'

Patsy hit him across the back of the head with the palm of her hand, ran away into the kitchen as he whirled around and ran after her. 'Don't you dare touch me!' she cried, grabbing the bread knife.

He roared with laughter. 'Murder!' he yelled. 'She's gonna murder me!' ran to the door of the kids' room and flung it open. 'See what yer ma gets up to!' he cried. 'See what kind of a ma you've got! Crazy woman!'

Patsy dropped the knife and started to sob. 'Leave them alone,' she cried, running into the centre of the living room. 'Oh, leave them alone, you hateful bastard! I hate you! I hate you now! You never really loved me! You don't love any of us, you only love yourself!' Her voice snagged and choked. She became hysterical, sobbing and talking together, how she had no one and she'd thought he'd be her family but he'd let her down, she tried, she tried to make things work, it wasn't her fault how she felt, she'd thought he'd help her but he was just a selfish bastard, he didn't care about anyone else's problems, just himself, he was just like his horrible mother, he was fucking it all up, her marriage, her life, she still had no one, no one, no one . . . standing wailing like a child with her mouth all square. The faces of the children appeared, pale and shocked, in their bedroom doorway.

'Dear God,' whispered Jimmy and tried to grab her and forcibly hug her, vicious and comforting, but she shuddered away as if he was covered in shit. Something snapped. He roared like a beast, hit her across the face, threw her against the wall and hit her again as she tried to rise, heard the screams of the children, flung her aside by the hair, yanking and twisting so that some came away in his hand, hurled the table over and sent everything flying, ran into the kitchen and dashed everything from the shelves, smashed all the crockery, ran back into the living room and stood shaking, teeth chattering, jaw clenched, fists clenched, a zombie, madness, saw Patsy crouching by the wall, her body and arms sheltering the crying children, the lower part of her face red with blood that dripped down over her hands.

'No,' he said, 'oh no, no, no, no,' and went to apologise, it wasn't me, wasn't me, but the kids screamed when he approached and she drew them in closer and hid her face and said in a strange deep voice: 'You leave my children alone.'

He stood dazed, turned and circled the room aimlessly, then went and lay on the bed and cried, a drunken, slobbering sot. Finally he fell asleep. When he woke up she'd gone, the children had gone, the place was all smashed up, and his head was killing him.

He dragged his way through the hangover, cursing himself for a fool and a bully, cleaned up the mess, wincing and sighing and listening for footsteps on the stairs. He stood gazing blankly at the bloodstains on the carpet and the wall. Christ, please, he thought, I haven't hurt her that bad, not that bad, it was just a nosebleed, but his memory was fogged, someone else's. What really happened? Nothing, nothing, they'd just gone out and they were coming back, he'd apologise. He saw Jesse's teddy lying half in, half out of the shadow under the window. One of its eyes was hanging out and he wondered if he'd done it. Jimmy Raffo, that nice bloke that makes everyone laugh, gouges the eyes out of his baby son's teddy bear.

His body felt sick, poisoned; he washed it, changed its clothes, combed its hair and took it out into the sunny street. The sun burned his eyes. He went to Joan's house and knocked on the door. Joan came out and told him Patsy was here but she wasn't well and she didn't want to see him. 'Go home, Raff,' she said awkwardly. 'Sort your head out. Don't pester her, she'll see you when she's ready.' He went to a shop round the corner and bought pen and paper and wrote a note saying he was sorry and he hoped she was all right. He got carried away, wrote how miserable he was, how he felt like a prisoner in a cage, wanted to break free from himself, burst out of this trap he was walking about in, burst out of his own head, he couldn't explain, he thought he was going mad. He tore the note up and threw it away, wrote another just saying he was sorry, stuck it through Joan's letter-box and went home.

Next day he called again, but still Patsy wouldn't come to the door. The next day she came out and closed the door behind her and walked on down the path, motioning for him to follow. Her face was pale and bruised, top lip still swollen; looking at her made something inside turn slowly over and over. Afraid to touch her, he walked beside her down the street saying softly, 'Oh, Patsy, forgive me, please forgive me,' but she said nothing until they reached the empty park and sat down on a bench near an avenue of trees.

'Well,' she said, gazing down the avenue, 'here we are.'

He said he was sorry.

'You've said that,' she said. 'You only need say it once. It's whether or not you mean it that counts.'

He talked stumblingly, desperate to say the right things. He said he'd do anything at all to make it up to her, nothing in his life had ever counted for anything but her and the kids, he was going mad there alone, he couldn't live, he'd make it up, he knew his mistakes and he knew what to do about them. She didn't look at him, and he ploughed hopelessly on, his mind racing. 'Say something,' he begged, 'please say something.' She opened her mouth and sighed, then closed it again. She's doing it on purpose, he thought, she's making me pay.

'I've been thinking and thinking,' she said finally, slowly. 'I've never in my life thought so much about anything.' She stopped. A cold breeze whished in the trees. 'I'd never stay with a violent man,' she said. 'Never.' He began to defend himself but she held up her hand. 'I still love you,' she said, looking away, 'I can't help it. I can't just think about you, though; you're good at heart, I know you are, but I have to think about the children. It's not just me and you. You did all that in front of the children and that's unforgivable, God only knows what harm that's done them . . . You're not a good father, Jimmy, it's a terrible thing to say but it's true. I've gone round and round in circles, and it keeps coming back to that . . .'

'Ask Luke,' he said. 'Ask Luke if I'm a good father.'

She looked at him closely for the first time. Her eyes were bloodshot. 'Luke thinks the sun shines out of you,' she said. 'That makes it worse. He cried all night. What do you think that night did to him? What do you think happens to kids who see their mother knocked about? How do they grow up? What do you think I told them about it? What could I say? Your daddy's sick. Oh, Jimmy!' Her eyes clouded over. 'It's so sordid!'

He sat silent, staring at the ground, dropped his head into his hands and struggled with his breathing. 'Oh, God, I'm sorry,' he mumbled, 'I'm sorry.' He couldn't believe that his life had degenerated so quickly. He had absolutely no idea what to do or say.

'You've got to stop drinking,' she said firmly. 'You can't get away with it. Some can, you can't. That's what did it the other night. I hate it, I hate it, you don't know what it's like, you change, you change into someone else and I don't know you any more, I start hating you—'

'I won't drink,' he said desperately, 'I won't touch the stuff. I'll never touch it—'

Patsy started to cry, put her arms round him suddenly and hugged him and made him promise never to drink like that again. 'We'll work it out,' she said. 'We'll work it out somehow, we'll both try really really hard.' They both cried. There was nothing that couldn't be solved, they said. Everything would be all right. But never again, never again. 'I'll leave if we have one more scene

100

like that,' she said. 'One more scene. I mean it, Jimmy, I mean it. I won't let the kids grow up scared. We've got them now and we've got to do the best for them.' He promised. He promised everything and he meant it. She showed him a raw patch on her scalp behind one ear, where he'd wrenched the hair out. He dimly remembered, like a nightmare, but it had the very quality of dream. It frightened him. He kept saying he was sorry, shaking his head in amazement. All of this was mad.

Six uneasy months followed. It maddened him how unhappy she obviously was, how transparently she tried to hide it, how it showed in so many different little ways. He blamed her bitterly as he lay awake at nights: why did she bother to come back, why didn't she just come out with it, say right out I don't care about you any more, I don't want to live with you . . . ? Sometimes they made love but it was worse than nothing, a pain, a pretence. He got drunk a few times but not too badly. An awful desperation began to swell inside him; they never talked about it, and he felt that a great well of loneliness waited to swallow him up. What she was feeling he could only guess.

They nagged and chipped away at each other. There was no happiness.

The day before Luke's fourth birthday Jimmy took the children out to buy a present for each of them: you couldn't get one without the other or there'd be hell to pay. In the shop, Jesse made straight for an enormous red fire engine. He was just two and aggressive, with a determination about what he wanted that was already becoming legendary within the family. The thing cost a fortune. 'You don't want that,' Jimmy said, trying to steer him away. 'Look at this nice milk truck.'

'Mine!' Jesse snarled, clutching the fire engine, which was almost as big as himself, to his body and running awkwardly away with it to the other side of the shop.

'Dad, why's he getting that great big thing?' asked Luke. 'That's not fair. It's my birthday, not his.'

They started to brawl over the toys. Jimmy told them both to shut up or they'd get nothing, but they took no notice of him. They pushed each other about, these two awful dark little brats that looked just like him, so everyone said though he could never see it himself. He was useless at saying no to them. In the end he spent about three times more than he'd intended to, just to keep the peace.

Patsy went mad. 'We can't afford *these*!' she cried. 'What do you think we're going to live on next week? Do you fancy starving, Jimmy, cos that's what you're going to do!' She showed him her purse with nothing in it and told him he had to learn to say no to them, it wasn't fair on her, made her always seem like the ogre, but God knows someone had to do it. 'You'd have them so selfish,' she said. 'Sometimes I wonder what the hell we're making of these kids, I don't want them to grow up fucked up in the head like everybody else.'

'You're asking a lot,' he said. They argued. 'Right,' he said sullenly, 'I'll go out and nick us some food, just wait and see, I don't let my family starve.'

'You do that,' she said, 'and you'll never see us again.'

He went out and put his last pound on a horse. To his amazement, he won sixteen pounds. He had a drink to celebrate, then went home and laid the money down on the table. She stared at it. 'Where did you get that?' she asked.

'I won it on a horse,' he said.

She didn't believe him. She said: 'You've done it, you've done it, oh, you've really done it this time. Did you steal this out of some old lady's purse?'

He grabbed the money and threw it at her, retrieved most of it and went out and got so blind drunk that he could never afterwards remember where he'd been or what he'd done, only that he came home at some point and took her by the throat and hit her across the face, this side and that, again and again with no mercy, that her eyes were shut tight so that he couldn't see her terror, but he could feel it and smell it, my God, my God, my God, my God, he thought, hitting her again and again and again, I'm really doing this, my God, and danced backwards away from her like some mad puppet, shaken by a rage against himself so great and terrifying that he would like to have stepped outside and kicked and smashed and beaten himself senseless. But he couldn't, so he ran out of the house and got on a bus and rode around in a trance, everyone looking at him strangely. When he came home, the flat was empty.

This time was different. This time she wouldn't come out when he called at Joan's, three times, four times, five fruitless visits standing like a lemon on the doorstep and being sent away with his tail between his legs. He got drunk and went round and tried to break the door down, yelling they were *his* kids too and she wasn't going to take them away, yelling insults, filth, hate, threats, yelling for all the street to hear how she couldn't screw, she was useless, she thinks it's for peeing with. They called the police and he was bound over to keep the peace. She wrote him a letter saying she was scared of him and wouldn't see him while he was drinking. He tried to stop drinking but he shook, his nerves raced, his heart kicked, his head felt full and bloated. So he drank again to straighten himself out.

She came to see him two weeks later, alone, and said she wanted to live apart from him for a while till he'd sorted out his drinking. Joan had said she could stay for a while. He could come and see the kids, of course. He hung around Joan's place too much, drunk sometimes, got thrown out a couple of times; he rowed with Patsy so often that they stopped letting him in. He tried to stop drinking so many times it was ridiculous.

Finally Harry Keyes dragged him up to Scotland to see some people that he knew near Inverness. They stayed for a couple of months. Harry's friends lived in a house up a track on a hillside miles from anywhere. They didn't drink. It rained for the first six weeks and it was eight miles to the nearest pub and they had no transport. Jimmy straightened out. Harry's friends were kind, understanding people and put up with him, talked to him, listened to him, kept him well supplied with dope, which he maintained kept him sane.

When the rain stopped, he took a tent and camped out alone on the banks of a small loch for six days. He always woke up just before it was light, scrambled from the tent still in his sleeping bag and watched the sun come up. There was a great serrated mountain, wrinkled and grey, looking in the haze of morning as if someone had shaken blue powder all over it and then blown gently. He felt the turning of the earth as a definite sensation. He decided there that everything was changing, that the upward swing of the wheel was in motion, that he would go home and patch up his marriage and get a job and stop being a fool.

He never trusted his feelings after that. It didn't happen. When he got back, Patsy told him as nicely as she could that she'd started going out with someone. 'Nothing serious,' she said. Truly, things had changed. He reached inside himself for the fighting spirit but it wasn't there. He was shocked. Somehow he'd never really believed it could come to this. A limbo time began. He hung around his old haunts, his old friends, getting drunk and stoned and doing nothing, took the kids out now and then, ate at his mum's and got his washing done there. Then he started turning up drunk to see the kids, until one time she refused to let him in and he smashed a window in Joan's side wall. They called the police, but he'd left before they arrived.

Asking around, he found out that Patsy's new bloke was from Dublin and that he worked on a building site. He only ever saw him once. Joan was away and he went round to her house sober, in the hope of catching Patsy and the kids alone. Before he even reached the house, he saw a yellow car pull up at the kerb and they all got out, Patsy, Luke, Jesse, and this big fair-haired bloke with a beard and moustache. He stood unseen, watching. He didn't hate the guy, nothing as simple as that. He looked at him with great curiosity to see just what it was she was leaving him for. He looked OK, probably a nice enough guy. They went up the garden path and in through the side door. He thought vaguely about smashing up the car later on, but couldn't see the point. It wouldn't make him feel any better. Funny, now that it was too late, how the anger was spent.

He went and had a few drinks then returned to Joan's house and knocked on the door. Patsy answered it. She said the children were in bed now, please don't disturb them, don't upset them, it upsets them to see you drunk. She spoke very gently, holding his arm. 'Why don't you come round tomorrow afternoon and you can take them to the park?'

'I want to see *you*,' he said.

'Mike's here,' she said.

'I know. I saw him. What difference does that make?'

'What is it?' she asked. 'We can talk here.'

'Why?' he said. 'Are you scared I'll have a go at him?'

'Oh, please, Jimmy,' she said wearily, 'I can't stand another scene . . .'

'No scene. I just want to talk to you. Five minutes.'

She went back into the house and he heard her voice, then she came out and closed the door behind her. 'We'll talk just here,' she said.

Of course he knew they were being watched from the

window. He really didn't know what he was going to say until he said it. 'OK,' he said. 'One last try. Look at me. I'm not sober but I'm not drunk. I'm OK. Why don't you come back with me and see how it goes? Don't you think this has gone far enough? He's new, you don't know him like you know me. It's got to be worth one more try. You can't deny—'

'No,' she said. 'No. There's no point in talking. The answer's no.'

For twenty minutes he tried to persuade her. 'You're not being fair on the kids,' he said. 'Anyway, you can't just do this. I must have some rights over them. How come it's always you decided when I can see them? Who gave you the right? How d'you think you got them? You didn't do it all on your own, for Christ's sake—'

'No,' she said. 'No. Tomorrow afternoon. Not now. I can't talk now. I have to go in.'

He said he was going to wait for her on the front. She was to get the kids and bring them now – 'They're *asleep*, Jimmy –' and we'll go home. It's as simple as that. He tried to make a joke of it. He laughed hopefully. 'You *know* it makes sense,' he said, the punchline of an advert on the TV.

'You're drunk,' she said. 'You're just getting better at not showing it,' and went inside and closed the door. A blankness fell on him. He went and sat on the wall at the front, rolled a cigarette and smoked it. The street was peaceful, leaves nodded in front of the street-lamps. He didn't know why he was sitting here. Not a very flash car, he thought. Well, that's something. He sat for an hour until she came out and told him gently, please to go, there wasn't any point in him waiting out here like this. He ignored her and she went away. He felt immobilised, drained, neutral, saw no point much in moving. He wondered if Mike would come out and get heavy, saw in his mind stupid scenes, fights, words, all acted out by performing monkeys going through the motions. He saw a light go on upstairs in the house, and then the lights downstairs went off. After a while the lights upstairs went off too. He rolled another cigarette. He had no idea of the time. It was a beautiful evening. A long time passed and the moon was bright and dramatic with clouds boiling around it. Eventually she came out and stood in front of him with her hands in the pockets of her dressing gown. He remembered the dressing gown. He turned his head to look at her, very tired.

'Jimmy,' she said kindly, 'this isn't going to be any use.' He noticed that her face had changed, it was leaner around the jaw.

'I know,' he said. He stood up and walked away, knowing that the stupid game was over and he'd lost.

A few weeks before Christmas he acquired a bent cheque book and card from someone he met one night in a pub, a friend of a friend. He went on a shopping spree, asked his friends what they wanted and got it for them, kitted himself out with new clothes. He bought Christmas presents for Patsy and the kids and went to Joan's on Christmas Eve but she wouldn't let him in the house. He said he wanted to say Happy Christmas to the kids. Patsy came out and told him they were asleep, he could leave the presents with her and she'd give them to them in the morning.

'You bitch,' he said. 'It's Christmas, how can you be such a bitch?'

'Mike's here,' she said.

Jimmy laughed. 'Oh, deary me,' he said, 'did I disturb something?'

'Please don't make a scene,' she said tensely.

'There's something I've been meaning to ask you,' he said.

'You've been drinking.'

'So,' he said, 'do you enjoy it with him? Yeah? Good at it, is he?'

'Oh, Jimmy, please.' She sagged against the door-frame. 'What do you want? What do you want! You think I'd tell you anything like that?'

'Oh,' he said, 'so you *don't* enjoy it with him, then? So you're so useless you can't enjoy it with anyone?' He laughed, mean and nasty, and she started to cry. He put the presents down on the ground and walked away. He hoped she'd feel terrible when she opened them. He hoped they'd ruin her Christmas.

He was sitting in Harry's place a couple of weeks later when the police busted in and searched everyone for dope, found the cheque book and card and took him in. The magistrate had not lied. He went to prison and did four months. It wasn't as bad as Borstal and he got on well with his cell mate, a boy just old enough for prison, in for stealing a packet of biscuits and some cheese. He became two people: this clown who died sometimes and became a weak and miserable wretch who in turn died and resurrected in the clown. The clown saved him. People liked the clown.

Patsy brought the children to visit him once. Confinement made him sentimental: when he saw them he felt he wanted to open his wings and bring them all under, his wife and his sons. His eyes filled with tears. He hadn't cared so much in a long time. There was a sheet of glass and a metal grille between them, it was like sitting in a post office. 'How are you, love?' she said. 'It's not long to go now.' They talked awkwardly for a while and the kids kept climbing about, touching the glass, calling through to him. He felt like a monkey in a cage. He asked Patsy if she still saw Mike.

'Yes,' she said. 'Well, actually, I'm living with him.'

'Then what are you doing here?' he said harshly. 'What are you trying to do to me?' and couldn't speak and put his head down, blinking hard. Patsy didn't speak. He was aware of the children watching, taking it all in. Oh, the poor little bastards, he thought, oh my God, the poor little bastards. He controlled his face and looked up, eyes very red. 'I've blown it, haven't I?' he said with a humourless laugh. 'I've blown it,' then trusted himself to speak no further.

Then they sat saying nothing, looking in tired bewilderment into one another's eyes. 'Oh, Pat!' he said sadly. There was a strange look in his eyes, humour and disbelief and the certainty of grief. He had a feeling he'd never see any of them again and was determined to imprint himself on her memory, like this, an eternal pain in the pit of her.

When it was time to go she said: 'Say goodbye to your daddy. Go on.' Her eyes were huge, transfixed, afraid even to blink. ''Bye, Dad,' Luke said and put his face to the glass to be kissed. Then Jesse. They waved as they left. Jimmy smiled and waved back, that ridiculous baby bye-bye wave you did for little kids, and watched them go, not Patsy, he wouldn't look at her any more.

This happened often. Someone's wife or girlfriend would visit and instead of cheering up, the guy would crack up very quietly. Jimmy lay on his bunk later and turned his face to the wall, dry-eyed but heavy with it all. She'd left him some tobacco. He rolled a cigarette and tried to smoke it, but a frightening lump rose up in his throat like a growth. Some time during the night that followed his cell mate came and held him while he cried, till it was over and they lay in total silence, kissing and rocking and gently embracing.

He told himself he could patch up his life. He was off the booze. It was the only possibility for the future: inconceivable that he should lose the past seven years like coins lost in a slot machine. He'd shake the machine.

When they freed him, Patsy and the children were gone without a trace. There was no message. Joan swore, everyone swore, that she'd left without a word to a soul. He didn't believe them. Someone must know something. But no one ever talked. 'She's telling you she doesn't want to be followed,' Joan told him as gently as she could. 'She knew you'd follow. This is the only way she can do it. I swear on my soul, on my mother's grave, she just left, she didn't say goodbye to anyone. Anyway, I hadn't seen her for weeks.'

He still didn't believe her. Bitch. 'She always wanted to go to Ireland,' he said. He imagined himself going over there and searching, but gave up the idea at once. It was over. They might as well be dead. It didn't seem possible that people could vanish so completely, but then perhaps it wasn't so strange. She had no family but Jimmy and the kids, no ties but those of friendship, most of which she'd broken anyway for him. She'd slept like a papoose against his back for years and never would again. His children, dead. It was inconceivable.

He went to stay at his mum's. She was living alone now in a council flat not far from the centre of town. He hung around Manchester for a while, got some boring job, went out with his friends, drank a little but not too much, stayed out of trouble. Somewhere at the back of his mind was the idea that he had to be there and stay straight in case they returned. Johnny turned up and tried to drag him into a fight outside a pub but he had no heart for confrontation, no heart for the pump of adrenalin, no heart for youth and folly. He went home and heard later that Johnny was in Strangeways.

Oh, God, he thought, where is my life going?

He went down to London to stay at Dave's place in Hammersmith, leaving an address with anyone who might possibly see her. She'd have to get in touch one day, he figured, even if it was only to ask him for a divorce. He tore up his photographs of Patsy breastfeeding, left some more of them all over the years in an envelope stuffed away at the back of his mum's sideboard. He kept one of Luke that he carried with him always in a very ancient wallet, for good luck. Sometimes, mildly drunk, he'd take it out and cry sentimentally over it. He had affairs with women and men but none of them came to anything. He was OK – still funny, still friendly. For a year he moved between London and Manchester, then he moved into Kinnaird Buildings and a new era began.

So they were all washed up together on this shore, Kinnaird Buildings.

Joe and Raff's place overlooked the yard where the boys played football. A nosy, friendly old lady lived next door and monitored all their comings and goings and those of their friends. She had a loud Cockney voice full of gossip and would catch you and keep you talking on the landing for ages.

Raff was a major distraction to have moving in on a person, insincerely looking for a job, drawing people like a magnet: the place was nearly always full, people would get stoned there and talk for hours. Joe was still cleaning cars; whenever he came in from work at least three or four people would be arguing about the class system or the closing down of the factories, or listening to music, or lighting paper bags and trying to float them to the ceiling. Judy was there a lot, Billy and Eric and the rest, and when everyone else had gone there was still Sharon, and Mandy who was seven now, very bashful, always hiding behind chairs.

Raff hung about on the edge of this unwilling part-time family, cooking, babysitting, sitting up all night talking. Sharon told him it served him right about Patsy and the kids. She told him men like him were wankers. Her old man had all these horrible sick books about torture and stuff and kept saying he saw demons in the carpet. He was barmy. She still had nightmares. He used to push her, trip her up, knock her legs from under her, pinch and prod and poke, twist the hairs at the nape of her neck, creep up behind her and yank her head back sharply and slap something revolting into her mouth, the scrapings of the sink, a ball of snotty tissue, a lump of slimy soap. Jesus Christ, said Raff. Somehow they became friends.

Joe and Raff both nagged Sharon, separately and together, but she just laughed at them or ignored them. They nagged her about food. 'You've got to stop living on oven chips and blancmange,' Raff would say, ladling rice, stew, spaghetti, tomato slop. '*Good food*. You like it, don't you, Mandy?'

'Yes, Raff.'

'Beefburgers!' Joe would say. 'Ah, that shit! Clogs the arteries.'

She'd laugh at them and tell them they were a couple of old grannies.

And they nagged her about smack, but she shrugged. When they nagged her too much she drifted back to her own flat for a while, drifting back a few days later. She was always telling them they had no idea of reality. Bit by bit, Joe's things gravitated into her place until in the end he himself was living there, and Raff had a place of his own. He wondered then if he'd been much in the way. He was not good at living alone, it became an open house for people passing through. Usually two or three were living there, and they all seemed to have names with qualifying adjectives: Australian Phil, Rasta John, Scouse Tony, Little Barry, Junkie Jean, Irish Cathy, Speedfreak Fred, Mad Pete. He'd developed an air of one who has suffered much but come bravely through, older and wiser than you no matter who you were. He had no secrets, would tell his tale to anyone who'd listen. He'd seen it all. No one pulled the wool over his eyes, not now. He was Jack-of-all-trades, the rake, the romantic outcast, a man wronged, one who'd loved not wisely but too well, the clown who cried in the alley, the fool in the deck, condemned to wander lost upon the earth. He enjoyed his image. He was completely transparent. Everyone liked him because he was such good fun to have around and sometimes it was a joy to hear him talk.

He did errands for the old lady next door. 'Here he is, my nice young man,' she'd say, take his arm and pull him into her hallway and whisper to him what all his friends had been getting up to and who'd been into the flat while he was out.

'It's all right, Betty,' he'd say, 'they're friends of mine. He looks a bit funny but he's sound,' then he'd go and tell them what she'd said and they'd all have a laugh.

And there were times between when he'd live alone and wander about looking for people to talk to. He liked the company of women and sought it out. He listened to Loretta's blues records and talked her head off, and went drinking with Judy. She was a good crack, he thought, you could have a laugh with her. She was absolutely vain, not that she was always looking in mirrors, it was more that she just knew she looked good enough not to have to bother. She was composed and distant and gave him close attention when he talked, and she was always telling him how much she liked living alone and how she was never going to carry anyone ever again. 'You're right!' he'd say cheerfully. 'I've had it all and it knocks you sideways.' Judy thought Raff was exactly the kind of man you didn't get involved with, not if you had any sense at all. She knew him as a type and it was a type she'd had enough of. And anyway, he'd beaten his wife. They always did it again. Didn't matter how nice they were, they always did it again. He may be all the kids' favourite uncle but he'd do it again.

One night Loretta and Billy left Littlejohn's and saw, parked below in the courtyard, a police car. It was quiet. Two policemen were walking up a staircase in the block opposite. Loretta and Billy didn't see until they reached

114

the third-floor landing how one of the walls over there was covered in blood, a great startling red splash against the cream-coloured paintwork as if someone had taken a bucket of it and thrown it up against the wall. It slapped Loretta in the eyes before she jerked her head away. 'Oh, Jesus,' she said, 'oh, Jesus.'

'Don't look,' said Billy.

'Oh, Jesus,' she kept saying. She felt as if the air around her had darkened and thickened and swooped in on her.

'Just don't look,' Billy said quietly and took her arm. They walked on down, out into the courtyard, silently skirted the open area where the car purred, slipped round the corner and on into the darkness between the buildings, towards home. 'Jesus Christ, Billy!' she said, horrified. 'What was it? Someone must've died to make all that blood, surely?'

Billy shook his head and sighed like an old man who'd seen too much of the world. 'God knows,' he said sadly, 'I don't want to know. Don't you think about it, just don't think about it.'

But Loretta couldn't think of anything else. Every doorway gaped light in their path and they passed in and out of the glow. She thought of herself bleeding, losing all that blood, where would it have come from? Which part of the body? 'I never heard anything,' she said.

'No,' he said, 'the music was on.'

'Someone must've died,' she said again. 'To make all that blood.'

'Don't think about it,' he said again. They reached their staircase. Judy's hall light was on. Loretta tapped on her door lightly before going into her own flat, but there was no answer. Sometimes you knew she was in but she didn't answer the door. Loretta wanted to talk to someone and Billy was never a talker; she felt jumpy, put the kettle on for coffee and started getting out her records to cover the silence, which now seemed to her unnatural

115

and menacing, chattering all the while to Billy who sat pulling his shoes off and rumpling his hair with his fingers. He said he was tired and didn't want any coffee, it'd keep him up all night, and soon he went to bed and left her alone. She turned the music down very low, sat back in her chair and worried. Life was a horror. Terrible things happened in it. Terrible things were being done to people, by people. That staircase, that was a terrible staircase, you heard screams from there, you saw smashed glass on its landings. Children lived there. She started to cry quietly. Sometimes it seemed to her that all these things were part of some deliberate plan to make her sad. I'm glad I never had one, she thought. Imagine bringing one up here. What's the matter with me? What's the matter with me? I shouldn't dissolve like this. She dried her eyes.

Some time after one o'clock she heard footsteps on the stairs. They stopped on the landing and someone knocked at Judy's door. Loretta jumped up, ran to the spy-hole and looked out; she saw Jimmy Raffo hanging around on the landing. He knocked again, louder, leaned against the wall and put his head back and studied the ceiling with a faint smile. She liked Jimmy. She thought Judy was a fool not to snap him up. He was often next door and Judy always laughed a lot when he was there. There was a natural ease between the two of them and Loretta couldn't understand why they didn't just stop circling around each other and get on with it.

She opened the door and he pulled himself up straight and smiled. 'Hello, lovely!' he said. 'I can't get an answer. Her light's on.'

'She doesn't answer sometimes,' Loretta said.

'I can't sleep,' he said, 'and everyone's gone to bed. It's too hot—'

'Were you at Littlejohn's? Did you see all that blood?' she blurted.

'Blood?' He frowned. 'Where? I never saw any blood.'

'On the wall,' she said. 'Oh, it was horrible!' She pulled the door wide and he came in and sat by the open window rolling a spliff while she told him about the blood and the evil staircase and how terrible it was, the things people did to one another. She talked nervously for ages and he couldn't get a word in. He looked down into the empty yard, lips apart, lids heavy. 'People are complicated . . .' he said.

'. . . I *hate* this place. I *hate* it. I want to get out. They won't give us a transfer. We tried again and nothing happened . . .'

'People are just people,' he said. 'It don't make no difference where you go. People aren't any better in some other place, not really, they've just got it easier.'

'I don't give a fuck about reasons,' she said vehemently, tears coming into her eyes. 'None of it makes it any better living here. Do you know how long I've lived here? Nearly seven years . . .'

'Lovely, there's people been here all their lives,' he said. Then he said, 'Ah, come on. You're getting yourself all upset. Let's go down the pie stall. Pointless sitting around here brooding.'

'At this time of night? It's too dangerous,' she said petulantly. 'It's one of those nights, it's got a dangerous feel to it, I don't like it. It's too . . . quiet.'

'Life's dangerous,' said Jimmy. 'We can't escape it, lovely.' He stood up, assuming a hulking stance and a booming tone: 'I'll protect you cos I'm big and strong,' he said and laughed and struck a match. 'Come on, I'm hungry. Honest, I go down there lots of nights. It's all right. All the muggers and maniacs are tucked up in their little beds by now. Come on, I'll treat you. Cup of tea and a gastroenteritis pie.'

Loretta shrugged, put on a thick jumper and her shoes, and they walked out into a very light, very soft night, full of unusual peace. They walked up to the junction where the lights winked on and off obediently for an

117

empty crossing, saw cats, but no people till they reached the pie stall under the railway bridge, where two ragged men and a ragged woman sat drinking against the wall. Jimmy bought two teas and two pies. As they ate he pulled out a very old wallet, took out a photograph and showed it to Loretta, saying that was his little boy. One of them, anyway. She saw a very dark-haired little boy of four or five, who looked just like Jimmy and smiled mysteriously sideways at the camera.

'Oh, he's lovely!' she said.

'Good little kid,' said Jimmy, putting away the picture quickly. 'I don't look at it very often. Still makes me feel funny.' He gulped his tea noisily, getting his upper lip wet. 'They'll come and find me when they're old enough,' he said. 'They won't forget me. It's a terrible thing to take someone's kids away. I mean, it's not just me, it's my mum and dad too, it's their grandchildren. She shouldn't have done that.'

Loretta suddenly wanted to cry again. Oh, don't, don't, she thought. She couldn't imagine losing a child after so many years, losing two – it was bad enough after five months and never seeing its face.

'How's your pie?' he asked. 'Mine's terrible. Look at this bit here, looks like a bit of windpipe or something.' He pulled something pale and revolting from the pie and flicked it away. They wandered back towards the Buildings. 'Are you getting tired?' he asked.

'No,' she said.

'Come up to my place. I'll never sleep tonight. I'll make you some *real* tea to take the taste of this crap away.' So they went up to the flat where he was living alone at this time, and talked until four o'clock. It was sparsely furnished, lonely, the walls lavishly drawn and painted upon, crowds of people, animals, buildings. He asked her what she thought his chances were with Judy and said he was trying to be very careful and time it all just right. She said she didn't know, Judy plays her cards

118

very close to her chest. 'Don't I know it,' he said. 'And a lovely chest it is too.'

'Judy, now,' Loretta said, 'she never seems to – what do I mean ? – nothing seems to get to her, if you know what I mean – very controlled, kind of – she never seems to – *feel* anything . . .'

'Oh, she does. She does. Still waters and all that. Sometimes the stiller they are the deeper they run.' He smiled. 'I keep dipping my stick in and still can't reach the bottom.' He grinned at Loretta. 'I try a longer and longer stick each time,' he said mischievously, 'but it makes no difference.' She giggled. 'Stop it, this is getting vulgar,' he said and laughed. 'You've got a dirty mind, you have.'

'Let me tell you a story,' he said. He told her about a time in prison when he was being goaded in the sewing room by a particularly hateful screw who'd taken a virulent dislike to him. They had a radio in there. All the other screws let them listen to it apart from this one, this big fat pink-faced screw with a little moustache, who always kept it at the front and turned it down so low that no one but himself could hear it. Jimmy was near the front, close enough so that the screw didn't even have to raise his voice. He kept on and on hour after hour in a low, caressing, insulting tone, savouring the words as if they were solid. Fool, bastard, wop, cretin. Jimmy was holding a pair of scissors. His hand trembled with rage. 'You do, wop,' the screw said, smiling. 'You do, wop. Try. I'd just love to see you try. You haven't got the guts, you stinking pile of shit.' Then he turned his back.

'I wanted to,' Jimmy said, 'I was shaking. I really wanted to, and he wanted me to, he was all ready. I mean, if I hadda gone for him, that would've been it – kaput! – me finished, really. And then this hand comes on my hand that's holding the scissors and it's this guy, this other prisoner, and he says: "Put them down, son, he's not worth it. Look at him, he says, the fat bastard, you wanna throw your life away for *that*? One move now and he's got you right where he wants you. You won't win, son. It's your life. You put them down." And he forces my hand down, and it's trembling, makes me put them down. And this screw heard every word he said and he just give him a filthy look but he says nothing. See, there was this feeling about him, this guy. No one messed with him. You just didn't mess with him, you know?'

He shook his head at the memory. Blue smoke curled at the side of his head. 'So what happens? Years later I read about him in the newspapers. Killed three innocent people and they shot him dead.'

'Jesus!' Loretta exclaimed.

'Yeah. It was all over the papers, you must've read about it. He breaks into this house and just kills everyone . . . unbelievable . . . really horrible . . . I think about that guy sometimes. He was good to me. Just goes to show. What, I don't know.' He laughed, twitching his eyebrows. 'Nowt so strange as folk, eh! But it's what I'm saying to you before, lovely. People are complicated.' He got up and went over to the window and closed it against the chill of early morning. 'I dunno,' he said. 'Look at me. I've done a lot of wrong things. I've been a right fool. I've been a complete bastard and an imbecile. I s'pose you could make a good case against me.' When he looked round at Loretta, his eyes looked sore and amused and very tired.

'You're OK, Jimmy,' she said, 'I'll not make a case against you.'

'You're a good friend, Loretta,' he said, smiling, 'I like talking to you.'

September came. Raff met Judy in front of the Buildings one day and said: 'Let's go to the National Gallery. Let's walk.'

She hesitated just for a moment then smiled. 'I haven't been in the old National Gallery in years,' she said.

'Hang on,' he said, 'just got to take this up for my old dear,' holding up a brown paper bag with a bottle of medicine sticking out of the top. She went up with him and waited on the landing while he knocked on the old lady's door and gave her the medicine, then nipped into his flat to get some money.

The old lady came out and gave Judy a good looking-over. 'Isn't he a nice boy?' she said. 'Ever such a nice boy. He's ever so good to me, he is. I've got five children and eight grandchildren and fifteen nieces and nephews, and they never come near me.' Raff came out wearing a bright red scarf around his neck, eating a blood-red apple and holding another which he tossed lightly to Judy. She dropped it. She always dropped things.

'She speaks very highly of you,' she said to him as they went down the stairs. 'What a nice boy you are!'

'Oh, I'm dead good with the old dears,' he said, smiling complacently.

They fell into step at the foot of the stairs and walked slowly in the direction of the river, to the South Bank and Hungerford railway bridge, where a train crossed the Thames with them, shaking the boards beneath their feet, through Charing Cross to Trafalgar Square. The gallery was almost empty. Raff was familiar with the place and conducted her about as if he owned it. His favourite picture was the one by Piero di Cosimo, the dead girl and the faun and the dog. He got very excited by the pictures and leaned towards them as if he was going to touch them or rub his nose against them. The men kept telling him to stand back.

They walked about for an hour or two, got hungry and went down Charing Cross Road for something to eat, then wandered back in the direction of home and at some point found themselves in a pub that played deafeningly loud Top Twenty music and was full of people who looked like gangsters. They got tipsy. An old tramp woman came in and sat down at their table and started to cry. Raff bought her a bottle of Newcastle Brown. She talked to Judy while he was at the bar, about the people who were following her, following her everywhere. She was well spoken, had a very high-bridged nose like a Red Indian and held her head haughtily. When Raff returned she turned her back on Judy and gave him all her attention. She said her son was a trapeze artist in a circus. Raff and the old woman talked for half an hour. He kept turning to smile at Judy, guilty because she was being left out, but unable to ignore the woman.

'Who is this?' the woman asked rudely, suddenly. 'This wife or girlfriend or whatever she is?'

'My very good friend,' he said. 'My very good friend, Judy. Don't you be rude now.'

'Ach,' said the woman, 'she'll be no good to you.'

'Oh, jealous, jealous,' he laughed, turning to Judy and smiling at her very warmly. He really liked her. It was this air of uncertainty lurking just below the surface, even though she sat and moved so casually, didn't fiddle or jiggle or poke at herself. And she was soft to him, he'd seen that straight away.

It grew late. He bought another Newcastle Brown for the old woman, and they left and walked back over the bridge towards the Buildings. Something is happening, she thought, and I can't stop it. Something will happen tonight. She felt panicked and exhilarated and totally fatalistic. When they reached home he came up to her flat and went into the kitchen and made coffee. He had this knack of making himself at home in anybody's flat, so that somehow he always knew just where everything went in anybody's kitchen, right down to the idiosyncracies of their cookers and heaters and so on. Judy sat on her knees on the rug in front of the fire, dreamy and drunkish, wondering what form his approach would take and what her reaction would be. She had no idea. She

122

didn't want him. But then he was so nice. Long, thread-like alternatives bloomed in her mind all in the space of a few seconds. She saw whole stories, beginnings, endings. She saw the terrible ties, acute, binding – scenes – jealousies, demands, violence, tears, recrimination, trouble – and happiness, simpler and less eventful, like a fairy tale that was sweet but not really believable. Not with someone like him. The end of this glorious loneliness. Knives to stab each other with.

He came back in from the kitchen with two cups of coffee. 'Milk's curdled,' he said. 'Yours is all right. Mine looks like the Antarctic, great crags and icebergs floating in it.'

Anyway, she thought, it's fate. Whatever happens or doesn't happen, it was all decided long ago. It makes no difference what I do. She withdrew and watched herself participating in this scene. What will she do? Wait and see. He sat and drank his coffee and talked about the schools he'd been to and his old mates and his mam. 'She's great, my mam,' he said, 'you'd really like my mam.' He never wants to hear about me, she thought, it's me, me, me all the time with him. She sat and smiled and listened to him, and there was so much that she sensed in him that made her soft, opening like a wound that hadn't quite healed, not yet. She sensed a great seething of dependency longing for an object. It was awesome and desperate and he'd pour it all over her like blood. Oh, I can't, I can't, she thought, a sudden sharp ache in her breast, please not again, not this, not him. It would be like refusing something that tasted delicious because you knew that in the end it would make you sick.

'Fancy you being a teacher,' he said. 'I never had a teacher like you. Maybe I'd 've liked school a bit better if I'd had a teacher like you. I know you don't think much of Johnny, but it was Johnny and one or two others that made it bearable for me.' Then he talked about his teachers, what a load of shit they were, wimps or sadists,

123

stupid gestures they had and how they always had these really irritating habits and made funny noises, a right bunch of crackpots, and there they are lording it over you, the stupid bastards. 'The one that used to get me by the short hairs, I hated that bastard, if I met him now I'd like to give him a right kicking for all the poor kids he's made life hell for. Every time I pass a schoolyard I shudder. I think, poor little bastards! I want to open the gate and break them all out and take them all away somewhere like the Pied Piper.' He mashed great cheesy lumps on the top of his coffee against the side of his cup. 'Why did you become a teacher?' he asked.

'I rolled there on a conveyor belt,' she said. 'I was good at French. I'm a good teacher, though. Was. Not like yours. I know all about them. My dad was a teacher and he was awful, but that's why I'm so good. One thing parents are good for – teaching you how not to be.'

'Will you do it again?'

'Oh, probably some time,' she said, 'but never for ever.'

He started to question her closely about her childhood and her parents, leaning towards her to listen as if absorbed. Judy couldn't tell him much. It was just a cold, unwelcome mishmash of impressions, moving sluggishly when she kicked it. She'd been an only child with strict, undemonstrative parents who'd always taught her to be independent and stand on her own two feet. Her father went out in the mornings in a dark shiny suit and came home in the evenings and ate and then watched TV or sat in the unused parlour with the stuffy smell, marking papers and exercise books. Geography. He was a teacher of the old school, tired, worn, sarcastic, probably incredibly boring – the sort who sat in front of a blackboard in a black gown, chalk-dust fingers, squeaky shoes, a stale syllabus. She could never quite understand her association with him, he thin and pale and pinched, she with her heavy features and good health. Her mother was large and sour and did nothing at all but housework, and complained all the time about her lot. Judy always knew that this was not her place. She grew up biding her time until she could escape. Sensibly. Life existed only outside the house and within her own room. There were three worlds. Outside, where she had friends and did well at school and went out to clubs full of loud music and nervous kids all trying desperately to get off with each other and feeling terrible if they didn't and pretending not to care. Home, the house, where friends were not encouraged and nothing ever happened to disturb the even keel. And her room, where often she went after tea and wrote terrible poetry in exercise books that she hid under the bed, and cried and dreamed of lovers.

She didn't tell him everything. Looking up, she saw that he was still watching her closely, a smile on his face. 'Go on,' he said, but she shook her head. 'I'm not in the mood,' she said.

'I can't imagine you,' Raff said. 'You know, I find that really touching, thinking of you there. It sounds so lonely when you compare it to how mine was, there was always people in our house, I can't imagine it any other way . . . Have you got any pictures of yourself as a little girl?'

She laughed. 'No,' she said. 'Not here, anyway. I hate looking at old pictures of myself.'

'I don't,' he said, 'I could look at old photos all day long, even ones of people I don't know. Sometimes you get good ones in antique shops, you know, you always wonder where they've all gone to and how they must've felt and everything when they were alive . . .'

'Other people,' said Judy. 'Oh, other people I can look at, it's just pictures of myself . . .'

'. . . and it kind of puts you in your place . . .' He took out a little container and looked down and messed with his eyes, and she realised after a surprised second that he was taking out his contact lenses. 'I tore up some nice ones of Patsy,' he said, standing up. 'Stupid thing to do.

125

But you know what it's like when you're feeling mad.' He took his clothes off, still talking. She watched in fascination, taken absolutely by surprise. His body was beautiful, slim and lithe and dark and arousing; she saw how comfortable he was with his nakedness, how he loved his own body and wore it much more gracefully than he wore his clothes. He didn't look at her, walked across the room and turned back the covers on her bed and got in, nestled his head back on her clean white pillow and stretched out his left arm towards her, open-handed.

There was a long pause. 'No, Raff,' she said softly. Oh, she thought. So that's the way of it. Shame. He said nothing and did not withdraw his arm. His eyes were grave and steady.

'Why not?' he asked.

She sighed and looked away from him. Why not? Why not? Because . . .

'Because I can't take you on,' she said.

'Can't take me on?' he said quietly. 'What does that mean?'

'I can't take you on. It – it means going all the way—'

'Says who?' His eyes covered over defensively and he withdrew his arm, bending it back behind his head.

'I can't,' she said. 'I can't get involved with anyone, it isn't just you. I don't want to.'

'What kind of idea is this you've got?' he said. 'It sounds barmy to me. Since when was there a choice?'

'Since I decided there was one.'

'What are you scared of?' he asked, with something cocky in his voice that angered her.

'You would say something clever like that,' she said testily. 'Why do people always find something clever to say? What's wrong with wanting to be on your own? You'd think it was some sort of perversion! For God's sake, Raff, you'd argue about anything. I'm saying no, nicely, and you want a three-hour discussion about it!'

126

'No, I don't,' he said, still cocky. 'What are you getting upset about?'

She made a sound of exasperation and went out to the kitchen and messed about in there for a while, excited and confused, sad and scared all at the same time. What is he? she thought. A drunken wife-beating waster. My very good friend. She gave him time to get up and dressed, then went back in. He still lay in bed, staring bright-eyed at the ceiling with his hands behind his head. His arms were strong and knotted with veins, shoulders narrow. She picked up an emery board, sat down and started brushing away at one of her nails, face non-committal. 'Really, Raff,' she said, 'I think you ought to go now.'

He sighed and stretched his arms and flexed his shoulders, turning his face towards her, but she wouldn't meet his eyes. 'It'll be OK, Jude,' he said seriously. 'We don't have to do anything if you don't want to. We could just sleep together. Like friends.'

She laughed a little but with no malice. 'Like friends, indeed! Oh, Raff! I couldn't do that. Maybe you could but I couldn't.'

'Well, then —'

'I'm too fond of you for that,' she said bluntly, 'I am very, very fond of you. I'm so fond of you that I won't sleep with you. If you can't understand that, I'm sorry.' She turned away. A long silence followed.

'Fond of me,' he said in a flat, faintly disparaging tone. Then, after another silence: 'No. Silly me. I *don't* understand. Thick, that's me.' And after another silence: 'And I thought I was being so good,' he said softly, 'holding back all this time.' Six months. They'd been counting. 'You're probably right. It probably is a daft idea, you and me. You're not daft. But I'll tell you one thing.' He paused but she didn't respond. 'You're involved. You can't help it. All this – sex and screwing and everything –

127

makes no difference. That's just a part of it. You're involved anyway. So you might as well come to bed.'

'No,' she said.

Nothing was said for a long time.

'You're not planning on staying there, are you?' she asked.

'Yeah,' he said, 'I'm waiting for you.'

'When will you take no for an answer?' she cried, jumping to her feet. 'I can't stand this kind of thing! No! I said no! I don't play silly games.' He turned his face away from her with an irritated frown as if she was merely being silly, closed his eyes and settled himself more comfortably against the pillow. 'Well, you'll wait a fucking long time,' she said and threw herself back into the chair in front of the fire. Good God, never again, never ever again, it'd be like having a stupid child tagging around after you all the time. 'What a baby,' she said furiously. 'What a big baby.'

Raff jumped up, startling her, got his clothes on and walked out of the flat without saying a word. Judy started to cry and hated him for making her feel like that. She locked the door after him and turned off the fire and the lights, undressed and got into bed and found it warm and full of his presence, curled up in it and tried to go to sleep. Oh, poor Raff! she thought. Poor Raff! I bet he's feeling awful. She hated feeling sorry for people.

It was an incident that neither of them mentioned again, and everything went on as before.

Loretta was sick to death of worrying about money. It was up and down, up and down, depending on the work, and Billy had just got laid off one job and didn't seem too mad about rushing out for another one straight away. He said he'd been working for years and years and years and it was time he had a rest. We'll manage, he said, and he talked about how nice it would be one day to run a little café or something, became quite voluble about it for him. He was sick of building sites and factories. Of course, you knew it would never happen. 'It's all right for you,' she said, 'you're not the one that sorts out the bills and all that.'

'But you're so good at all that, Loretta,' he said. There were times when Billy was immovable. He wouldn't even argue, he'd just let everything wash up against him and roll off like waves around a rock.

Loretta got a couple of hours cleaning here and there to tide them over with the dole. She looked for something more. She got the rent arrears down to twenty-eight pounds and the electric down to fourteen. Billy didn't think they were doing too badly because he didn't know that Loretta took things out of shops; he had no idea of the value of most things and didn't really notice that they had more than they should. She was bolder now. She took, at various times, blankets, sheets, cups and plates and saucepans, a pair of bathroom scales, groceries, cosmetics, a hat, an embossed mirror, a skirt she never wore. It still gave her a thrill. She was scared of getting caught, always intensely so at the actual moment of theft and again when leaving the store, but it was something she now felt she had to do. Each time was a little point scored, against something she couldn't define.

Out of the blue one morning an unseasonal electricity bill came dropping through the letter box. £89.60. She just stared at it blankly at first, thinking it was some mistake, but no, their name was on it – then she saw that it was dated two years back and that it was from their old flat. She was sure they'd paid it off. A great anger began to grow in her and she wanted to rip it up and stamp on it, it was just one more aggravation she could've done without. She grabbed her coat and umbrella and went out through the Buildings. The walls were growing in graffiti and swastikas. This place, this place, she thought,

129

it's enough to do you in. You heard things. Sometimes at the weekends there were gang fights in the spaces between the buildings, a rape you'd heard about, weapons on the roof, a suicide. You just walked through it, walked through it.

She went down to the Electricity Board, through an awful nagging of wind and rain and biting cold, but they insisted that the bill was correct and that she had to pay it. She argued. She couldn't believe it. It was all so long ago and she was sure they'd settled up before they left that flat. In the end they said they'd add it on to what was already outstanding and she could pay it off at an extra pound a week. She left and walked towards the Elephant and Castle distractedly. Her umbrella blew inside out and two of the spokes broke. She dumped it in a wastepaper bin, ran and got soaked. In the precinct she wondered whether to buy a birthday card for her mum or some apples and custard for after tea. She bought apples and custard. Sod the fucking calories. Then she thought she'd go and see Rita and Keith, took a bus up to Clapham Common where they were living now in a small room in a bed and breakfast place, waiting for a flat.

Keith got angry when she told them about the bill and started ranting. He said he never worried about money any more, he'd decided it was all just too ridiculous, he just presumed at all times that he owed somebody somewhere something even if he never moved out of his room. You pay for being there, he said, for breathing, it's like tax, you just seem to run these things up as you go along without knowing you're doing it, it's like stamps, I've never understood about stamps, I got pulled once for not having stamps, I said . . . At the same time, Rita talked. Their voices cruised along together side by side like bicycles along a country lane. Rita said the terrible weather was because of all the nuclear testing and all the radiation leaks they didn't tell you about, and the polar

130

ice caps were melting and when it came it would be sudden, very sudden. She sat at the table laying out cards. She talked of financial collapse and social chaos and overpopulation and this rogue cancer that was much worse than ordinary cancer, which they had in some laboratory somewhere, and if it ever got out it would wipe out three quarters of the world's population in . . .

Loretta lost her temper. 'Oh, shut up!' she snapped. 'I'm sick of all you prophets of doom! What's it to be? Nuclear war? The Ice Age? Pollution? Or everything all at once? Make your fucking mind up!'

'But, Loretta,' said Rita reasonably, 'I see no sense in closing your eyes to these things, that's what everybody does and that's why—'

'Well, why don't you piss off and do something about it then?' she said angrily. 'Go and *do* something instead of just bringing everybody down. Sitting on your arse reading the cards! It's like Nero fiddling while Rome burns . . .'

'We all do what we can,' said Rita calmly, drawing in the cards and laying out another spread. 'For some it's action. Others try and improve their own immediate sphere. Human aggression starts at home—'

'Oh, crap!' Loretta said. 'You know what your immediate sphere's like? Fucking depressing! I mean, you're not exactly a barrel of laughs, are you? You don't uplift anyone! You're like fat Rob. Don't you think I've got enough on my plate with this stupid bill, and you start telling me about the end of the world?'

'But Loretta, it's all connected, don't you see . . . ?'

Loretta stormed out and ran down all the narrow dingy stairs, out where the rain still fell. A mist covered the far side of the common. She walked heavily down the road with her scarf wrapped around her head, had an idea and ran back and knocked on their door again. She was still very angry but calm now. 'Lend us a tenner,' she said, 'I'll give it you back on Friday.' Rita sighed, looked stiff and martyred and muttered pointedly how they weren't exactly rolling in it themselves, but Loretta knew she alway kept a little stash for emergencies in one of her shoes stuck away at the back of the wardrobe, a habit she'd had since childhood. Loretta waited until she gave in, then got a bus to Nina's.

Nina lived in a flat half-way up a tower block, full of loud wallpaper and brass, the radio playing and women's voices talking. Nina was pulling red socks onto Stephen's wriggling feet and an older sister that Loretta had never met talked loud banter on the phone. After a while Nina took Loretta into her room and started reading aloud a letter from her boyfriend in St Lucia. She had one in St Lucia and one called Wilfie who lived in Stockwell and always ignored Loretta. Loretta listened, half interested, restless, and when it didn't seem impolite to interrupt she asked Nina if they could go and get ten pounds worth of dope from her uncle; she wanted to score away from the Buildings so that Billy wouldn't know, she'd keep this for herself, stash it away somewhere and have a little smoke now and then when she was feeling down. Then she took out the bill and showed it to Nina. 'I don't know what to do,' she said, near to tears, 'I feel like it's all getting on top of me.'

'Ach,' said Nina, making a movement as if she was flinging some nonsense over her shoulder, 'you don't want to worry about it. Let 'em wait. Tell 'em you can't afford it.' She jumped up and brushed herself down briskly. 'Money problems,' she said, 'not as bad as heart problems. Believe me. That's when you really got trouble. Tell you what, we'll take Stephen. You can give him an airing while I do the business.' And she scolded all the time she got Stephen ready, muffling him up like an Eskimo, telling Loretta she didn't know what real trouble was. She seemed strong and vital, and Loretta felt silly and shabby and frightened.

The rain had stopped and the sun was out, shining brightly on the wet pavements as they walked to the flats where Nina's uncle lived. Stephen hung out of the side of his push-chair, watching puddles ripple as his wheels crossed them. At the flats, Nina said she'd only be a tick and ran up the stairs three at a time, whistling very piercingly; Loretta walked on with the push-chair till she came to a long row of shops, where she slowed down and sauntered, looking in the windows. At the end of the shops there was a low wall in front of some flats and she sat down on a reasonably dry bit and wheeled the push-chair to and fro gently. Stephen started climbing out clumsily, watching her mischievously from the corner of his eye. She laughed and caught him and hauled him up onto her knee. He was very heavy. He laughed too and put his arms round her neck. 'Oh, you're my little love,' she said to him, 'yes, you are, you're my little love.' Then he sat comfortably away from her, resting his back against her arms, and they smiled at one another wordlessly for some time. Her eyes filled with tears.

It grew colder and rained lightly. She settled him back in the push-chair and put the plastic cover on to shelter him, then walked again for warmth, down to the big road and through a deserted courtyard, out into a small street where a tiny old woman in a grey coat came up to her and said that she was lost and could Loretta please take her home. 'I just came out for a bottle of Guinness,' she said. She had long grey hair like thin frayed wires, skinny mottled bare feet in old slippers that had soaked up the rain like blotting paper, and she clutched a carrier bag of clinking bottles.

'Where do you live, then?' Loretta asked and the old woman gave her an address she'd never heard of. Jesus, Loretta thought. 'Come on,' she said, 'we'd better find it.' The woman placed a frail wasted claw, the hand of a starved child, in the crook of Loretta's elbow and it sat there like the cold hand of time. They walked back towards the big road. Traffic roared past them like dragons, splashing the pavements. Stephen was falling asleep under the clear plastic, with a look of distant peace as if he were lying in a warm bed listening to rain outside the window. It must be lovely to be in there, Loretta thought. The old woman barely came up to her shoulder and walked with quick small steps, talking all the time in a thin apologetic voice: she didn't know why, her usual shop was closed, she'd just popped out for a bottle of Guinness, she thought she'd crossed two roads but she couldn't remember which one it was, where they all joined, they all go different ways. Loretta stopped everyone who came along and asked for directions but no one knew. Oh, Jesus, she thought, why do these things happen to me? They walked on and on.

'We'll have to go back,' she said, 'I've got to meet my friend. She might know, I suppose.' If not, it's hang around all day getting soaked or take her down to the police station. With a bag of dope in my pocket. Oh, marvellous.

Nina was just coming down the stairs. 'Who's she?' she asked.

'She's lost,' Loretta said and told her the address, but she'd never heard of it either. They walked slowly along the pavement and the rain grew heavier and skipped in patterns in the road.

'You must be mad going out in those slippers!' Nina said sternly, walking on the other side of the old woman. 'Look at your feet!'

'I only popped out for a bottle of Guinness,' said the old woman shyly.

'Not like that, you don't. That's stupid!'

A girl of about fifteen came out of a shop in front of them. 'Dolly,' she said, 'are you lost again? You left your door open.'

'I only popped out to get a bottle of Guinness,' the old woman said, letting go of Loretta and taking the girl's arm, forgetting Loretta entirely. 'Can I come home with you, darlin'?'

The girl smiled and made a long-suffering face at them. 'Aren't you lucky I came along?' she said. They walked away like mother and child, the girl bending her head slightly in indulgence to listen to the old woman's voice.

The rain fell harder and they ran most of the way back to Nina's and stood talking in front of the lift. Nina handed Loretta a paper bag of ganja, rich in seeds and stems, and shook her by the shoulders and told her not to look so worried. 'I bet all those poor old bags never dream they'll end up like that,' said Loretta, 'I bet they just wake up one day and there it is—'

'Now stop!' Nina said. 'You stop right there!'

And that same night they were busted in Littlejohn's and it was a miracle that she didn't have it in her pocket at the time. They never found out what triggered the raid. Johnny had gone missing about the same time and at first everyone thought it might be something to do with him, but when he did turn up again he strenuously denied all knowledge. There was a bizarre feeling about the incident, as if she'd suddenly found herself taking part in a TV drama, the door bursting open, the big men in big coats, 'Freeze!' hands on heads like naughty children back at school, the bluff, malicious humour, the search, in the kitchen with the policewoman, frisked, men talking in the hall, confusion, orders, the woman's voice like a cracked whip, fat legs in boots, the place turned over, Willie coming home in the middle of it, pushed up against the wall with his arms up his back. Loretta trembled. She tried to square all this with memories of Andrea's dad, the chief superintendent, sitting with the dog on his lap watching football on the TV. And then the camaraderie in the back of the police van, the station, the hours of waiting, and getting strip-searched when she wanted to go to the toilet. She was clean. Everyone was, apart from Littlejohn and Eric, who each had dope in their pockets. And, of course, they'd found a couple of old syringes in the flat, but these were legal.

This was nothing, just another dope bust, a pathetic, dreary little fizzle of an adventure. Littlejohn and Eric were in court just before Christmas, fined, the usual. But Loretta took the world too seriously. These incidents, these games that had to be played, the rules of which she never quite got the hang, crept into her dreams at nights: the police came to the door; there was a van waiting; they were at the door, at the window; sometimes they took Billy away; they read your letters; they found all your secret things and laughed about them. She never learned to take these things in her stride. Things touched her too much, the insult in a policeman's voice, the cries in the courtyards, the blood on a staircase. She should have lived in some safe and sheltered part of the world, but she lived in Kinnaird Buildings.

Judy went to stay with friends in Newcastle for Christmas. A man from the Council was supposed to be coming to fix her water heater some time, so she left her spare key with Loretta and Billy. Rob reappeared and tried to move in with Jimmy Raffo, but Jimmy had heard all about him and was firm. 'No offence or anything,' he told Rob, 'but I just don't think we'd get on in the same flat somehow.' Rob latched onto Judy's place next and kept pestering Loretta for the key, but she wouldn't give it to him. In the end he moved into an awful gloomy flat that had been burned out when some glue-sniffing kid knocked a candle over. It was covered in soot and scorch and there were boards at the windows, but he tore them down and could be seen looking out of his burned-out window with tear-filled eyes.

*

Judy was gone for three weeks. When she got back the first person she saw as she came into the Buildings was Jimmy Raffo coming down his staircase with Sunny on his back, her skinned knees sticking out from under his armpits. Sunny had fallen head over heels in love with him and sometimes followed him about like a dog. 'Hey, Sunny!' Judy heard him say. 'Look who's here,' and he smiled and waved to her and came running down to meet her at the bottom. 'How's it going, lovely?' he said. 'Good Christmas?' Sunny stared over his shoulder, a frail ginger-haired child, unsmiling and unwelcoming.

'Oh, it was fine,' Judy said. 'You should've seen the snow! Saw lots of old friends, you know, got pissed a few times, the usual . . . What was it like here?'

'Great!' he said, setting Sunny down on her feet, taking her hand and walking along through the Buildings beside Judy. 'This geezer called Rob's turned up. You've heard about him, course you have. The most miserable person in the world. Christmas bloody Day and you're sitting there with your paper hat on and your cheeks feeling all funny from blowing up balloons for the kids, and everyone's having a good time, and this guy sits down next to me and starts –' he made a sudden and perfect transition into someone else, voice, looks, everything, '– "They're going to drop the bomb on us, they're all mad, all the people in power are insane and there's no stopping it now, mumble, mumble, mumble" – went on for *hours*, ruined my Christmas, the bastard.' Judy laughed. He hoisted Sunny up into his arms and walked along with her in the direction of Eddy and Dee's, calling over his shoulder as she turned away towards her flat: 'Might see you later.'

She was tired. There was no hot water because of course the man from the council hadn't come. The flat was strange and musty and unwelcoming. She knocked on Loretta's door but there was no answer, so she lit the fire and had something to eat and made coffee, pottered about messing things up and breaking the place in to her

137

presence, wondering if anyone would call – she thought Raff might turn up with a bottle of wine or something, looked forward to it somewhere in the back of her mind. But no one came, nor did Loretta and Billy come home. She boiled up some water on the stove and had a wash, then went to bed and fell asleep straight away.

Some time in the night she was hurled out of deep sleep into a terrible nightmare: someone was in the room, moving towards her under cover of pitch darkness. It was no dream, a sound had awakened her. A board creaked. In the fearful space between the two worlds, she heard a quick indrawn whimpering sound and realised with horror, as her senses cleared and she came fully awake, that she really had cried out so pitifully, displaying her childish weakness to the intruder. The shame of exposing her fear was foremost in her mind, stronger even than the fear. It was like one of those dreams where suddenly you're naked in the street.

'Oh, my sweet,' a voice whispered close by, 'don't be scared, it's me.' It was Raff. He was drunk and trembling and lay down on the bed beside her and tried to crawl into her arms. She was naked under the covers, vulnerable, badly frightened and furious.

'You fool, Raff!' she spat at him, pushing him away, almost in tears, all disoriented in the dark. It was happening in a lost place, a vacuum, outer space. 'You nearly frightened me to death!'

He was some warm threatening presence in the darkness, sighing and dogged and impatient, groping blindly back at her as she pushed him away. 'Oh, God, Raff, not like this!' she said wearily, and her tone riled him.

'What's wrong with you?' he said testily. 'You're being ridiculous,' then tried to mount clumsily on top of her, breathing alcohol fumes down into her face. She gave a great heave and dislodged him but he came rolling back like one of those very persistent cats that won't stay off

138

your knee. 'Please, please,' he said forlornly, 'we don't have to do anything.'

She could have cried. How many times have I played this game? No more, no more. Weaken just once, give in, feel sorry for him, put your arms round him and pull him close against you, just once. You'll carry him always like a stone in your chest. She was stiff, wouldn't hold him. Be firm. Be firm. Someone else will give him a good home. He lay hard against her. Both their hearts beat very loudly, she could hear them and feel her own pounding through to her back. 'Oh, Raff,' she said too harshly, afraid her voice would betray how close she was to tears, 'please go home.'

He jerked up on his elbow and she sensed his anger like a little moving cloud in the darkness. 'I can't understand you!' he cried. 'You're being so stupid! This is ridiculous! Here we are, two healthy animals, male and female! We *should* do this! It's the reasonable thing to do! Why don't you just stop being so bloody stupid?' He yanked at the covers with great strength, she felt cold air, then his hands big and clumsy and groping on her shoulders and face, and she hit out, furious.

'Don't you *ever* try and force me!' she yelled and punched as hard as she could with her fists and feet, felt him weaken at once and fall back and roll heavily from the bed. He hit the floor and lay there, swearing and sighing. 'You get out of here!' she shouted, drawing the covers protectively about herself. 'You get out of here right now!'

'Oh God,' he murmured on the floor, 'Oh God, oh God, oh God.'

'Out!' she cried. 'Out! Out, for Christ's sake!' groping about near the end of the bed for clothes, intending to get up and kick him out physically if she had to, somehow; she was endowed with the strength of fear and fury.

'Ssh!' he sighed from the floor, subdued. 'Ssh! My head aches.'

'More than your fucking head'll ache when I've finished with you if you don't get out of here,' she said fiercely.

'Ssh. Ssh. I can't move. Just let me lie here,' he said. His voice was flat and tired, all the fight gone out of it. There was a long silence. Judy fought tears, furious with herself, deeply disturbed. Nothing happened. She thought he'd fallen asleep and despaired of getting rid of him tonight, lay back down stiffly on her side, knees drawn up defensively, waiting. 'Let me stay here,' he said weakly, 'I can't move. Just let me stay here.' The room was very cold. 'Hold my hand,' he said, 'there's no reason to, but do it anyway.' She reached out into the darkness, felt air, reached and reached and felt only air. Then suddenly her hand connected with his, the palms clasped and the fingers locked.

He fell asleep soon. She heard his breathing change and felt his grip slacken. After a while she withdrew her hand, got up in the dark and gave him her good thick quilted eiderdown, settled it around him and got back into bed and lay trying desperately to sleep. She masturbated, then wept quietly, utterly wretched. Maybe she was being too kind. Maybe she should just fuck him for the sheer urge of it and damn the consequences. And if she did, one day she'd break him, she knew she would, she was stronger than him.

She fell asleep. When she woke up the room was light and she saw Raff sleeping on the floor, his face troubled. He looked somehow raw, as if all his nerves were too close to the surface. Oh, dear God, she thought, where do they come from? The world's full of them and they all come to me. These charming weak men she had taken and taken and taken, and would take no more.

He woke in confusion and found her watching him from the bed. His eyes passed through several emotions and ended up with humour. He smiled, 'Am I a ridiculous person?' he asked.

'No,' she said.

'She says that,' he mumbled, closing his eyes again and wriggling under the eiderdown, 'she says it but she doesn't mean it,' putting his hands around his head and wincing. 'Jesus Christ!' he groaned. 'I feel as if someone's been kicking me all over all night. Have you been kicking me, woman?'

'Of course I haven't been kicking you. Why would I want to kick you?'

'Oh,' he said, 'I'm sure you've got your reasons.' He lay for a while holding his head, breathing loudly between his teeth, then got up all clumsy in his wrinkled clothes and lurched out to the toilet. Judy jumped out of bed and got dressed quickly and stood in front of the mirror snagging a comb through her hair. Her eyes looked tired and puffy, deeply shadowed. Raff called through from the hall: 'Shall I make a cup of tea?'

'No,' she said, 'I'm going down to the café.' She went and threw him out of the kitchen and got herself washed with cold water. 'You'd better give me my key,' she said, coming out and lifting her coat from a hook. He was standing by the front door, all ready to go. 'How did you get hold of it, anyway?'

'Loretta,' he said, feeling in his pocket and handing over the key. They left and walked down the stairs. 'She had to go out somewhere and she thought the repair man might come so she left it with me. He never came.'

'I know,' she said.

They walked down to the market and sat in their usual café watching the cold, unlively market outside, two teas and a plate of soft, underdone toast on the red table top. The big silver urn hissed and the fat Italian man in his white apron mopped the counter, searching his back teeth with his tongue. He winked at Judy. She wasn't quite sure of her relationship with Raff now. He was acting as if nothing had happened, lolling against the wall drinking his tea thirstily and telling her some daft story about how he'd locked himself out one night and gone round the back and climbed up the drainpipe (they're dead flimsy, don't you ever try it) and started to climb in through the toilet window. He knew it was the right window because he always left the light on in the toilet so it'd look like someone was in. Anyway, half-way through the window he sees that there's a bottle of disinfectant and some Jeyes fluid on the windowsill. 'Then I think, hold on, I haven't got wallpaper in my toilet –' He laughed, 'Can you imagine if someone'd been sitting on the toilet – I'm stuck half-way through the window right next to the cistern and I get the giggles—'

'Raff,' she said, 'we haven't said a word about last night . . .'

'I know,' he said, coming to attention and sitting up straight, 'I know exactly what you're going to say. I can even say it for you. Save you the trouble. Shall I say it for you?' Reasonable and cheerful. 'We have a good friendship, we get along, we like talking to each other, why change anything? Why spoil it?' He smiled. 'The other's just – well – I don't want to be a fool and spoil a good thing. I was pissed, that's my excuse. Don't worry! I do take no for an answer. I'll never do anything like that again. It's all right, it's no big deal. I mean, I'm not heartbroken or anything – and neither are you – so – in fact, it's a funny thing really, I'm not even all that sure that I fancy you in that way, no offence or anything, I mean, you're a lovely-looking woman – anyway – but, I tell you what, I'd be very upset if I couldn't come up and see you any more.'

Oh, my God, she thought, this one's devious. She looked out of the window and rolled a cigarette. 'Do you realise what you're doing?' she said. 'You clever swine. You're wriggling out of it without admitting that you were a bully last night. That's all. You were just a bully.'

'Oh, Jude!' he said seriously. 'I'm sorry! I really am sorry. I don't know what to say. Forgive me. I'd never

142

hurt you, you know that, don't you? You must know that! If you only knew how much I value our friendship . . .'

'It's OK,' she said, 'you don't have to make a speech. No more games, that's all.'

Raff put his head down for a few moments, then looked up and smiled fully and held out his right hand, like one amiable stranger meeting another. 'Friends,' he said. 'Right?' They shook on it.

In spring Loretta went to work in the china and glass department of a big store in the West End. The money wasn't very good and they treated you like schoolchildren, but she worked hard and was happy there.

From the point of view of the customer she was the ideal sales assistant: she liked people, she was helpful, she never tried to make you buy anything you didn't want. From the point of view of the management, she was not ideal: she always turned a blind eye to shoplifters, and after the first few weeks she started taking money from the till. Hundreds of pounds passed through her hands every day. In the canteen she heard stories: this method, that method, how some supervisor got away with a fortune, how they never checked the till rolls. She held out for a while, weighing up the various methods in her mind. One night her till was tenpence short and they made her stay three quarters of an hour late until the error was found. They wouldn't let her just stick tenpence of her own in and call it quits. She was tired, the evening was shot. Sitting on the tube half asleep going home, feet aching, she began to fume. Sod them. Off they go on their expense-account lunches. Strawberries and cream. Duck *à l'orange*. Wine. She knew. She had a friend in Accounts. Tenpence. Three quarters of an hour. So tired. Sod them.

She started fiddling the till. She had a credit-card fiddle that worked well on crowded Saturdays when so much money went through the system that a few quid here or there wouldn't be noticed. She'd build up a surplus in the till and when she went to the chute in the store room to send up for change, she'd take out the extra and stuff it in her bra. Here a fiver, there a tenner. Half of what she took she kept for bills and clothes and little luxuries; half she put in a Post Office account which she vaguely thought of as the escape fund, the nest egg, the bulwark against whatever lay ahead. She couldn't see very far ahead. Whenever she looked there, she felt frightened.

Mondays she got an afternoon off. She'd walk up to the rent office on her way home from work, pay off some arrears, make a note in her diary, buy a big bag of fruit and go home and rest her feet and read a book. One day, settling down with her latest romance and an apple, feet up, she was startled by a single hard slam on the door knocker, sudden, unheralded by footsteps. It had the effect of a gunshot. Loretta jumped to her feet and dropped the book and stood for a moment with her fingers to her mouth. Jesus, my nerves are bad, she thought, pulling herself together and tiptoeing nervously to the door to peep through the spy-hole. She'd seen a film once where someone put their eye to a spy-hole and a big spike came through and poked it out. This was in her mind now. But it was only Jimmy, standing there with a stupid grin on his face.

'Don't knock like that,' she scolded, opening the door, 'you gave me a fright. You must've crept up the stairs.'

'I never creep,' he said gaily, coming into the living room. 'It's my shoes, they don't make any noise.' He carried a bottle of gin in one hand and a very large black book under one arm. She saw at once that he was very drunk. 'What's all this?' she asked, indicating the bottle. 'You celebrating something?'

144

He swung the half-full bottle up in the air, smiling at it. 'Yeah, I'm celebrating,' he said, 'I've been in the George,' put the arm with the bottle around her shoulders and pulled her close and kissed the side of her head resoundingly, then let her go. 'A present for you, lovely,' he said, handing her the book, a very expensive one about the treasures of Britain, full of shiny colour photographs.

'What?' she said, amazed.

'Nicked it. The bookstall on the station.'

'Oh, Jimmy!' she cried. 'You shouldn't. Oh, you silly fool!'

'Ah, go on,' he said, sitting down and sprawling, uncapping the bottle, 'living off the land.'

She scolded on for a while but she was pleased. She gave him a lecture about getting caught, but he laughed it off and flicked through the book, pointing out to her the places he'd been and the places he'd like to go. She tried to give him coffee but he waved it away and went on drinking from the bottle, talking all the time. Nonsense, it seemed to Loretta. She heard him pacing up and down with the bottle, talking to himself when she was in the kitchen. Later he became agitated and talked for a long time about some distressful incident, whether real or imagined she couldn't tell, perhaps something he'd read in a book or seen in a film or on a newsreel. Whatever it was, it had got inside him and he couldn't let it go. Again and again he stumbled through a scene: he was dying, this boy, they shot him, soldiers, fell on some steps, his arms out like this, his face, his eyes . . .

'What was this, Jimmy?' she asked kindly. 'Was it something you saw on the TV?'

He sat hunched and awry in the corner of the settee, a hurt look in his eyes, breathing unevenly, hugging the bottle to his breast as if it were a child and nuzzling its mouth softly with his cheek. 'What bastards they are,' he said thickly, 'what fucking bastards they are,' and he was off again on a ramble of sorrow and outrage at the atrociousness of mankind, the soldiers shot him, arms out like this, blood on the steps, faces, machines, rifles, his face . . .

'Who?' she asked. 'Who was this, Jimmy?'

'What does it matter?' he said. 'Me. It was me.'

'Something got in your mind and—'

'No!' he said, shifting his eyes to look at her. They were wet and hooded, full of misery. She was afraid of them. It was as if he'd gone out and let someone else in. 'Don't you understand? It really did happen. They shot him. He's dead now.'

'Who, Jimmy?'

'This kid. What does it matter?' He stood and paced the room again, throwing back his head to swig from the bottle and sometimes spilling it down his chin and neck. 'Have a drink!' he said.

'No,' she said, 'not in the afternoon. Don't you think you ought to give it a rest? Sit down, for God's sake. You're going to be so sick. Why don't you save that for tomorrow?' He stumbled against the fireplace and lost his footing, flung his arms out and spilled more gin, fell down into a chair, looked startled and annoyed. 'Oh, come on,' she said briskly, 'come on, Jimmy! I've got things to do.'

'Nothing's that important,' he said, struggling to stand again, 'nothing's more important than talking to a friend.'

'Right,' she said. 'You put that bottle away and I'll talk to you,' and approached him with a hand held out for the bottle. His face transformed: it could have been hate or fear, she didn't know, but it was violent and sent a chill through her.

'You talk to me like that!' he cried, his voice savage and snagged. 'You're not my fucking mother!' Then he drank very defiantly, a long determined gargle, his brow churned like rippled sand. For the first time ever, Loretta

146

felt afraid of him. She walked out into the kitchen and stood looking down into the sink, shaken, wondering what to do. He came after her and stood in the doorway, his jacket off and his hair wet somehow at the front. 'Guess what day this is?' he said with awful forced cheer, and when she looked she saw that his eyes were his own again, soft and tired and humorous.

'What?' She moved about getting vegetables from a rack, lifting saucepans from hooks, filling a bowl with water.

'What are you doing?' he asked.

'Making soup.' She peeled an onion carefully, kindly, as if it were a creature that could feel each stripping of the skin.

'Make soup later,' he said. 'Come and talk to me. Come and talk to me. Come and talk to me, Loretta, I'll get a complex if you make soup; every time I go and see people they go off in the kitchen and start making soup. Can this be coincidence, I ask myself? I need to talk to you. Please. Come and talk to me.'

She gave up. They went back into the living room and she settled herself on the settee to listen as he talked and paced and stumbled and drank. 'This is a special day,' he told her several times. Then he said it was Luke's birthday, eight today, he was drinking to his son. 'Have a drink with me,' he said. 'We'll drink a toast to Luke.'

Loretta went and got two glasses from the kitchen, took the bottle from him and poured a little into each one. He smiled very gently at her. 'You don't think much of yourself, Loretta,' he said, 'but *I* do. I think you're a priceless jewel among women.' He plucked the bottle back from her, laughing. 'And you don't steal my gin that easily!'

They drank to Luke. Loretta hated neat gin but sipped away bravely. Jimmy knocked back what was in his glass and returned to the bottle. He swayed about in front of the fireplace. 'They do all right,' he said, 'yes, they do, the women, they just like complaining. She did all right out of me. I give her two good sons. She's got them now. What have I got? My blood. She's stolen my blood.' He liked the phrase and said it again. 'She's stolen my blood.' His eyes filled and his face changed, tears overflowed and rolled down his cheeks and he dashed them roughly away. 'They could be in Timbuctoo,' he said, 'or they could be in Brazil. They could be in fucking Bognor Regis. What does it matter? *I* don't know where they are.

'I want them,' he said, 'I want my wife. I want my little boys. What can I do?' He sat down, shook his head and closed his eyes, his brow knotted and shiny, tilted the bottle and drank until there was only a bit of slosh left in the bottom. Then he broke down, rested the bottle against the wall, put his head in his hands and cried weakly, speaking through his hands: 'What can I do, what can I do, what can I do, Loretta, everything fails, it's just a heap of shit, my life's a heap of shit I'm crawling through, I can't understand why they're throwing all this shit at me. Oh God – oh God – oh God – what's wrong with me – what's wrong with me – what's – I have nothing, nothing! – I don't want it, I never wanted this, I never wanted – what shall I do? – Where do I go? There's nowhere for me to go! – oh, please, please, give me a break, I never asked for any of this – oh God – I'm some walking joke, hah! Hah! Let's make this one, this stupid one, let's stick him down there, see how long he lasts – fuck, I've lasted pretty well, considering – Jesus. Oh, Jesus – I'm dead, I'm dead, I'm all dead, I'm all dead —' He sobbed and dropped his head lower, spoke in a terrible low voice that seemed to come from some drunken lower level of purgatory. 'I'm just mud on someone's boot, that's what I am, mud on the road, mud on the road! What else, what else? – I hate it! – I hate it, I hate their fucking bastard eyes! – I hate my life! – I hate my life! – Why should I care? Hah, no one else does – it's all just rotten, rotten, rotten, a rotten fucking fruit and

148

I'm the maggot – we're all the maggots – people are fucking bastards, I hate them, I hate – the good ones get killed, it's true, oh, Christ, it's fucking true, man! – The good ones, the good ones go mad or they kill them or something – I hate this fucking horrible shitty world – I close my eyes, I close my eyes – we're all the fucking same, scared all the time, horrible and stupid and pathetic, I'm as bad as anyone, it's in me, all of that, all the shit's in me, there's nothing I couldn't do, nothing, nothing! – Oh, my God, my God! Oh, I hate it, I hate it, I hate this world! – This kid, you shoulda seen this kid dying, it's like you have to watch, you have to see this thing, they shot him and his back went up – fancy dying with all the cameras on you! – He's looking into the camera and he knows! A show! My God, a show! – A kid! – It could've been my kid, it could've been me – why are we killing kids? – Who says it's OK to kill kids! – They're saying it's OK! – They're really saying it's OK! – We're rotten, all of us, the fucking lot of us, I hope they drop the fucking bomb tomorrow, I hope they blast the fucking evil lot of us to kingdom come! – Oh, Jesus, I know, I know, I know, I do because it's me, oh, Jesus! I know all about it now! Oh yes, I do!'

He jumped up, grabbed the bottle again and stood at a weird angle like a scarecrow pinned against the wall, his face wretched and wet. 'I know what she's about now. People just get between you and your own rotten core, that's the only real thing, it's a big ache, that's all – that's all I am – a big ache – it's me!' he lurched forward and Loretta jumped up. 'Some fucking stupid life after death!' he said. 'I don't want that! I wanna be gone! Just not there any more!' He shouted: 'I don't want it! This!' looking down at himself in disgust, as if he'd just found himself to be covered in shit or contaminated in some way. 'How can I get rid of it!' he cried. 'I can't take it off!' and looked about wildly as if looking for a hidden exit.

'Stop it!' she cried, shaking him. 'Stop it! That's enough, that's enough, Jimmy!' She was afraid, trembling slightly herself. He slunk away from her and stood still and stiff for a moment before sinking down into a corner of the settee and covering his face with his arms. 'Oh, I'm sorry, I'm sorry,' he cried abjectly. She sat down beside him. Distantly she heard Judy going into her flat across the landing, and noted it.

'It's OK,' she said, 'it's the gin talking. It's just like a nightmare. It's not that bad, Jimmy, I promise you it's not that bad. You're OK, really.'

He took his arms down and looked at her with eyes that looked smaller than before, red-rimmed and half asleep and partly dead. 'Oh no,' he said quietly, 'you don't know. I'm not, I'm really not OK.' Then he put his head down on her breast and cried very deeply. She didn't think she could bear the weight of it. She held him and rocked him and mumbled nonsense and wiped his eyes and nose, and he was a terrible warm heavy trembling weight. He cried for a long time, then was quiet with closed eyes as if falling asleep.

'My head aches,' he said. Loretta got up carefully, propped him against a cushion and went out to the kitchen to get aspirin and some water and put the kettle on for tea. She'd get some hot sweet tea down him, God knows why, it was what people did in situations like this. When she came back he was lying on his back on the floor, mouth open, face dead white, one hand gracefully arched upon his chest. She knelt and shook him. The hand flopped from his chest like a dead fish. Nothing moved anywhere and she couldn't hear him breathing. Oh, God, oh, Christ, she thought, he's dead, he's dying, and ran from the flat, hammered on Judy's door till it opened. She babbled. Judy came running over without a word and they crouched over him.

'Raff!' Judy shouted, started pulling him up by the shoulders, then got behind his back and pushed. 'You stupid bastard, get up!' His eyes opened, dead. They got him into a sitting position with his back against the settee and Judy pulled and shoved and slapped him, shouting at him so furiously that Loretta cowered. 'How dare you do this!' she cried. 'You get on your feet now! How dare you put people through this! How dare you upset Loretta with your whining! How *dare* you do this to your friends! We could all be so weak! Don't you ever pull a trick like this again!' She hit him across the face, harder, Loretta thought, than was necessary. Tears came from his eyes. 'You are so boring,' Judy said, standing and trying to pull him to his feet, 'so boring, just a stupid, boring, little shit. Help me, Loretta. We'll get the stupid bastard into my place and he can sleep it off there.' They dragged him up and tried to support him, but he weighed a ton and the three of them staggered about in a crazy dance. His eyes flickered and his head rolled and his voice mumbled, but his feet were useless. 'On your feet!' Judy ordered like a sergeant major. 'On your fucking *feet*, you stupid bastard!' They dragged him up and down till his feet started working, then got him out onto the landing and over to Judy's. She slapped him about with an ice-cold and none-too-clean dishcloth, which made him cough, just for the hell of it, shoved him into her bed and took his shoes off and left him to sleep it off. He turned onto his side and started to weep softly into the pillow.

'There's nothing in the world more boring than a drunk,' she said, standing back.

They were panting with the effort of moving him, arms akimbo. Loretta was crying a little. 'His nature,' said Judy, 'is to make others share his misery. Oh, Loretta, don't cry.' They went back to Loretta's and talked while Loretta made soup, bustling, hard-faced, shocked at the callousness of Judy's manner. Judy sat on a high stool and smoked, leaning back with arms folded and brows lifted, head thrown back, fast-talking and snotty and casual: 'It's the stupidity of it that gets me. The sheer stupidity. The absolute ridiculous waste of time of it. Don't let it upset you. We could all do that. Any human being in the world could do that. I can just see you mollycoddling him, I can just see you making a great big fuss of him, that's just what he wants, everyone crying all over him, everyone feeling as bad as him, spread a little misery, the selfish bastard, spread a little misery and he feels he's done his bit for the day. Oh, what a creep, he'd bring us all down if he could. Drunks are such selfish bastards. The last thing you should give him when he's like that is sympathy.'

'That's horrible,' Loretta snapped. 'That's really horrible. What's wrong with you? Where's your − fellow feeling? So what if he is a pain in the arse at times, everyone needs sympathy.'

'I mean,' said Judy, smiling a little, 'it's all right to *feel* sympathy but it's pointless to *show* it to him. Not when he's like that. Just makes him worse. Good kick, that's what he needs. So he's had his troubles. Who hasn't? I know people who've had far worse lives than he's had and they don't go around spilling crap like this all over people.'

'For God's sake, he just got drunk! Haven't you ever been drunk?'

'Anyway. It's pointless being nice to him because he probably won't remember a thing about any of it when he wakes up.'

'It's when he talks about his children . . .' Loretta said.

'I know. I know, I know. But what can *we* do about it? We can't make any of it any different for him, not now. So why should we have to suffer for it? I tell you, Loretta, I tell you. If ever I was tempted in that direction, and I never really was, *that*' she jerked a thumb over her shoulder, 'just put the lid on it. I hate all that.'

'You know what you want,' Loretta said, pointing severely with the knife she used for chopping vegetables, 'you want a good dose of suffering. You want to get down off your pedestal. *You*'ve had it easy, it's all right for you to talk. *You* never lost any children, *you* don't know what it's like. You don't want to make judgements when you don't know what it's like.'

'No,' said Judy stiffly, sliding from the stool, 'I'm not one of the club. You're quite right. Of course I've never suffered. I've lived a life of total ease and contentment. Since when did you take it on yourself to pronounce on other people's suffering? Don't *you* judge. You've got a monopoly on it, have you, you and him? What do you know? See. Now we're arguing over the stupid brat. Oh, he'd just love that!' She walked out.

Raff snored and twitched in her bed, arms hanging down, face hidden. The sky was darkening at the window and it was turning cold, so she put on the light and the fire and sat down in the chair by the fire with a notebook and a pen, started writing letters but ended up scrawling poetry and didn't stop for the next two hours. Then she sat back and read what she'd written, and it was so awful she tore it up and threw it in the bin, and started on a letter to a friend very far away, one so distant in time and space that it was like writing to herself. She'd never send the letter. She wrote everything that had happened to her since she came to live in the Buildings, very fast and heedless, crying sometimes with the intensity of it. Of what? she thought. Nothing's happened. But she ached. Then she wrote more poetry, gazing at the wall, scribbling a few words, gazing at the wall, scribbling again, scoring lines through it, starting again, scribbling and gazing and scribbling. It was very badly written but it stung in places and stammered in others and sang in one or two. She ran down to the shop before it closed and bought a whole load of cold stuff that she could eat as she wrote without any messing about, came back and ate and had coffee and smoked some dope and went on scribbling and scrawling. She felt as if her heart were breaking and healing at the same time. Around mid-

153

night, Raff opened his eyes and mumbled and she went over and sat on the bed looking down at him. 'Water,' he croaked. She got him a mug of water and he glugged it all down and fell asleep again instantly as if someone had hit him on the head. How did I ever get lumbered with him? she thought. Good God, never in a million years. Poor Raff! Who'll take him like this? He wanted someone to fall in love with him and he was absolutely the worst kind of man for anyone to fall in love with, an alcoholic baby, potentially violent.

She wrote all night in the chair by the fire. At half past six it started to rain softly and steadily and a wet pigeon came and sat on the windowsill. Raff woke up and asked in a sick voice for a bowl, and she ran and shoved the one from the kitchen sink under his hanging face just in time. For an hour he was utterly wretched, vomiting and retching and groaning and heaving, trembling all over in great spasms. Finally he rolled onto his back and sighed as if he were dying. 'Oh, I'm sorry, Jude,' he said, 'I'm so sorry, I'm so sorry.'

She went over and sat with him. 'I've changed my mind,' she said. 'You *are* a ridiculous person. Oh, Raff! What a terrible thing to do to yourself. That's a really corny old story, young man, good looks, good friends, talent, drinks himself to death by the age of thirty. Not you, Raff, please. It's not even original.'

He laughed. It was one thing about him, he never cared if you laughed at him, he'd laugh with you. 'I know,' he said, 'I know. I'm an idiot. You don't have to tell me,' then groaned and held his head. 'They're hitting me with hammers,' he said.

She gave him something for his headache, made him comfortable and took away the sick bowl, telling him he could lie for as long as he liked.

'Where did you sleep?' he asked.

'I didn't.'

'Stretch out here beside me,' he said, 'I won't touch

154

you. I'm in no shape to touch anyone.' So she did. 'Funny,' he muttered, his lips all dry and sticky, his breath foul, 'I always seem to have trouble with birthdays.' She fell asleep without intending to and woke to find him gone.

It was a strange, stormy day, full of heat and thunder and sudden bursts of angry rain. Judy wandered about barefoot in her dressing gown in the afternoon, tired and restless. Loretta came over and asked after Raff, and they drank coffee and talked and apologised for being rude to each other yesterday, said not at all, not at all, it didn't matter at all. Raff called. He'd changed his clothes and washed his hair and looked fine if a little pale. 'Was I a pain in the arse yesterday?' he asked, smiling at Loretta. 'I apologise if I was. Honestly, my head when I woke up! Ask her.'

'Who's her?' said Judy. 'The cat's mother?'

Everything was normal, so normal. None of it had happened. He doesn't even remember, Loretta thought. He went to the window and cried: 'Look at that sky!' Loretta went and stood with him. The sky was black. Thunder like the rolling of a massive stone above the earth rolled over the Buildings, and lightning flashed. Jimmy whistled.

Judy watched their outlined figures with the light of Armageddon beyond them in the window, till it happened: a ball of lightning hurtled down between the Buildings, she saw it pass the window with a fierce clap of sound as the rain began. They ducked and laughed and came away from the window.

155

Those last summers, hot and violent, when the cities simmered. For so long they'd been talking of pulling the Buildings down, but nothing had come of it. Now it began. They moved people out of the end block. Boards appeared everywhere, in all the blocks, doors and windows, and a ghost building loomed opposite Dee and Eddy's. The Buildings were left for decay but the people still lived there. Wildlife in a landscape: people and pigeons and dogs and cats and beetles and fleas, many fleas, a plague of them. The graffiti grew in hate. The Council no longer sent cleaners to do the staircases, which became soiled here and there with piss and shit and puke and blood that everyone hated but no one wanted to clean up. Rubbish piled up in some of the stairwells and out by the bins, and the summer made it stink; kids set fire to it to see the fire brigade come out.

A heat haze lay over the Buildings. On Friday afternoons, an old junkie called Ken would come around and play the Man in Dee and Eddy's to a roomful of nervous, slightly sick junkies who gave him all their money. Ken was so typical it was ridiculous, fat and soft and waxy-skinned, with little eyes and a fruity laugh and pale pudgy hands that liked to touch people, to knead a shoulder or knee or thigh. No one liked to be touched by Ken but no one there on a Friday afternoon would have dreamed of offending him. If you weren't a junkie you avoided Dee and Eddy's at these times. It was a crushingly boring place to be, and full of tension, like a dentist's waiting room. The kids cruised in and out and people snapped at them to close the door. The TV chunnered. Eddy moaned and Dee grumbled and everyone looked fed up or tired or just plain stupefied. Johnny was always there, Willie, Rob, Littlejohn, Sharon.

Littlejohn's place, which had evolved through many changes and locations within the Buildings, had shaken down into a slow, early-morning twilight sort of a place. An old blanket hung across the window. It was messy, undisciplined, turn by turn lazy and noisy. They liked an audience and would sometimes give you the whole show: a needle poking at a bruisy mess in the crook of an elbow; a bloodtrail on skin, carefully smeared with a cigarette paper; a raised ridge of needled skin on a thin white arm. They fixed casually, without drama, like you'd pick your nose or clean your teeth. But Littlejohn was the artist. This was his calling. His teeth were turning rotten in his good-looking face, his mouth was always tense. He knew his veins well and was full of panache, deft with either hand, tied up swiftly, pumped the vein, hit it at once. A thin red line would appear in the syringe. You never saw him make a false move.

Jimmy hung around with everyone that summer, moving from scene to scene: lolling at Littlejohn's, drinking with Eric, going around with Billy and Loretta, and Judy, with whom he talked for hours. He was completely self-centred, constantly analysing himself out loud. Whenever he got too boring she'd tell him to shut up, and he'd laugh and make fun of his own boringness. They went out together, the four of them, to Hyde Park, to the Carnival, to Crystal Palace; late at night they'd end up in someone or other's flat, watching TV or listening to music or just talking, feeling close and sentimental and not showing it. Jimmy was good company but he changed all the time, drifted between spheres. When he was depressed he took his misery and poured it all over Loretta. Then he'd go into a drinking spree that might last for days, and everyone would avoid him because of his sarcasm and aggression and a certain unpredictability that felt dangerous. And then he'd shake it all off his shoulders and come round and apologise for anything he might have done or said, he couldn't remember, and they'd forgive him, of course, and everything would go on as before. As summer turned to autumn he drank more and more. His worst benders were pure hell, gin and misery, raw and unrestrained. Judy saw him one day by the shops, stumbling and incoherent, and tried to take him home, but he told her to fuck off. The next day he was in the courtyard, bruised about the face. She ran up to him and held his arm, looking anxiously into his face; his eyes were heavy and distant. 'What happened?' she asked. He said he'd fallen over, shook her off sulkily and walked slowly away. Then he seemed to recollect and came back and talked restlessly for a moment before asking her if she could lend him fifteen quid, he had to pay off some electricity or they'd cut him off.

'No,' she said, 'you'll spend it on booze.'

'You know, you really are an incredibly stupid woman,' he said to her with a great show of deep, controlled dislike. 'Oh, you're high and mighty now all right, but you'll get yours. You wait. You wait.'

'Why don't you just stick your tongue out?' she said. 'Nyaah-aah! It's about your level.'

'Stupid cow!' he spat and jerked away. She walked rapidly away, stiff with rage. Oh, what a pain in the arse he is, she thought, almost grinding her teeth, why is it my fate to meet so many of these people? Why don't they just go off and kill themselves and have done with it?

He went up to Dee and Eddy's and borrowed the money from them after half an hour's haggling, left and bought a bottle of gin and went looking for someone to drink it with.

At some point, he came to on the floor in his flat, with

158

no memory and his face in a pool of vomit. He didn't know who he was or where he was. He was just a chunk of aching misery. Then he discovered that this was home, this room that towered above him. This was the old blue carpet on his floor. That was a relief. He lay frozen to a stone, desperately ill. One nostril burned, clogged with vomit. His dry mouth splatted open into a cold brown pool of it. He tried to move his face away from it but a knife came down in his brain, tried to groan but had strength only for a faint whimper.

For a long time he lay working up to the effort of pushing his body up, did it finally in easy stages till he was on his knees panting weakly against the wall. A sickening tide swelled slowly in his head and the room ebbed and flowed with it. He coughed, which made him retch, cleared his nose into his hand and wiped it in disgust on the foul sticky front of his jacket. He could smell himself.

The world had come back to him from a great distance. He tried to think, groping, remembering nothing. He'd bled from a cut on his head and a cut between two fingers that ached diabolically, and the blood had dried on him. He shivered, his teeth chattered, his bowels griped. The back of his head ached hotly, steadily. A dream memory came: he was in the bar of the George and the place was rowdy. Who was he with? Johnny? Johnny? He went out into the night, a lot of people standing on the pavement, drizzle, a bridge, railings. The scene faded. Nothing took its place. It seemed an awful long time ago. There was darkness at the window. Not last night? When? It seemed he reached out over miles of interstellar space to find that wavering dream memory. His eyes ached.

He got to his feet and staggered with shaky knees out into the hall, bent nearly double, holding onto things, realising as he moved that he'd shat himself at some point. The hall had pools of vomit. He needed liquid. He got to the sink and drank from the tap, stuck his head under the stream of water and gasped, then hung there crying listlessly from pure self pity. Raising his head, he saw his face in the mirror, wild-eyed, bloody from an old nosebleed, one eye badly bloodshot. Looking closely, he found that one of his contact lenses had lodged itself tightly as far as it could go under the upper lid. God knows how long it had been there. The other was gone.

He staggered into the hall again, shed all his clothes carefully, rolled them into a ball and slung them in the toilet. His pants were caked with slimy greenish shit. He couldn't understand why it was that colour. Then he cleaned himself, shaking and sweating, sank to the floor and probed his sore eye tenderly, wincing, till he got the lens out, got himself to bed and lay trembling under the covers, full of pain and sickness, enduring. A parcel of time was gone. He had no way of knowing how large a slice of himself was gone. Later he found out that it was three and a half days. None of his friends had seen him during that time so he never found out where he'd been, with whom, what had happened. He was frightened. Never again, he thought, never ever again. Oh, no, not down this road, please not down here.

He was going on the wagon. This time for sure.

He found himself alone in his flat, weak in body and mind, cleaning up vomit. He began to shake: a large rat appeared in the fireplace and he heard someone beating on the front door. When he looked there was no one in the spy-hole and he was afraid to open the door. He heard laughter in another room and it sounded insane. He sweated and panicked. When he lay down he saw a column of cockroaches come marching across the ceiling. One fell down – CRACK! – on the bed beside him. He jumped up in terror, searched every pocket in the place, every lining, and got together enough for a couple of cans of beer and ran down to the off-licence, which, merci-fully, was open. He drank the first can as he walked back home and felt much better, hoping not to meet anyone he knew. Who had he insulted? Who wasn't speaking to him any more because of something he couldn't remember? He felt scared and emotional in a very basic way, felt like crying and suffering as freely as a child. When he got home he got back into his cold bed and placed the other can on the floor beside him, ready; he bundled about for a bit making a nest around himself, wanted another animal to share it with and was then so lonely that he started to cry. He didn't even know who he wanted. It was just raw want. Oh, God, this is hopeless, he thought. Maybe he should just go back up to Manchester, nothing was happening for him here. He could stay at his mum's until he found a place and then, and then . . .

He turned up at Judy's late one night and paced about the room jerkily, scowling.

'Oh, sit down,' she told him. 'You make me nervous.'

'You've been avoiding me,' he said sullenly, sitting down.

'Oh, really? As I remember it you told me to fuck off the last time I saw you.'

'Oh, you don't want to take any notice of what I say!' he said. 'You ought to know me well enough by now. Anyway, I'm sorry.'

'Everyone's got to forgive you all the time, isn't that so, Raff?' She walked out to the kitchen indifferently and made coffee, tired, unsure how to treat him and unsure of her own feelings. How stupid, she thought. When I saw him, I was glad I was wearing the red kimono. This is all a great nonsense.

'You made me angry,' he said when she came back in. 'You're always making me angry these days. You're just like a bloody schoolteacher.'

'Not interested,' she said coldly. 'Not interested. You

161

can go if you want a fight. You won't get one here. Or you can drink your coffee and behave like a human being for a change.'

'God!' he said disgustedly. 'The self-control!' He picked up his coffee and sat back and drank. 'I'm edgy,' he said, 'I'm on the wagon.'

'But I can smell it on you,' she said and laughed.

'Two pints!' he said, aggrieved. 'Two pints!'

'Two pints isn't on the wagon!'

He leapt up, spilling his coffee and making her jump. 'You!' he cried. 'You bring everything down! What do you expect, miracles? You ought to be encouraging me, not making fun of me all the time!'

'I wasn't making fun of you, don't be silly!' She was slightly afraid of him in this mood and spoke with a mixture of sharpness and sympathy. 'Sit down, for God's sake. You won't get me into a fight, so stop it.'

'Stop it!' he mimicked, sitting down. 'You won't get me into a fight, so stop it! You're so boring and complacent.'

'Oh, for Christ's sake, Raff, why don't you just go somewhere else? You're not coming in here and doing this to my time—'

'Aha!' he said triumphantly. 'Now she's getting riled.'

Judy scowled and turned away. She rolled a cigarette quickly and angrily. 'I don't know why they let children out on their own,' she snapped at the wall.

He stood up and started walking about the room nervously, all his movements arrogant. 'Do you want to come to Scotland with me?' he asked.

'What?' She turned and looked at him as if he'd just asked her to jump off the roof.

'I said, do you want to come to Scotland with me?'

'I'm boring and complacent and you want me to come to Scotland with you?'

'I know these people,' he said. 'Near Inverness. We could stay with them. Really nice people.'

162

She didn't know what to say. She lit the cigarette and tried to figure it out. 'Won't it be getting pretty cold up there this time of year?' she asked.

'You don't want to go, do you?' he said sharply, and then before she had time to reply: 'Would you miss me if I went away and never came back?'

Yes, she thought. 'What kind of a question is that?' she said, and was seized with an inexplicable urge to cry, as sudden as a blow.

'What kind of a question is that?' he cried, strutting and quivering before her. 'Talk straight for once! Talk straight! Why can I never get a straight answer out of you? You *think* about everything. You're stupid! You're full of crap just like everybody else, only you think you're so fucking smart and so cool, but you're not! You're not! You're fucking pathetic!' He moved towards her but she jumped up, and he backed away. 'If you could see yourself from where I stand. You know what you are? You're stupid and boring and vain and stuck up and *cold* and selfish and nasty—'

'You *dare* talk about selfish!' she shouted, advancing on him. 'You *dare*! The *hours* I've spent listening to you rabbit on and on about your own stupid, boring little self, your pathetic, moaning, creepy little self – You want to know about selfishness? You don't have far to look!'

He walked away from her and stood at the door with his head hanging. 'Fuck off, you silly cow,' he said quietly with such depth of hatred that she went cold. 'I don't even fancy you any more. I didn't even like you. You were just *there*, so I thought I'd have a go. Everybody thinks you're stupid. Everybody thinks you're a poser. We have a good laugh about you, you and your stupid poems. They're not even good. Everybody knows they're no good.'

She stood stiffly, watching him watch her for reaction. 'Get out,' she said.

He smiled evilly. 'Hurt, aren't you?' he said. 'Nasty,

163

aren't I? Well, that's what I'm like.' Then he flung one hand to his brow and staggered about in vicious parody, crying: 'I vant to be alone! I vant to be alone! Huh, what crap stupid image is that you've got? That's all it is, just a stupid fucking image, you let it get a hold of you and you think it's you but it's not. You're just a poser like everyone else. You're no different! Just a stupid bloody poser!' He laughed exaggeratedly, doubling up and holding his stomach. 'Oh, God! One woman's search for herself! One woman's voyage of discovery! Cue heroic music! A man's godda do whadda man's godda do! Oh, that's rich, that's rich!'

'Get out!' she yelled. 'Get out!' flinging her mug of coffee at him. It hit him on the chest and the liquid sloshed up into his face.

'Hah!' he cried. 'Hah!' and hurled the door open and stormed out.

She saw him in the market the next day and crossed the road to avoid him. As she did, she saw that he'd seen her and pretended not to, and she hated him. She caught a tube to town, met Loretta coming out of work for her dinner hour, and they went for a drink. Loretta was in high spirits; she had money and insisted on buying a meal for them both, and talked for ages about how she was going to adopt some kid that nobody wanted – she was going to find out about it, anyway – she wasn't sure, she didn't know if they'd let her and Billy adopt, really, but maybe they could give them some difficult one that nobody else would want. Oh, they'd be all right, so long as they didn't find out about Billy's old dope rap. Anyway that was years ago. And later they parted outside the tube station.

Loretta went back to work and was taken off the floor and told to count stock in the stock room. She had a notebook and pad and started making a neat list. After about fifteen minutes a personnel manager called Mr Seton came to the door and called her. 'Loretta?' he said pleasantly, hovering in uncertainty, a dark, pale-faced man in the gloom. 'You are Loretta, aren't you? Could you come with me, please?' She slid down from her stool, smiling, and followed him through the store. Diversions were always welcome.

'We've got these inspectors in,' he said as they walked. 'They're just picking people out at random and talking to them – you know – they just want to ask a few questions, find out how people are getting along and so on . . .' They took the lift up to the sixth floor where all the offices were.

'Will it take long?' she asked, looking at her watch.

'Oh, no, I shouldn't think so!' The lift doors opened. 'It's just a formality really, they're just, you know, talking to a few people.' Loretta's senses sharpened. She thought there was a touch of artificiality about him, a dropping off of joviality as he spoke the last words. She was wearing her old boots, newly dug out a week ago for the rainy weather, ideal for stuffing money down. They needed heeling and snagged in the blue nylon carpet as they walked down a long corridor that smelt like a hotel. Voices and machines hummed in big glass offices. No, she told herself comfortingly, it can't be. Don't worry. How could they know? They never check, they never check, they haven't checked for years. Mr Seton opened a door at the end of the corridor and ushered her politely into a small room with naked walls, a lonely grey filing cabinet and one old desk. A fat man in a grey suit sat behind the desk, and an empty chair awaited her before it. Against a wall another man shuffled papers and did not look up as she entered.

'This is Mrs Booth,' Mr Seton said to the fat man, who stood and smiled, holding out a large pale hand. 'Mr Pritchard, who wants to ask you a few questions.'

'Hello, Mrs Booth!' said Mr Pritchard heartily. 'How are you?'

'I'm fine, thank you,' she said, shaking hands with him and sitting down. The man by the wall, she now saw, was Renshaw, something high up in Security, an ex-policeman. No, her mind said. No. Stay calm.

'Loretta,' Mr Seton said, 'would you like me to stay while you talk to Mr Pritchard? It's up to you.'

'No,' she said, 'it's OK.' When she saw how relieved he looked, she knew. He left gratefully and her heart began to beat a little too sharply. Her stomach tightened. She wanted to be out of this poky little room, downstairs working the stretch before tea break, talking to people, everything sane and normal.

'Now, Loretta.' Mr Pritchard spread his hands out flat and wide on the papers on the desk in front of him, flexing them like a concert pianist limbering up for a performance. He was pale and small-eyed, friendly and efficient, instantly dislikeable. 'You don't mind if I call you Loretta, do you? Now, Loretta, you've been here – ' he consulted something on the desk, ' – eight months, is that right? Are you happy in your work?'

Maybe they don't know.

'Yes,' she said brightly, 'very happy.'

'Good.' He smiled. 'Now, I'm told that you had training in till procedure and so on when you started work, is that right? Yes.' He nodded encouragingly and asked if she'd be good enough to explain till procedure to him as she understood it. She sat with her hands folded in her lap, composed, telling him clearly all the stages involved in ringing up a sale.

'I see,' he said, studying a list in front of him. She couldn't read the words or the figures on it. 'And what if someone wants to pay by credit card?' he asked.

This is it.

'Yes,' she said eagerly, dry of mouth, 'oh yes, credit cards.' She told him how to make a credit-card sale.

'I see,' he said again, 'I see.' He was silent then, clenching his fingers under his chin and looking down sternly at the list. She could hear the scritch-scritch-scratching of Renshaw's pen but did not dare turn her head to look at him. The scratching stopped and she wondered if he was now looking at the side of her face, the bulge of her stomach as she sat. Her face reddened.

'I see,' Mr Pritchard said again, looking at her and smiling faintly. 'Well, that's very interesting because we've noticed one or two irregularities in your till procedure. Perhaps you'll be able to explain them to us. Now . . .' he opened a drawer and pulled out briskly a great sheaf of sections of old till rolls, stapled together, marked with red ink here and there. Loretta's nerves raced. Like a magician pulling a rabbit out of a hat, he pulled forth with a flourish a slim red vase very much in vogue for ruby wedding presents, placed it on the desk and kept his hand upon it, smiling faintly still as if it were a thing he was tremendously proud of.

It was through. She was caught. He produced item after item and placed them all on the desk, showed her all the proof, all the till rolls, all the credit-card dockets with her initials on. They'd used fake customers to get her. She made a weak show of denying it at first, said she couldn't understand why the amounts hadn't shown up on the till rolls, maybe she'd just forgotten to ring them up. Mr Pritchard laughed. Then he was quietly hostile and incredulous and full of an obvious dislike for her, the kind one stranger could hold for another purely because of a situation, the kind that had always confused and frightened her. 'You forgot to ring them up!' he said. 'But everything balanced at the end of the day. Isn't that a little bit strange?' His voice hardened: 'Can you explain that!'

She began to stammer and her voice broke. Inside she felt a deep hollow sickness.

'Make it easy for yourself, Loretta,' Renshaw said

167

sympathetically from his chair by the wall. 'Just tell us everything you know and don't try to hide anything. You know there isn't any point. If you're straight with us and we can tell Mr Barber you were co-operative, it *may* influence him not to call the police.' She looked at him for the first time. He was tall and heavy with glasses and a big chin. 'He'll make a decision on the strength of our report,' Renshaw said, leaning back and appearing to doodle boyishly on the paper in front of him. 'The more you co-operate now, the better it'll be for you.'

She looked down at her hands in her lap, very still and pale. The police, oh God, she thought. A workman outside somewhere on a scaffold sang. She thought of Mr Barber, a round, white-haired, elderly man with a permanently pleasant expression, who patrolled the store with his hands behind his back once a day, looking at everything but speaking to no one. His decision. 'OK,' she said quietly, playing with her fingers. 'Well, you know. You know I was taking money out of the till.'

Mr Pritchard shuffled papers on the desk, then started shooting prices and dates at her, his voice high and impatient and his look very piercing. He said he wanted to know how long this had been going on, how often, the exact method she'd used, how much she'd stolen altogether, who else was at it? Her mind was a racing blank. She tried to think but there was never enough time before he hit her with another question: 'How? When was this? Go on, go on. How much? And who else was in on this with you? No one? No one! Come on, you expect me to believe you worked all that out on your own?' Loretta mumbled and stuttered. Renshaw sat with one leg cocked over a knee, head on one side, doodling and throwing in a comment or asking a question now and then.

This discomfort, she somehow knew as she talked, groping from moment to moment, would be far-reaching

168

and vital. But she could not think beyond this moment and this room. She stumbled onwards over the wasteland. It went on for so long she lost track of time and didn't bother any more to check her watch, it was no longer relevant. Her stomach heaved and her dry mouth crackled as she spoke. Mr Pritchard watched her closely. She detailed her method clumsily, fog in her mind, going over it again and again. She said she'd been fiddling the till for about four months now but only on Saturdays, and not every Saturday – different amounts, sometimes ten, sometimes fifteen, whatever turned up that was easy. She wasn't sure. She'd never had more than twenty-four pounds at any one time, she remembered that. She thought she must have fiddled about a hundred and sixty pounds altogether. Maybe. Maybe less. Maybe . . .

'Fiddled,' said Mr Pritchard coldly. 'You call it fiddling, we call it *stealing*. Believe me, we take a very serious view indeed of *stealing*.' Then he stared at her with indifference, till her face burned and she was afraid to look anywhere. She was no good at this kind of thing. Her eyes felt dry and stinging. She'd given up by now, gone on automatic. She just wanted to get out of here and go home and talk to someone nice, worry in peace, work it all out. What now? What now? What now? flashing on and off like a neon light. All that money. All that money gone. She looked out of the window at a cold white sky above ornate rooftops. She'd told them the truth, everything.

'No, no, no. You'll have to do better than this!' Mr Pritchard said, then laughed shortly. 'A hundred and sixty pounds! You don't seriously expect us to believe that, do you? Oh, I sincerely advise you not to play games with me! Look here,' he leaned towards her gravely like a doctor about to inform her that she'd got terminal cancer, 'I know when I'm being lied to. It's my job to know and I know my job. I get very angry when I know someone thinks they can pull the wool over my eyes.' He stared coldly into her eyes without blinking, watching as she quietly panicked.

'I don't know what you mean,' she said.

'What would you say,' he said, leaning back and swivelling gently in his chair, kneading his fingers together under his lip, 'if I told you we have proof beyond doubt that you've stolen at *least* eight hundred pounds?'

She gaped. He was mad. 'You're joking!' she cried weakly. 'It couldn't be anything near that! I'd know if I'd had that much!'

'Don't lie to me,' he said.

'I *know* I didn't—'

'Come on,' he said briskly and scornfully. 'Why, only last Saturday we know you took twenty-five pounds in one day.'

'But I didn't do it every week! And it was only Saturdays! No. No. No. Nowhere near eight hundred—'

He slapped a sheet of blank paper and a pen down on the desk and swivelled them towards her. 'Right!' he said. 'Now you're going to sit here and think carefully. You're going to write me out a list of every single occasion you can remember when you stole money out of the till. I want amounts. I want dates. I want to know what items were involved in the sales. We can check. We'll find out in the end, anyway. It'll take a little time but somewhere there's a record of every penny you stole. Did you really think a store this size would let a thing like this go unnoticed? The more you give me now, the easier it'll go with you.' He stood, shaking his sleeve back to look at his watch, his face stern. Renshaw crackled his papers. 'We're going to leave you here for a while to search your memory. Twenty minutes or so. You just think very carefully.'

As they left, Renshaw placed two cigarettes and a book of matches down on the desk solicitously.

'Thank you,' she said solemnly. The door closed. She

170

sagged. She didn't smoke but she lit a cigarette and let it burn away between her quivering fingers. The man was mad. She put her head down on the desk and crossed her arms over it. It was impossible. Did he think she kept a diary, a calendar in her head? Dates, amounts. He was mad. She thought desperately. She'd have to make it up. She could stick a few 11.95s down, those little tea sets, there were always lots of them. One 24.99. She wrote one or two things down and tried to count back the days in her head. It was ridiculous. She leaned her head against her hand and sweated, felt sick, wanted to go to the toilet. Her mind raced: they'll call the police. They'll stick eight hundred pounds on me. Prison. Oh, God. So that's how it ends up! But maybe they won't, maybe they won't call the police in. They never do, do they? I want to go home. I hate that fat bastard with his great fat belly sticking out the front of his suit and his horrible fingers and piggy little eyes. Bastard. You can see he enjoys his job. She gave up and looked out of the window and waited, trying to calm herself by breathing deeply, her brain simmering. The cigarette burned out and she ground it out in the ashtray and lit the other one, pulled on it and blew the smoke straight out again, remembering with scorn how she had used to feel, so warm and secret hauling back her pathetic loot and counting it in her flat in Kinnaird Buildings. She looked at her watch about fifteen times, the fingers moved from quarter past three to twenty to four. By now she would have had her tea break and be getting into the home stretch. A long and terrible fantasy unrolled before her – a sinister court, an echoing prison, she confined, keys and bars and voices in the distance, removed from the world and everyone who cared about her. She couldn't stand it, she'd go mad. And then another thought came into her head. They won't let me have a child now, she thought. Will they?

Mr Pritchard and Renshaw returned and resumed

their positions. 'I can't do it,' she said, pushing the paltry list across the desk, 'I can't remember anything. I told you, it was just a bit here and a bit there, that's all I know.'

Mr Pritchard glanced at the list then tore it up and threw it in the bin. Suddenly she felt dangerously close to tears. This was endless. 'Who else on your floor is stealing?' he asked.

'Who else? I don't know.'

'Oh, come on,' he said. 'You spend all day chattering to one another. You go to lunch together. You talk in the canteen. We know you're not the only one. You expect me to believe you thought this up all on your own? Who else?'

'I don't know. No one talks about it.'

He shot names at her, one after the other.

'I don't know,' she said over and over again.

More names.

'I don't know.'

'You hesitated there. Why? Is she a thief too?'

'*I* don't know. I didn't hesitate—'

'Will you answer the question.'

'I don't know anything . . .'

He hurled his pen down on the desk with great violence, threw himself back and swivelled in his chair, turning his furious face towards Renshaw and making a gesture that implied: What can you do? She's done for. Loretta jumped. 'I *don't* know,' she said, 'I really don't know!'

'Loretta,' said Renshaw, 'we don't want to prolong this any more than you do. We know you're not the only one. I don't think you realise quite how much we do know.'

'If you know so much,' she said, 'why are you going on at me like this? I've admitted everything. I don't know any more, I can't remember anything.'

'What about the black girls?' Mr Pritchard asked.

172

'What about them?'

'How many of them are stealing?'

'I've no idea.'

There were more names, questions. How did this one afford to go to the West Indies this summer? How did that one afford to buy a motor scooter? Loretta gave up and just stopped speaking. Mr Pritchard's mouth snapped shut and he scribbled angrily in a pad on the desk in front of him. Loretta didn't care what they thought any more. She tossed her head and scowled, put two fingers in her mouth and sucked them, looking out of the window. Renshaw lit a cigarette and offered her one. She shook her head.

'Your friends have dropped you in it, Loretta,' Mr Pritchard said drily, sighing wearily and stretching his back. 'They've dropped you right in it.'

She didn't speak. Tears came into her eyes but she didn't care.

'We've already spoken to the others on your floor. Quite a little gang of you, isn't there? I wouldn't bother protecting them. Do you know what my information is? My information is that you're the ringleader. Oh, yes! The ringleader!'

Loretta started to cry.

It was Mr Barber's decision to call the police. She had to wait in another office, with a secretary at work on a typewriter in the corner, and Mr Seton, who gave her a cup of tea and asked her if she'd like a biscuit. But she couldn't eat anything. Mr Barber looked in once. He just stuck his head through the door, looked at Loretta, said, 'Ah!' and smiled vaguely, then went out again as if he'd got the wrong room. She felt that he'd just wanted to look at her. He'd never looked at her before, though he'd passed her many a time.

173

Two policemen in plain clothes came and arrested her and walked with her to the police station, staying considerately a few paces behind her all the way so that it didn't look as if she was being taken in. It was tea time and the streets were crowded with people getting out of work. One policeman was young and grave and polite, the other older and bluffer. The grave, polite one, whose name was DC Mitcham, took her up to a room with tables and benches, where a friendly little Cockney woman, who joked with her and called her lovey, helped her to take out of her bag all the embarrassing old crap that she carried around, lay it on the table and itemise it – dirty tissues, tampons, ancient envelopes and bits of paper, chewing-gum wrappers and Christ knows what – put it all in a clear polythene bag with her rings, her earrings, her cross, her watch. She was taken into a smaller room and photographed with a number, full face and profile, then had her fingerprints taken. She'd gone into a kind of daze and didn't believe that this was finally happening. This had been a nightmare long before it came true. The sky grew dark in a window. She sat at a table opposite DC Mitcham, who got his ashtray positioned and lit his first cigarette, asking her if she wanted to make a statement.

'I don't know,' she said. 'I did it. What can I say?'

He said he thought she ought to make a statement, he'd help her. He got out the form and his pen and took off his jacket and settled himself, yawning. People came and went vaguely in the room.

'They said eight hundred,' she said. 'It was nowhere near that. There's no way I'm admitting to that.'

'They've got to prove it,' he said. 'If you didn't take it, they can't prove it. All we want now is your own estimate.'

'Could I go to prison for this?'

'Put it this way,' he said with the hint of a smile, 'I'd be very, very surprised if you did.' But it was technically

174

possible, he added. Anything's possible.

'They said I was the ringleader. I don't know what they were talking about. I'm not the ringleader of anything.'

'They were trying to frighten you,' he said, 'to see if you were holding anything back.'

He yawned. Both of them kept yawning. She had to go over the whole thing again. It was amazing how long this took, how many details there were, how slowly her brain was working now, how slowly his seemed to be working too. He was quiet and very serious and wrote diligently, his hair hanging in his eyes, and it dragged on and on, cigarette after cigarette, yawn after yawn, and she fiddled with the bare place where her wedding ring had been and wished it was there to turn. It felt like three o'clock in the morning.

'Don't look so worried,' he said, smiling faintly. 'You're not a dangerous criminal, you're just a silly girl.' Then he told her nothing much would happen for a while, they needed time to sort out their evidence. She'd be in court for about a minute in the morning, just to set a date. And then he picked his nails while they waited for her things to be returned to her.

She got home about half past eight. She had to be in court at ten the next morning. Telling her not to worry was like telling her not to breathe. She felt sick and couldn't eat anything and kept talking about prison. Billy laughed outright. 'Don't be silly,' he said. 'As if they'd send *you* to prison.'

'First offence,' said Judy. 'A piddling hundred quid or so – well, a hundred and sixty then, even two hundred, it's still piddling. These people deal in thousands. Millions! This is chickenfeed to them. You've got nothing to worry about.'

No one seemed shocked or bothered by what she'd done. But she started to cry, rummaging frantically in drawers and in the wardrobe, trying to find something

175

decent to wear in court. Everything she had was either tatty or gaudy. Any of the extra she'd spent on herself had gone on make-up and short skirts and coloured tights and Crazy Colour for her hair.

'What d'you want to wear something decent for?' Billy asked. 'You're skint. It's true, it'd look funny if you went in looking all posh.'

'I've got to look *respectable*,' she cried.

'Oh, fuck 'em,' he said.

She didn't sleep. She wouldn't eat breakfast for fear of being sick. Billy and Judy went to court with her. She wore her straight black working clothes and her winter coat and the boots that needed heeling, even though the day was quite warm, and sat sweating miserably on a hard bench in a hot, bleak, yellow basement full of nervous people, awaiting her turn for an hour and a half. There was much coming and going through the heavy double doors that led into the court. People consulted in side rooms, and sighed and smoked and wandered about because there weren't enough chairs. DC Mitcham and Renshaw were there. It was impossible to tell who was a criminal and who was not.

She was called.

The very idea of a court was sinister to Loretta. She hated quiet, shiny, official places. The big wooden doors opened for her and a man whispered, telling her where to stand. Billy and Judy slipped onto the public benches. The room was bright technicolour and everything seemed polished, even the faces of the people. A young man stood in the dock with his back to her, facing the high bench above which three grey, bespectacled male heads looked down. There was mumbling. The young man left the dock and went out by a side door and Loretta was prompted by gestures and whispers to take his place. It reminded her of speech day at school. Stepping into the dock was like walking out onto a stage. She stood lonely, exposed, surrounded on four sides by people who watched, figures positioned by ritual. She stared straight ahead, hands clasped, face burning, unable to take in what was being said, unable in fact to hear much of it as it was directed not to her but to the bench and mumbled. Renshaw spoke. DC Mitcham spoke. Her heart beat stupidly fast and she cared about nothing but getting out of here and going home. The faces were neutral when they looked at her and she knew exactly what they saw: shop assistant, light-fingered, common. They gave her a date some time after Christmas, nearly three months distant. Someone gestured her silently out of the dock towards a side door, someone else took her place. Round and round we go.

It was like one of those punishments at school where you had to stand on your chair or out in the aisle or at the front in assembly, so that everyone could look at you and know you for the wrongdoer you were. You needed panache for a thing like that; if you didn't have it, you were dead. And if you were awkward, shy, fat, ungainly, spotty, unsure, your blight stood on show.

They met her out in the corridor. She smiled. 'Jesus,' she said, 'it's gonna be a great Christmas.' They went searching for the office that gave out legal-aid forms.

Joe hated Ken. He considered ways of doing him over, even thought about tipping off the police but gave up the idea because he didn't want to risk getting everyone involved and bringing the police down on the Buildings in general. No one needed that. He reasoned it would take two people, himself and an accomplice. They'd wait until he left Eddy and Dee's, after dark, lie in wait and give him a good kicking and take all his money. Joe had never done this kind of thing before but he thought about it a lot. He imagined himself Robin Hood-like, giving the money back to all those poor stupid junkies, his friends. And he thought about keeping the money himself and buying a car, telling no one, they wouldn't thank him for it, anyway. But, no, he'd need a partner, he'd never do it on his own. Johnny was the man for the job really, but Johnny, of course, had a vested interest in keeping Ken healthy. Joe had mulled over the idea with Raff a few times but all they ever did was talk. 'I hate that fat bastard,' they said to each other. 'He wants his legs broken.' Sharon, Ken's regular customer, would listen undisturbed; she knew they'd never do anything.

At Christmas Eddy and Dee hired a video and ran films constantly in their darkened front room. The place was always crowded, and always, from somewhere, you'd hear kids' voices and the bleeping of computer games. Someone was always fixing up in the toilet because it wasn't allowed in front of the kids. Someone was always nodding off in a corner. Eddy was always yelling out the door at the kids. When Ken arrived on Friday afternoons, all attention would turn to him, and if

Joe was there he'd get up and leave. Later Sharon and Joe would have a row because Joe would rabbit on all night at her about how stupid she was, how stupid they all were, how someone ought to kneecap that fat fucker.

Christmas was over. Sharon stood at the ironing board smoothing out a dress for Mandy. Wilted Christmas decorations adorned the wall behind her. He'd been going on for an hour. 'I wish you'd shut up,' she said disinterestedly, pushing her hair, darker the longer it grew, behind her ears. Her detachment in argument infuriated Joe and spurred him on to yet more invective. She listened for a while. 'See, the trouble with you, Joe,' she said knowingly, 'is that you see everything in one dimension. It's all goodies and baddies with you. You don't know anything about the man. Ken's all right. You don't know him. Everyone's just getting through same as everybody else. I mean, really, you're just intolerant.'

'I'll swing for that bastard,' Joe said grimly. 'So help me, I don't care, I'll swing for him.'

'You can't,' she said. 'They abolished hanging. Don't you remember?'

She wore a self-satisfied smile. Joe hated it and felt a desperate need to make her lose her temper, just to break that complacency; but he never could. Not unless she was sick, and then he kept as far away from her as possible. 'Stupid,' he muttered, 'I hate stupidity.'

'I hate intolerance,' she said smartly.

'Better than being stupid like you,' he said in a juvenile tone.

'You know, you're so middle class,' she said. 'Really, really middle class,' then added with an air of understated superiority, 'I'm too seedy for you. You can't take it.'

He always lost his temper first. He started yelling:

179

'Wake up, you stupid idiot! You're not even seedy! You're neurotic, the way you clean this place up all the time, you're worse than me! You buy all those stupid women's magazines, for fuck's sake! You're more middle class than just about everybody else round here, what is this ridiculous class fetish you've got?'

'Ssh!' She dumped the iron on its stand. 'Do you want to wake Mandy?'

He strode about the room angrily, taking out his pipe and blowing down it. 'You want to talk about kids!' he said. 'Talk about kids then. All be junkies or tea leaves by the time they're fifteen. Sooner. Colin. Tom. Sunny. Mandy. Colin's nicking things. Eddy wallops him. Great child psychology! What about your poor little fucker? Someone should take her off you!'

'I've heard it before,' she said, 'I've heard it before, Joe. None of it touches her. She sees nothing. Anyway, I'm coming off soon.'

There was a knock on the door. 'Sure,' he said sarcastically. 'Easy.' Sharon went and looked through the spy-hole. She saw the pale, gaunt face of Ian, Mandy's father, and she jumped back as if slapped. She looked again. The full fussy mouth, the straight dark hair, the knitted brow, a face she'd lived with for years and now saw only in nightmares. He knocked again, harder.

'Who is it?' Joe called impatiently.

She ran back into the room and crouched foolishly behind a chair. 'It's Ian!' she whispered. 'Don't let him in, don't let him in!'

Raff, on his way round to Littlejohn's, heard the shouting before he turned the corner, didn't fancy walking slap into some fight, and thought about going round the other way and over the roof. But it was just one voice. Sod it, he thought, and walked on into the courtyard, where a single figure in a black leather jacket weaved about and yelled boomingly up at a window on Joe and Sharon's staircase. 'Fucking bitch!' he roared, cupping his hands round his mouth so that his deep voice was hollow and impressive. 'I'll break yer fucking neck, yer fucking bitch, yer! Yer fucking cunt! Send yer man out! Coward! Coward! They're mine! Mine! Mine! Yer fucking bitch, yer!' Raff ignored him and went on up to Littlejohn's.

'Was Ian still there?' Littlejohn asked as Raff sat down. Littlejohn sat cross-legged in front of a flickering fire, gaunt and spiky with gappy teeth.

'Who?'

'My brother,' Littlejohn said. 'Big scene round at Sharon's. He's a nutter.'

'Oh, yeah,' said Raff. 'Yeah. Tall feller? He was shouting up at the window.'

'That's the one.'

'Your brother? How come he's so tall?'

Littlejohn shrugged. 'He was round here first but we didn't let him in. Standing on the doorstep burbling on about how he's made a pile of money and he's come to take his kid away to a better life. Load of bullshit. If he's loaded, how come he's looking for a doss for the night?'

Raff said nothing.

'Maybe he really has got money,' Eric said. 'Maybe we should let him in and roll him.'

'Huh!' said Littlejohn. 'You don't know him. He's always got some story. He's not getting in here. Give him a foot in the door and you'll never get rid of him.'

A couple of hours later when Raff was going home, he saw Ian swinging gently in the playground. These nights were windy and very cold and the courtyard was just beginning to spot with rain. 'Hey!' Raff called on impulse as he passed. 'You looking for a place to crash? You can stay up my place if you want.' Afterwards he never knew why he did this.

181

'Who are you?' Ian asked bluntly. He looked suspiciously through the gloom, a long ghostlike face with small eyes. Raff said he was a friend of Littlejohn's and walked on with a show of indifference, already regretting that he'd spoken. But Ian followed and fell into step beside him, launching into a long moan about Littlejohn that lasted all the way home and a while longer: 'He's gone very strange! I suppose he always was a bit.' He was surprisingly well spoken and personable. 'Seems to be hanging round with a lot of very heavy people. I presume you know Sharon? Very bad influence on her, he was. I used to warn her when we lived in Brixton but you just can't tell some people. Very naïve, very easily led, you know, but wouldn't take simple good advice. There isn't a lot you can do for someone like that. Did you know he was a poofter? He never lets on about it and it's made him go funny. Well, I know he's got serious problems but his big failing is in trying to make everybody else pay for them. That's where him and me always fell out. I don't take shit, you see. Wouldn't even let me in!' His voice rose in mild indignation, 'I mean, he is my fucking brother after all, and it must be at least four years since I saw him. Not even a cup of tea, I ask you, talk about bitter! God, he looked awful!'

Raff was tired and just grunted now and then while Ian talked, thinking, Oh Jesus, what have I let myself in for?

'No electricity?' Ian asked as Raff lit the candles.

'They cut me off a couple of weeks ago.'

'That's a drag. No decent sounds.' He looked around as the room appeared in a ghostly glow. 'This your place?' he asked. 'Nice little place. Who did all the pictures on the walls? You did? Well, you're prolific anyway! You wouldn't have a bite to eat, would you?'

'There's some bread and cheese in the kitchen,' Raff said, lighting the fire, 'help yourself. You can bring me some while you're at it. You'll have to take a candle. And put the kettle on.'

'What did your last servant die of?' Ian said jovially, getting up. 'Here. Roll one.' He placed a tiny fragment of dope on the table, took a candle and went out. It was such a small amount that Raff had to stick a bit of his own in too, to make it worth bothering. He was smoking a lot lately, maintaining that it helped to keep him off the booze. Ian came in laden with everything in the kitchen he could get his hands on, which wasn't very much — bread, cheese, onions, Marmite and tea. Ian talked and Raff, who was only half there, drank gallons of tea and smoked and grunted, sometimes listening, sometimes turning off and drifting. It didn't make any difference. Ian was one of the biggest bullshitters Raff had ever met, so transparent and overblown he was pathetic. He talked and talked and ate and ate and kept rolling spliffs with Raff's dope. 'Do you mind?' he'd say politely, going ahead and doing it anyway.

Sharon, he said, was insane. However, he'd be prepared to take her back if he thought he might be able to help her, although that didn't look likely. She was in it too deep, this veil of maya, illusion. She was a naturally dependent person, he said, all this nonsense with heroin was just a replacement for him. She seemed to have a *need* for slavery, it was what did him in in the end, her need to be constantly abased. Of course, that was why she was living with a darky now. It was just her way of getting back at him. She *revered* him. He used to say to her: Darling, don't grovel. Very strange person. Wouldn't listen to what was good for her. She had some filthy habits. Used to pee in the sink and wipe big bogies on the bed sheets.

He lit a cigarette and smoked it with fussy lip movements, squinting at it, trying to blow smoke rings and failing. 'She hates men, you know,' he said. 'I don't mean like the feminists. I mean on a much deeper level than

183

that. She's out for nothing less than the absolute destruction and eradication of the entire male sex.'

'Jesus,' said Raff. 'Someone ought to tell Joe.'

'This lot round here obviously haven't got her sussed,' Ian went on. 'She's laying low, not letting on to her real nature. Mind you, she's very cunning. It took even me a while to suss her and I'm usually very perceptive. Sometimes I just find that I know all about a person as soon as I meet them, it's a kind of clairvoyance. But *her*. She's like one of those missiles that pass underneath the radar. You take note. Start watching her. She's not human sometimes. Even her face isn't human – you seen it in some lights? You look at her sometimes and she's demonic. You ever hear of Kali, the Goddess of Destruction?' He shrugged, leaning back and pushing his long hair from his brow gently. 'I suppose all this sounds crazy,' he said. 'Well.' Another sad shrug. 'She has her problems. But it worries me that my kiddiewink's growing up with such a person.' He looked sideways thoughtfully for a long, dramatic pause, blowing out smoke in a listless trickle. 'Worshipped me, the nipper,' he said softly. 'She screamed when Sharon took her away. Hung onto the banisters and screamed. She didn't want to go with her.'

'I always thought it was the other way round,' said Raff.

'What?'

'I thought it was you that left her.'

'Oh, yeah, I did. This was another time.'

Then he started to criticise and analyse Raff's pictures. He said they had energy but lacked discipline. 'You ought to stick at it, though. They do have a certain individuality. I like the one over the window.' He said he knew some art dealers he could introduce Raff to if he ever got it together to do anything serious. 'There's big money in it if you know the right people,' he said. 'That's where I might be able to help.'

'Fuck off,' said Raff.

Ian ploughed on. He talked about the people he knew and the life he'd been leading 'these past three crazy years'. He'd made a lot of money on the international art scene but right now he was working as a photographer – fashion, mainly. He'd done a lot of stuff for *Vogue* and the *Face*, you've probably seen it. Of course, he didn't use his own name. Oh no! He laughed. He liked to cover his tracks. He'd been living with this model but they'd just broken up; beautiful woman but terribly insecure and desperately jealous of every other woman he came into contact with. Always comparing herself, why the hell are women like that, for Christ's sake? She resented being kept. Poor Lisa! She had problems.

He'd had an offer to edit this poetry review in LA. He was mulling it over. The money was lousy, of course, but, then, money wasn't everything and he had a few other strings to his bow to bring the shekels in, ha ha. His own work was being published quite widely now. LA, though! Have to think about that one. 'Do you know LA?' he asked. 'You should go there, just for the experience. I was there on and off all last year, keeping tabs on the galleries. Crazy place. Plenty of money in LA. Plenty of good pharmaceuticals too. Half of Colombia must have gone up my nose in the past few years.' Course he kept it all under control, not like some. Then he started on about drugs. Coke, sulph, meth, acid, hash in the apple crumble, Diconal in the milk shake, the time he saw God, the time he experienced nirvana, the time they had to take him away in a straitjacket and pump him full of Largactil. He was one of those crashing drug bores; he'd go on and on like the Ancient Mariner.

At two o'clock Raff stood up and said he was going to bed. 'Turn the fire off,' he said, going into the back room. 'I'll chuck you a couple of blankets out.'

Raff didn't sleep well. He kept waking up and hearing Ian prowling about the flat, seeing the flickering of

185

candlelight under his door, hearing laughter and small sinister banging sounds. He dreamed fretfully that the flat was on fire. About nine he gave up and woke fully and got up. Ian was still prowling and he knew it was imperative that he get rid of him without delay. Emerging, he saw with tired disbelief that the furniture was slightly rearranged and that Ian was sitting smoking in Raff's favourite jacket. The place was fuggy. The rain drizzled at the window behind him and his presence was large.

'Put the chairs back where they were,' Raff said, heading for the kitchen.

'There's more room this way,' he heard Ian say indolently.

'Like fuck there is!' Raff called over his shoulder. 'Put them back!' He stood in the kitchen, tired and frayed and hungry. Ian had eaten everything, down to the last crumb. 'Jesus!' Raff muttered, stomping back into the living room. 'You greedy bastard,' he said. 'Couldn't you have left a couple of slices?' He slammed about the place, anger rising in him, his head heavy and his nose stuffy. 'I'm going down the caff now,' he said. 'You'll have to go. Give us my jacket.'

Ian didn't move. He was smoking another cigarette and picked a fragment of tobacco carefully from his big red lower lip. 'Yes,' he said slowly, 'this'll do me nicely.' It was unclear whether he referred to the jacket or the cigarette or the flat.

Raff started getting his shoes on. 'Come on,' he said, 'no pissing about. I'm wearing that jacket now so give it here. Come on, you've got to go now.'

Ian seemed to have grown larger and more solid with the morning light. 'Well, I tell you what,' he said, standing, laying his cigarette down in the overflowing ashtray on the table and slowly taking the jacket off, 'why don't you go and have your little snack while I clean up in here a bit—'

'Like fuck you will,' said Raff. 'Fuck off. Now!'

'OK, OK, OK!' Ian turned away, looking slightly hurt and very reasonable. 'Obviously you feel I've intruded enough on your hospitality.' He shrugged himself into his own black leather jacket, turned and frowned wearily down his long pale nose, took from somewhere a sharp thin blade that he drew slowly down his sleeve and studied with pursed lips. Raff watched, on guard, furious, unafraid because he felt instinctively a lack of danger, that this was just some stupid elaborate show. 'Do you think you could see your way to lending me a little cash till later today?' Ian asked politely, buffing the blade gently against his elbow, 'I left my cheque book in my other coat . . .'

'Fuck off,' said Raff in his most dangerous tone. 'You scrounging bastard.' He gave Ian a great shove that sent him tottering backwards in the direction of the door. 'You threaten me and I'll stick the fucking knife right up your fucking nose!'

Ian put the knife away quickly and nipped out into the hall as Raff advanced. 'Keep your temper!' he said in an uncertain tone. 'Who's threatening anyone? I'm not threatening anyone.'

'Get out of my fucking house!' yelled Raff, and shoved him again, harder, so that he fell against the door and made it shake. He straightened hurriedly, opened the door and slipped out onto the landing, then retreated a safe distance to the stairhead, poised to run.

'You're paranoid!' he called back shakily.

'And you're a coward!' jeered Raff from the door, exhilarated because he was coming out on top and it was so easy. 'You've got the knife and you're still scared!'

'Shit on *you*, cuntface,' said Ian. 'You're not right in the head.'

Raff lunged forward but Ian ran away down the stairs, boots clattering. Raff turned and closed the door, made a show of giving chase until he reached the second-floor

187

railings, stood looking down till the tall figure appeared in the bright, drizzly courtyard below, then shouted abuse down, telling him to keep his ugly face out of here if he didn't want it kicking in and to leave Sharon alone too. Ian walked away through the drizzle. At the bar gate he turned. 'Heavy friends she's got!' he yelled. Raff started down the stairs at a run but by the time he'd reached the bottom Ian had gone. Raff walked off in the direction of the market, weaving a story to tell in his head: He came at me with a knife, but I . . .

That day he was moved along by an extreme restlessness that pushed him about from place to place, in search of something to take his mind off how badly he wanted a drink. In the afternoon it pushed him edgily into Eddy and Dee's. God knows why, he might have known there'd be no encouragement for him there. The money he still owed was a thorn between them. Earlier he'd met Joe. 'Sharon's really pissed off with you,' he'd said. 'What d'you let that creep stay at your place for?' God knows how everyone knew, but everyone did. Joe was snappy about it. Later, Littlejohn was lethargic and hostile: 'You shoulda listened. I told you he was a prick.' So he told himself he was in Eddy and Dee's to sort things out with Sharon, who was there with all the other junkies, but now that he was here he didn't know what to say and she was refusing to look at him.

The room was tense. Ken hadn't given out yet. Raff felt nervous, as if his presence had somehow helped produce the tension, as if they'd all been talking about him before he came in. No one took any notice of him, apart from Sunny, who came and stood between his knees and looked up into his face. Ken presided with his flabby chuckle and endless voice and they listened as if he were a sage, laughing at all his stupid jokes. Sharon sat beside him, looking frozen. His swollen hand moved against the side of her breast. A balding Christmas tree dropped its needles. The kids argued in another room. The colour screen chunnered away in the corner. Raff was so nervous he started making snide comments about the crap on the TV, the Christmas decorations, Ken's baby-blue jumper. Everyone knew that Raff and Ken couldn't stand each other, it was like an invisible ray that crossed the room between them. No one took any notice. Ken looked indifferent and Raff went on exuding hostility. His guts were convulsing for a drink. Suddenly Eddy turned in his chair and started berating Raff about the money he owed, his voice high and aggrieved. Raff blinked, surprised. 'I'm getting it,' he said. 'Soon.' Dee made a long crude blowing sound and Ken laughed, a fruity chuckle that made Raff want to leap across the room and smash his face in. This fat greedy slob, he thought, can get anyone to suck his cock.

Sharon had had a terrible night and was all fidgety and twitchy. Ian had raised old monsters. Mandy had been awake listening to the voice below, saying nothing.

Sharon had had a big row with Joe, who kept saying if she didn't pull herself together he was going to see to it that they took Mandy off her. The poor little bastard, he said, torn between the devil and the deep blue sea. Joe was just mouth, Joe would never do anything, but still he was a bastard to say it. Mandy heard him. She kept crying. And this stupid bastard had given the great creep a place to stay right on her doorstep. And there he sat making clever-clever comments as if nothing had happened.

'You,' she said darkly, trembling, pointing at him, hoping to make the best of the little drama for the listless onlookers, 'you are no friend of mine. You better stay away from me in future.'

'I'm sorry, Sharon,' he said aggressively, 'I didn't know what he was like—'

'Course you did!' she yelled. 'You knew enough! You knew what he did to me! But you didn't think it

189

mattered. You're like him. You're on his side, you think it's OK to hit women. You come on all nice but you're just a miserable little creep that hits women. I'm finished with you!' She started to cry.

Ken's hand moved up to her shoulder. 'You let it out, love,' he said.

'Jesus, Sharon,' Raff said miserably, moving Sunny aside and leaning forward, 'it wasn't like that. Take it easy!' He looked around. No one looked back at him, not even Willie or Johnny. 'Bloody hell, what's the matter with you lot?' he said. 'Come on, Sharon, I made a mistake, for Christ's sake. I'm sorry. What do you want — flesh? I even got rid of him for you in the end. I threw him out. He won't come back now, I scared the shit out of him.'

'You?' Dee said quietly. '*You* couldn't scare the shit out of a two-year-old.' She had a way of making her voice an insult in itself. Some people laughed, some stoically ignored what was going on.

'Why don't you just fuck off?' Eddy said to Raff. 'You're upsetting people, can't you see? Go on. Fuck off.' And everyone waited to see what he would do. He made a quick chopping gesture with his arm and jumped up awkwardly, went to the door and turned there briefly. 'You stupid bunch of wankers!' he said, quietly and emotionally, and left before anyone could respond. He hoped he'd left a bad atmosphere. He was close to tears. He hated them all. He ran down the stairs and stood in the courtyard wondering where to go, not wanting to go home. The sky was dark. He was a miserable little creep that hit women. Nothing had worked out. He'd ended up here and he didn't know why, this place, these people who cared nothing for him. He went up to Loretta's, as he always did when he felt the self-pity rising in him, but she wasn't in. He considered knocking on Judy's door, but all they ever did these days was argue and upset each other and he couldn't face any more hostility today. Anyway, he hadn't seen her for ages.

190

So he went downstairs and stood in the courtyard watching some pigeons strut and peck, fighting a feeling of panic and hating this flat, post-Christmas feeling everywhere. He'd go home, he thought. Back to Manchester. Stay at his mum's and get fed and let her make a fuss of him. God, he thought. How long is it? Going on for two years, must be, and he never wrote letters. He'd never written one in his life. He figured he might last a couple of weeks before she started driving him mad. Then his feet carried him away, to the pub, which was open by now, where he spent the last of his Christmas dole.

Loretta's solicitor told her not to lose too much sleep. He said he was practically sure that she wouldn't go to prison, such a thing would be outrageous and he'd lodge an immediate appeal if it came to it. But anyone could be unlucky. You might get some old codger who's got indigestion or he's just had a row with his wife or something, or someone might decide that this kind of thing was rife and it was time to make an example of someone. Don't forget, he said, most magistrates are employers themselves. Theft from a fellow employer. Who do you think they're going to identify with? I'm being honest with you, he said. I can't promise that you won't go to prison, but I can promise that it's highly unlikely.

That was all she remembered, that she might go to prison. No one took it seriously. She'd meet people and they'd joke with her about it: Hello, Loretta, still on the loose? How's the criminal, then? Ma Booth, the woman who broke the Bank of England! In the end they'd only stuck her with a hundred and forty-six pounds odd and everyone knew she wouldn't go to prison for that. She laughed along with them. But she didn't sleep nights. She lay awake counting the days to that time when she would have to stand once more in that shiny sinister room with faces on four sides. It wouldn't go away. The faint chance of prison swelled and swelled till it drowned the world. She clung to worry like a rock. 'Forget it,' Billy said. He had no idea – all this was quiet, internal, nocturnal – her brain ran a treadmill and he didn't see. She'd look at him sometimes and think, My God, it's like living on separate poles, and want to scream at him: Look, look, look, I'm cracking up! And if she did try to talk about it, to him or to anyone, it was always the same: Don't worry. Don't worry, don't worry, don't worry. It'll be all right. For heaven's sake, this is nothing, nothing at all!

Long nights, mornings, afternoons sometimes – she spent too much time in bed, even though she didn't sleep. There was no urgency about getting up in the mornings; she missed working but couldn't face all the effort of getting a job, maybe an interview, having to make up some story about why she'd left her last job, what she'd been doing this past year, references, all that. Oh, no, she couldn't face all that, not till this terrible time was over, this weight on the brain gone. Prison. She'd have to tell her mum and Auntie Bren. Everyone would know. A cell, the clanging of iron doors, locks, bars. Shut away. Incarcerated. For her sins.

She spent her savings on bills and dope, ran out of money, went to the doctor's when she couldn't afford to buy as much dope as she would have liked and asked for something for her nerves, she had this court case coming up and it was doing her in. She held out her hand, showing the doctor how it shook. He prescribed some pills to make her sleep, said that was all she needed, a good rest and to try and stop worrying, gave her tips on how to keep the mind positive. The pills didn't work so she went back and he gave her Valium, but she hated them, they wiped her away and made her feel like nothing at all. She stopped taking them after a couple of

192

days and stuck them away at the back of a drawer somewhere. She went to her mum's and cadged a few strong sleepers. They didn't work either, so she went back to see the doctor again and he tried her with something else. When she went back again and told him they didn't work, he told her she was probably imagining it and that she must be sleeping without realising it. But Loretta knew that those disturbed limbos she fell into now and then, day or night, didn't count as sleep. They were just occasional fade-outs. In the nights she'd listen to the loose doors in the flat open by themselves.

From her immediate fears she'd pass to greater ones: war, illness, loneliness, cruelty, death, the whole caboodle. She'd feel as if she were living on an unexploded bomb, ticking relentlessly under her feet, and it would begin to seem that life and the world itself existed just to frighten her to death. And sometimes during those endless nights she'd listen to the sounds in the courtyards, the screaming and shouting and puking and sobbing, and think: My God, my God, this is a funny world. What am I doing here?

A couple of days before New Year she met Jimmy in Littlejohn's place. He was sitting quietly drunk in the corner, crouched and awkward. There was a rash on his neck; his eyes were moist and sore and the look in them, full of humour and misery, stabbed her. 'Jimmy,' she said anxiously, sitting beside him, 'you OK?'

He smiled and said she was just the person he wanted to see, he had all these really good tee-shirts round at his place going dead cheap, did she know anyone who might want to buy one? 'Come up and have a look,' he said, scrambling up. He'd got an old suit from somewhere and wore it roughly and elegantly.

Back at his flat, he produced armfuls of baggy tee-shirts

193

in Cellophane wrappers and started pulling them all out to show her. He said she could have one, any colour she liked, she was his very good friend and he wouldn't take any money from her. Two fifty to anyone else.

'Where did you get them from?' she asked.

He laughed and tapped his nose.

It was cold in the flat and he lit the fire, then cleaned up all the mess in the grate, old ash and dog-ends. 'I've been feeling lousy, Loretta,' he said quietly as he worked. 'It's ridiculous. You think going to another place'll make a difference, but it doesn't. It follows you. I think I'll go away.' He squatted on a small stool with his head and wrists hanging, a little red brush dangling from one hand. He yawned. It was tea time but felt very late and the sky was black at the window. Loretta had not slept for so long that every period of the day had assumed a kind of wrung-out quality. Jimmy talked about his plans: he'd go home for a while and sort himself out, see his old mum, then come back to London and get a job and some money. Get back on his feet. He could do it, he'd done it before.

Then Dee came knocking on his door. She came in and stood sternly in the living-room doorway with Colin aimlessly behind her chewing gum and looking hard, a huge love-bite on his neck. Dee looked as if something had made her very angry very recently, as if she'd been brooding on it all the way over here and couldn't wait to let it out. 'Hello, Loretta,' she said, short and polite, getting that over with, then snapped at Raff: 'All right, where is it? Today, you said. What excuse have you got this time?' Colin made a cynical sneering smile at Loretta and crossed his eyes at Dee's back.

'I'm getting it, Dee,' Raff said. 'Honest, it's just taking a bit of time. Look, I've got all these tee-shirts, I've got someone coming round to buy some tonight and you can . . . '

194

Dee said he could stick them up his arse. She'd heard it all before, she was sick to death of hearing it, he was a scrounge and a bullshitter, useless, she was sick of asking for the fucking money. Why the hell should she have to keep asking for it all the time? Why should she have to come traipsing all the way over here anyway? 'Don't show me tee-shirts, man!' she cried. 'Show me cash!'

'I'm getting it, I said!' He turned his back on her and knelt by the grate once more, looking at the fire, 'I've told you, I'm getting it. I'll be getting a *lot* of money soon.'

Dee laughed without humour, turning sharply to go and pushing Colin before her. 'Oh, yeah?' she jeered over her shoulder, 'Oh, yeah? You? *You*'ll never have anything. You're pathetic!' She left, slamming the front door behind her.

Jimmy closed his eyes. His throat convulsed. Moisture oozed from beneath his lashes. 'And all I've done for them,' he said mysteriously; then his face crumpled and he cried in earnest for a moment into his hand. It was disturbing, inappropriate, and gave Loretta the feeling that he'd come to the edge of a pit and was swaying on the rim, looking into the depths. She didn't know what the feeling meant and was afraid for him and wanted to help so badly that she knelt beside him on the rug for a while and put her arms around him. She didn't know what else she could do. He cried listlessly, his face white and sheened with a fine sweat, then pulled himself together and went on tidying the room. 'So what d'you think of the suit?' he said, becoming jaunty. 'Not bad, eh? East Street market. Coulda been made for me.'

She saw him again down by the shops the next day, hanging around near the phone box. He was in a good mood. He said he'd got rid of a few tee-shirts and had enough money to go home now, tomorrow, he was just ringing his mum to tell her he was coming. 'Wait for me,' he said, 'I'll buy you a drink. I'm gonna give her a surprise. I'll pretend to be someone dead official, I'll say, I'm ringing about your son . . . and she'll think, Oh no! What's he done now? She hasn't heard from me for two years, you know. I'm a fucker for not writing.'

All the windows were out in the door of the phone box and Loretta heard everything.

'Hello?' he said in a deep crusty voice. 'Is that Mrs Raffo? Mrs Agnes Raffo? And do you have a son called James Michael Raffo? You do? . . . Well – this is him . . .' His voice thickened and there was a long pause. Looking, she saw him wipe his eye clumsily. 'Yeah,' he said, smiling. 'How you doing, lovely?' She moved away and browsed at the paper-shop window. A few minutes later he came out in high spirits and they went to a pub in the market and sat in the back room and talked for a while, drinking lager. 'Look,' he said smugly, 'only one drink. That's my lot for today.' He played the fruit machine and lost. 'Bastard,' he said. 'They're rigged, these things. I'm starving hungry. Fancy something to eat in the caff?'

Loretta said no, she had some shopping to do. 'I may not see you again before you go,' she said as they left, 'I'm going to my mum's in the morning.' She was going to sneak a few more sleepers, not that they'd do any good.

'I'll see you in two weeks, then,' he said.

'If I'm still free.'

'Oh, cobblers!' he said. 'Course you'll be free, you daft bugger.' He laughed. 'And if not, I'll come and break you out, guns ablazing!'

They stood in the cold street market. 'You've been good to me, Loretta,' he said. 'You've saved my life. You're a diamond, babe.' Then he swept lightly down towards her like a courtier to a queen, taking her hand and kissing it with wonderful smiling gallantry. She laughed, and then they hugged, kissed quickly on the mouth and went their ways, she to the bread shop in the next street, he to the café.

Judy was sitting at the table near the window. She saw him as soon as he opened the door, he saw her, it was too late for either of them to pretend they hadn't. They hadn't met for a while and didn't really know whether they were supposed to be avoiding each other or not. Neither knew whether to smile. He stood at the counter, waiting for toast and coffee, then came and sat down opposite her, grim-faced.

'Want some toast?' he asked.

'OK,' she said. He tore it with his fingers, the soft, warm, underdone toast, and gave her half. They didn't know if they really liked each other but had missed the friendship. Behind his head was the lace in the window and people going by huddled in their coats in the grey, inactive market. The silver urn steamed and hissed. The fat Italian man was cleaning up behind the counter and talking loudly to someone at the back of the room.

'I'm going back to dear old dirty Manchester tomorrow,' Raff said.

'For how long?' she said sharply, taken by surprise, sure, somehow, he meant for good.

'Oh,' he said, 'about two weeks, I suppose. Going to see my old mam, haven't seen her in two years. She'll be dead pleased to see me. I just phoned her and she started bawling.' He smiled, suddenly full of the old friendliness, and Judy smiled back. 'She'll drive me barmy,' he said, 'I'm her favourite. I'm her big son, I can't do any wrong.'

'Do you good to get away,' she said sympathetically. 'This place is just too much at times. It's driving everyone crazy. You know what I saw the other night? I heard this noise and I looked out and there's this guy down there taking a running kick at someone's head— '

'Someone's head!'

'Not a head! Yes, a head, but with someone attached to it. This poor man lying on the ground and this other man . . . .'

197

'Thank God for that!' he laughed. 'I had awful visions of someone booting a head around the yard.'

She laughed too. 'See,' she said, 'we're laughing about it. Poor bastard gets his head kicked in and we laugh.'

'It's a funny old place, right enough,' he said, rolling himself a cigarette. 'I've been in worse, though.'

Judy made patterns with slopped tea on the scratched red Formica. 'I've been thinking about going away too,' she said, 'right away. Out of London. I don't know.' She shrugged and pulled an awkward face. 'I was thinking of looking for a teaching job somewhere. I don't know. I have to start *doing* something. Time's a-wasting.'

He looked at her seriously for some moments. 'Do you remember,' he said then, 'all those awful things I said to you. Well, I never meant them. Sometimes I'm just a horrible bastard. You never want to take any notice of anything I say when I'm being a bastard.'

'I know,' she said coolly. 'It's past. Forget it.'

'You serious? You're really going away?'

'I dunno. Just ideas.'

'It's this grey time of year.' He turned and leaned back against the wall so that he could talk to Judy and look out of the window at the same time. 'Everyone's at a low ebb. You should never make a decision when you're at a low ebb.'

Loretta walked past the window, hurrying along the pavement with a preoccupied air, pale and drawn and worried. Raff jumped up and gawked after her through the lace curtain, pushing his chair clumsily aside with one hand resting on the back, bent sharply at the wrist. 'She looks bad,' he said, sitting down again and shaking his head a little, 'Loretta looks bad. It's a shame, this court thing. So stupid. They shouldn't do that to someone like Loretta.' His roll-up had gone out. He struck a match and touched it to the ragged, burned paper and inhaled deeply, frowning, shaking out the match. He said he had to see Rob. He was going to let the daft bastard stay in his flat while he was away and

198

keep an eye on things. 'I'll never get rid of him when I get back,' he said. 'I'll have to move in with you.' And then he was gone, leaving the door ajar slightly and the cold coming in.

'They never teach your friend to close doors?' the fat Italian man grumbled. Judy got up and pushed the door to, then bought another coffee and sat on for a while, stricken suddenly by a terribly idle and sentimental mood. She heard the cold traders shuffling and hawking out there, and thought of the summer that was past: it seemed distant, romantic, sharp and treacherous as a childhood memory.

Raff packed his things early next day, left them by the door, went to Eddy and Dee's to sweeten them with a fiver and make peace, then took Sunny to the park and watched her play on the swings and slide till both of them were freezing to death. After he'd taken her home, he went up to his flat and on the landing met Betty, the old lady from next door, all bundled up against the cold, her cracked red fingers fiddling with a purse and an enormous shopping bag. 'There you are, darling,' she said. 'I thought you'd gone. Your lady friend was up looking for you. I told her you'd gone. She looked ever so disappointed.'

'Oh, *shit*.' He looked at his watch. Quarter to two. Not much time. Let her stew, he thought, but he turned anyway and ran back down the stairs, round to Judy's, where he knocked confidently on the door. After a moment the spy-hole darkened and he pulled a face at it, then she opened and stood looking pleased to see him, holding a piece of bread that dripped honey over her fingers.

'The old lady said you'd gone,' she said.

'Not quite. Can I have one of them? I'm starving.'

She turned, smiling, and walked before him into the

kitchen. 'Close the door,' she said. He came in and lounged against the fridge with his hands in his jacket pockets, watching the knife slice soft bread, talking fast. He'd been to the park with Sunny, he said, he'd stood at the foot of the slide to catch her as she came down; then he'd gone up and she'd stood at the bottom and stretched out her arms. 'I'll catch *you*, Raff!' she'd said. He thought that was very funny.

'Just think,' he said, 'this is your last chance to make me a cup of tea.'

'Put the kettle on.'

'Honestly, you're terrible the way you treat your guests,' he said. He put the kettle on, muttering to himself, then started pulling things down from shelves and poking around generally to see what there was for him to nibble on. They began to argue amiably, carefully, hoping at least for a happy parting, then loaded things onto a tray and went and sat by the fire in the warm, curtained room. The radio was on, silly music, and he got up and walked about the room eating and talking about himself, breaking into a dance every now and then. He said he was back on the wagon. Again, ha ha. New Year's Eve with his mum, see, and he never drank with her, it was an unbreakable rule. Suppose he might see Patsy and the kids up there, but he didn't think it was likely. And if he did he wouldn't know what to say to her any more. Hello, I suppose. 'I don't really blame her now in a way,' he said, 'I mean, I wouldn't stay with me if I wasn't me. If you know what I mean.' He talked and talked, nervous, quick of movement, then started pulling at his knuckles and making them crack.

'Don't!' She cringed. 'I hate that!'

He grinned and got cocky. 'Don't you like that?' he said innocently, pulling away, crack, crack. 'Why not? I bet it's possible to play your own bones like a musical instrument. I knew this girl once that could dislocate her jaw at will, she used to pop it in and out, it was horrible.

200

I bet you could go on TV. Make a fortune! Listen, I can do my toes too, they're really long, my toes . . . ' He bent down and made as if to take his shoe off.

'Stop it!' she yelled.

'Listen.' He came and stood by her chair. 'Beethoven's ninth concerto for bones,' and cracked a knuckle loudly right by her ear.

'God!' she said, flinching away. 'I can just imagine what sort of horrible kid you were. I bet you were a right awful, irritating little bastard, weren't you? You still are. You must be one of the most irritating people in the world, you know that?'

He listened smiling, as if she was praising him. 'I know,' he said. 'It's awful but I can't do anything about it. I was born like this.'

'That's no excuse,' she said.

'Terrible, isn't it?' he said. 'And the worst of it is, you really do like me, don't you? You can't help it. That's the awful thing about me.'

She turned in the chair to clout him, but he laughed and grabbed her head very firmly between his large splayed hands, planted a quick hard kiss on the hair that covered her forehead, and walked away. 'Can I have an apple?' he asked, taking one from a bowl of fruit on the windowsill, lying down on his back on her bed and taking a big bite. A silence came down. He chewed and swallowed, then recited slowly, looking up at the ceiling: ' "The wind was a torrent of darkness among the gusty trees . . ." ' broke off and swivelled his eyes towards her and grinned. 'Aha!' he said softly, 'I seen the look in your eyes then. Surprised, weren't you? Didn't think I'd know anything like that, did you? See, you're just an old snob really. Think I'm thick. See, you don't know all there is to know about me. You'd be surprised.'

'One thing I've always known about you,' she said, 'is that you're not thick. Go on, what comes next?'

'I don't know, I only know the first line. I know lots of

bits. I only ever remember the first lines. I know: "He clasps the crag with crooked hands", and "Oh what can ail thee, knight at arms", and "If I should die think only this of me" . . . We did all that at school. And I know: "The boy stood on the burning deck, Picking his nose like mad. He rolled them into little balls, And flicked them at his dad".' He burst into loud laughter and she laughed with him. Then he stared at her until she became self-conscious. 'I have to go in five minutes,' he said. She looked back at him with a vague half smile but he couldn't read her expression at all.

She was regretting the end of their friendship. Something had changed in the past few minutes, she felt it like the first tang of a new season in the air. Whatever happened now, the old was at an end and something must replace it. The moment grew and grew. Something should be said; each wondered what it was and who should say it, till the moment was gone, missed.

He jumped up and threw his apple core at the bin and missed. 'Christ, I'll miss the bloody bus, I know it!' he said. 'I'll have to run all the way. Victoria! God, you know what Victoria's like, takes about ten hours to find the bus,' stretching and getting himself to the door, 'I can't let her down. I bet she's got all kinds of goodies in for me. Great! Wait till you see me when I get back, I'll be all fat and spotty.'

'Have a good time, Raff,' she said, following him out into the hall, 'take care.'

He opened the door and stood in the cold doorway working out his final words. They would leave just the right impression. He was good at this kind of thing. He gripped the doorframe and leaned in towards her. 'All the mistakes I've made,' he said, 'I never tried to hide them. I know them. Some people don't know their mistakes but I know mine. I *know* them. Do you know what I'm saying?' As he spoke he remembered saying words like these before, to Patsy years ago, and his brain clicked

202

like a cog. Judy said nothing for a moment, pulled up short by an urge to laugh at him and also to cry. He would be thirty in June. The lines about his mouth were deepening pleasantly.

'You're so nice when you're sober,' she said, then turned, ran back into the room and returned to fill his pockets with apples and pears. 'For the journey,' she said.

He laughed. 'You're pulling my jacket out of shape,' he said.

Before she could think any more about it, she put her hands on his shoulders and kissed his mouth. He was ready, parted his lips and received her avidly, sticky and sweet and clinging, pulling her closely against him. She hadn't wanted this. No, not the old game, please not the old game. Such beauty there was about it, such pain. She started to cry. 'I know,' he said gently, 'I know, I know, I know.' They stood for a long time in the doorway pressing their crotches together hard, nuzzling and fondling and kissing deeply. It had been so long since either had done anything like this that there was a kind of innocence to it, as if they were very young and discovering these sensations for the first time.

'Oh, you bitch,' he mumbled against her eyelid. 'You wait till I'm running for a bus.' They began, slowly, to disentangle. 'I *can't* let her down now. She'll have been shopping and everything . . . ' They kissed again and pulled away, smiling and excited, hugged quickly once more then stood apart.

'Safe journey,' she said, touched his shoulders and kissed his cheek, turning him and pushing him on his way. He went smiling, without another word or look. His footsteps faded. She missed him already. When she realised just how much she missed him, she knew it was useless and hopeless and that she would do the foolish, the unforgivable thing as soon as he got back. She'd take him on.

*

203

'I don't sleep,' Loretta would tell Billy.

'Yes, you do,' he'd say mildly, 'I've seen you.'

'How do *you* know?' she'd snap. 'Just cos someone's got their eyes shut doesn't mean they're asleep.'

'Oh, you can tell,' he'd say, and she'd throw down whatever she was holding and stamp about the place with tight lips, wishing she could crack his complacency like a head.

She counted off the hours, day and night, and waited for relief. In fifty-one hours, all this will be over. In forty-eight hours, all this will . . . And she couldn't eat anything.

Billy wasn't coming to court this time, he had a few days' work with Joe, so she went with Judy. She was sick twice the morning of the ordeal, drily and politely, in Judy's toilet before they set off to catch the tube. She felt a fool. Her forehead and upper lip sweated under her make-up; she'd put on too much and knew it, but it was too late to do anything about it. Judy made her sit down for a few minutes, then gave her a slug of brandy from a little bottle. 'No, it won't make you sick,' she said. 'I promise. It'll settle your stomach and calm your nerves.'

Loretta sipped the brandy and tried to make a joke of it. 'Can you see it?' she said, giggling. 'Throwing up in the dock! Whoops! All over the side!'

She wore her old boots and a coat of Judy's that had some buttons missing, but she thought it looked better than her own. 'I'm really scared, Jude,' she said as they stood on the crowded tube, hanging on straps. 'It's ridiculous. I feel really frightened.'

'You'll be all right, Loretta. Think how good it'll be when all this is over. You'll wonder what on earth all that worry was about.'

Loretta smiled with her mouth but her eyes were somewhere else. Someone stood up and she slipped quickly into the vacant seat, got out a little mirror and checked her face. Her eyelashes were spiky, overdone. A searching anxiety appeared in her eyes whenever she looked in a mirror. 'I hate my face,' she'd said once to Judy. 'If I could have just one wish in life, it would be for a new face.'

The yellow basement was more crowded than before, and too hot. Many of the people were damp from the morning rain, many had colds, sniffed and coughed and sneezed as they sat drearily or walked up and down. It was as if the room itself were running a temperature. Loretta had another slug of brandy and Judy had one too, and they waited, waited, talking and running out of things to say, waiting, watching the people, watching the big doors open and close, wondering who in this crowd would go down, who would go free, who was innocent, who guilty, waited and waited and waited. Real time had no meaning. Time was a sludge, a stagnant pool.

They called her name. It began again, like a film rerunning. This time it was a middle-aged woman in a red coat in the dock in front of her. She was waved off and Loretta was waved on. Bright lights and pink faces on all sides; so taken was she by the brightness and strangeness and the effort not to be sick, that she felt quite elated. Her heart pounded. Too big, too sharp, too real, three heads above a dark, forbidding bench, two male, one female, all grey, the woman's hair very tightly curled. The man in the middle was pink like a well-cured ham and wore glasses that reflected the light, obscuring his eyes. The man on the end was forgettable. Someone told her to sit down, so she did. There was a great deal of muttering. The three heads looked at her with no apparent animosity or sympathy or curiosity. Other faces looked at her in the same way. And the mumbling, undramatic process began. Her statement was read out, sounding incredibly stupid and making her flesh creep. The muscles in her face tightened up. A list of her thefts was handed up to the bench and the three passed it about among themselves, studying it with care. The man in the middle said something to the woman and she chuckled, then all three conferred in hushed tones like people on a quiz show. Any minute now, thought Judy, someone will say, I'm going to have to hurry you up . . .

Loretta's solicitor stood up. He said that Loretta was of previous good character, a hard worker, as her references would show, and that she had been under extreme pressure at the time the thefts were committed. She lived in a deprived and demoralised area, in sub-standard housing, her husband was unemployed and she herself was also unemployed at present but was seeking work. She had been suffering from depression but was now receiving treatment for this. She was very sorry she had acted as she had, now realised that what she had done was disgraceful and was determined that she would never do such a thing again.

She could see it in the local paper. A few lines. And as he spoke she knew beyond all doubt that she would do such a thing again. Her face burned. To her horror, her eyes filled with tears. There was nothing she could do, the tears ran down her face, her nose began to run. She took a tissue discreetly from the pocket of Judy's coat and dabbed at her face with it. No one took any notice. Her character references were passed up to the bench and the magistrates read them, sharing them out and passing them round, and a soft murmuring and rustling of paper descended on the court. Soon, she thought, this will all be over, staring straight ahead, her clasped hands comforting each other, shaking a little. Faces looked at her directly from time to time, neutrally. The three heads conferred again, then the one in the middle, glasses winking, announced an adjournment for them to reach a decision, everyone stood, rustle, rustle, they filed from the bench and out of a door at the back and everyone sat down again and started to talk softly among themselves like untroublesome children in a school break. Loretta didn't move or look round. Her solicitor came over and leaned against the dock and said softly to her, 'Don't worry. This doesn't mean anything. They just fancy a coffee break every now and then.' She smiled at him. She didn't believe him. They were out there arguing about how long they were going to send her to prison for.

Ten minutes passed. It lasted forever. When they returned, the one in the middle told her to remain standing. He gave her a little lecture about the gravity of the offence, for which she could be sent to prison; to have stolen was bad enough, but to have abused the position of trust in which her employers had placed her showed a disregard for standards that must not be excused by her situation. There was altogether too much of this kind of thing going on and the tendency was often to underplay it. However, in view of her previous good character and the fact that she appeared to realise the seriousness of what she'd done, the court was prepared to be lenient. She would see a probation officer to determine her suitability for community service, and appear before the court again in two months' time. 'I hope you understand,' he said, 'that this is an alternative to prison.'

So I don't have to go to prison? she wanted to say, but was too scared to open her mouth. She felt as if she were on her knees on the floor, begging for mercy before these people. There was a shuffling and a mumbling in the court. Someone waved her out of the dock and she aimed herself at the side door. Someone else stepped up and took her place. Round and round we go. Outside in the annexe there was a table and a very highly powdered woman, fat with blonde hair, who gave her an appointment to see a probation officer. 'You are very fortunate,' the woman said sternly. 'Very, very fortunate to have been given this chance.'

'What does it mean?' Loretta asked.

'It means the probation officer will talk to you,' the woman said. 'Try to discover how you *fell into crime*.' She lowered her voice regretfully at these words. I don't

207

believe this woman, Loretta thought, she's like something on the TV. Another bad drama. 'Then the court will decide what sentence to pass.'

'Oh. I thought that *was* the sentence. I don't understand. Do you mean I could still go to prison?'

'It depends on the report,' said the woman.

Loretta began to walk. Her solicitor walked with her and told her not to worry. People were always telling her not to worry. 'Yes,' she said. 'Yes. Yes, I know.' He was very kind. She walked along with her bit of paper clutched in her hand, rushed down the corridor looking for Judy. She felt awful, horrible, six years old again, frightened and shamed and chastened. It wasn't over. She was starting to cry again and couldn't help it. It wasn't over.

Judy came running up to her. 'What's the matter?' she asked. 'It's all right. What's wrong, Loretta?'

'I thought it'd be all over,' she said. Her brain reeled, trying to imagine how many hundreds of hours she had to start counting off now. 'Why are they taking five months out of my life?' she asked plaintively. Her eye make-up ran. They sat down on a bench while she fixed her blotchy, feverish face. 'God, look at me!' she moaned. 'Oh, my God, the state of me, have I been standing there looking like this in front of all those people?'

'They don't matter. They don't matter at all.'

'If they send me to prison after all this,' she said, 'it won't be fair. I'm already paying.'

'Don't be stupid!' Judy said. 'You heard him. They're not sending you to prison. You do things like painting old people's homes and stuff like that . . . '

'No,' she said. 'This woman said. It still could go either way. It all depends on this probation officer. Oh, my God! I'll have to make a good impression!' She spoke as if this were a desperate impossibility.

'Loretta,' Judy said sternly, 'you're being ridiculous. Now you're being ridiculous. Now just stop it, stop it right now, I'm beginning to lose sympathy.'

'You don't know,' she said. 'You don't know what it's like. It isn't you it's happening to. You just don't know, you don't know, you don't know.'

In four more days she reached a state of Valium calm, having sought out the old bottle from the back of the drawer, moving slowly and acquiescing in everything that happened, anything for a peaceful life. Judy and Billy kept trying to shake her up and get her involved in things, so silly and kind and ineffectual. They kept dragging her to films she didn't want to see and they took her out for a beautiful Indian meal she couldn't eat. By now she must have known she was being a fool and overdoing all this but it didn't seem to make any difference, it had become a habit that had taken over her body and wouldn't let it eat or sleep. So stupid to jolly up the mind when the body went its own sweet way. In the end, stoned one day, they started talking about a day out in the country, quite a ridiculous prospect in the middle of this bitter winter. 'Oh, come on,' Loretta said, stirred by this from her lethargy, 'now you're really going over the top. I've never heard of anything so stupid in my life.' But they'd got hold of the idea by now, they were laughing and making plans and saying how lovely it was to be out in rotten weather. She told them they'd gone completely mad.

She sat on the settee taking up a hem, her fingers quivering finely. 'Well, I'm not coming,' she said, but they took no notice. they said they'd get Willie in on it so they could use his van, then they got it down to a choice between upriver, Pangbourne or Goring or somewhere, or Brighton.

'Brighton's not the country,' she said.

'Well,' said Billy, 'it's the seaside, isn't it?'

'You must be bloody mad,' she said. 'I'm not walking

209

up and down Brighton sea front in this weather, I can't think of anything more ridiculous.'

'Fuck the weather,' Billy said. 'It'll be a nice day.'

'A good winter day can be better than anything,' Judy said. She was standing looking out of the window, as if the weather out there were any indication of the weather to come. This wasn't for Loretta, it was for her. She wanted more than anything else to be out of this place, out under a big sky, just for a day. Down in the bleak back-window place between the buildings some children wheeled around an old supermarket trolley. It was a still, white-skied day, very cold, but crisp and bright. I wonder why I'm still living here? she thought. I wonder why? It's different for me, she thought, I don't have to be here. I don't have to be here. And she turned and looked at Loretta and knew that Loretta couldn't get out. How could Loretta get out now?

Loretta had had enough of the silly pair. Oh, let them waffle on about how nice it is to be freezing cold on a river bank in the dead of winter, how great to miss the crowds, how lovely and subtle the colours are this time of year. She made some excuse about having to get something from the shop to get away from them for a while and ended up having a cup of coffee in Dee and Eddy's. They were in front of the TV watching a video of some war film full of exploding shells. There was a kind of perpetual Sunday feel about the place although it wasn't Sunday. Sunny lay on Eddy's wide lap, asleep with her mouth open, and the boys sniggered about the room making fun of his flared pants. The smell of cooking wafted in from the kitchen. Dee yawned grotesquely. It was like being at home with your parents.

The phone rang and Dee stretched out a worn languid hand and picked up the receiver from its niche. 'Hello?' she said, 'nine two — Oh, hello. Yeah? OK. Hahahahaha . . . It's Raff,' she said. 'Tom, find me a pencil or something. Hang on, Raff.' He was ringing from his mum's in Manchester with some message for Rob, something about the flat. Dee wrote something down on a piece of paper. 'You'll never get rid of him,' she said, 'never. He's well stuck in there now, you know,' and laughed.

Loretta leaned towards the phone. 'Hello, Jimmy,' she called. Dee gave her the receiver.

'Hello, lovely,' he said. 'How's life in the palace?'

'OK,' she said. 'Just goes on.' She told him about her court case. As she did she was overwhelmed by the fear that something dreadful was going to happen to her, that they would take over her life, her freedom, for what she had done. She didn't say all this, she didn't even think it, it was just a cold mist engulfing her from the inside out. Jimmy was very cheerful. He told her not to worry and then he said he had to go, he was running up a bill, and rang off saying he'd see her soon. She went out into the wintry courtyard where some council workers were loading a truck with old debris from some flat — pots and lamps and a broken guitar, sticks of furniture. A craggy old man in threadbare clothes hovered, ready for anything worthy of salvage but finding nothing. The yard was ghostly, full of boarded windows. She walked home alongside an iron fence that had created a narrow alleyway to the shops, where no one dared walk after dark.

It would be nice to see the country.

Willie took them in his white van to a place where the riverside fields went on and on and they walked for miles under a wide sky with trees upon a skyline and a sharp white line defining everything. It was bitterly cold, but clear and bracing, the reedy Thames still and shiny, silver ahead. There were Friesian cows, woods, rutted fields and gateways full of frosted hoofprints, tyre tracks, a peaceful spire and a stark rookery in dark spiny trees. Some boys were fishing along the bank, the maggots

211

motionless, frozen in the tins. Willie stopped and talked with the boys about the fishing. One had caught a big silver fish that lay dead beside him, one great desperate eye devouring the sky. And later there was a warm half-timbered pub with a stuffed fox in a case, drink and food and good conversation, and later still the long drive home in the dark, the lights of London, the old familiar streets. Willie dropped them off at the foot of their stair-case and drove away.

Going up the stairs they met Johnny coming down, his face strange and tight. 'Oh, man,' he said softly, looking at Judy. 'Raff's dead.'

When Agnes came home from shopping, Jimmy was in the kitchen, she could hear him moving about. She called to him but he didn't answer. Instead he came and stood in the doorway that linked the kitchen with the living room, his eyes small as if he'd just woken up, one hand to his head.

'Oh, mam,' he said, 'I've got a terrible headache.'

He swallowed and blinked and took two steps into the room, then cried out in a way that chilled her to the bone. He fell with a suddenness she'd remember for ever, as if the puppet master had just let go of the strings, striking down the framed pictures of desperate smiling schoolboys and grandchildren she never saw, striking the bone above his right eye a crashing blow on the edge of the tiled grate. She dropped her bag and everything rolled out, packets of tea, sugar, Jaffa cakes, cigarettes and matches and strawberry-flavoured ice cream and a little bottle of whisky. She ran to the phone and dialled 999 and asked for an ambulance. He lay face down, breathing too loudly. She said her son had just collapsed with a terrible headache, he was unconscious, what should she do? Her voice was calm but her hands trembled. A voice spoke to her, steady, taking details, instructing, promising help, then clicked into the void. She ran into her bedroom and returned with a pink flowered duvet and covered him gently, then sat down on the floor beside him to wait, afraid to touch him in case some touch of hers should hurt him more. He breathed noisily, puffily, his face flushed and troubled. There was blood above his eye.

'It's all right,' she said, 'I won't let you go. You'll be all right, lovely.' But he knew nothing of her, never regained consciousness, and in a few hours he was dead.

At first Judy didn't believe in Raff's death. Death was too harsh a word and Raff was still Raff, still cracking his bones in her room. He was away, in Manchester, at his mum's. Of course she knew really that he was dead because wherever she went people were shaking their heads and saying, Oh, isn't it a shame about Raff! I can't believe it. Good old Raff! My God! They spoke to her gently, as if she were a widow.

'I can't believe it,' she said.

'I can't believe it,' they said back to her.

Dee and Johnny and Loretta were prone to tears. Judy didn't feel like crying. She thought she ought to and she tried, but she couldn't. Oh God, she thought, he's gone, he's gone, what does it mean? All she felt was a deep restlessness that kept her walking about her flat, roaming the Buildings, visiting people, going to the shop when there was no need to. But there was no emotion. She thought there must be something wrong with her.

After three or four days of rambling she suddenly realised that where she really wanted to go was Raff's old flat, to see his pictures on the walls. She thought Rob was still living there so she went up and knocked, but there was no answer. It seemed she'd stood a million times outside the familiar door, nothing had changed. He was looking at her now through the spy-hole and would open to her at any second. But instead she heard a sound behind the door across the landing and knew that Betty was preparing to come out and nail her and talk on and on and on about what a shame it was, that nice young man, and she couldn't face it, any of it, the pictures, the old woman, those bereaved rooms, whatever might be lying around in there. She fled. Next day she found out that Rob had in fact gone, no one knew where, and then it was too late: the Council went in and smashed the meters and some of the pipes and boarded the doors and windows.

There was no trace remaining. No one had a picture of him or a letter he'd written. This is sad, she thought, I should cry. She lay in bed in the dark, eyes wide open, trying to force tears. He was dying all the time. I could have made his last days happier. What did it feel like for him to die? Was he scared? Was there a moment when he knew? She listened to the trains at Waterloo. Time passed. In the early hours a woman started screaming in one of the other flats. That went on for a while and then silence returned, disturbed only by a rising breeze that dully banged the door to the roof. Someone had forgotten to wedge it with the rope. Later some kind of battle took place below, involving hordes of people who roared and yelled until the police came and broke it up. Nothing remained then but occasional furtive scurryings and the weary banging of the door. She turned over, pressed her face into the pillow and pulled the blankets over her head. I don't want to live here any more, she thought. An ambulance went by, siren blaring.

In the morning she went out and bought a few magazines and scoured the Opportunities columns for teaching jobs, ringing a few that looked likely. Later she started working out the blurb for the applications. It took her mind off things.

A week passed. The place was different now. Johnny and Willie had gone up to Manchester for the funeral. They'd asked her if she wanted to go, but she had a horror of funerals and couldn't go through with it. It made her feel guilty, though she didn't quite know why. What did any of it matter when a person was dead?

Suddenly, late one evening lying on her bed, she

215

started to ache persistently, frighteningly, deep in her chest. She'd been drifting, building futures, wondering what would have happened if he'd come back. She imagined making love to him, how he would feel and sound and look, imagined it slowly and completely till they reached the climax, together, of course, and perfectly, and then she pulled away in fear of his ghost, jumped up and ran across to the table, opened her notebook and scribbled boldly on a clean page, as on a gravestone, his name and the dates of his life. Finished. Nothing she imagined would ever come true. He was dead and that story was over.

Then she started crying. It went on for so long she was afraid it might never end. She went to bed crying, fell asleep, woke up crying. When she had to go out or talk to anyone, she found she could stop, but it would start again whenever she was alone, something her body had to do, like sweating. By the third day she didn't even try and fight it, just let it trickle on as she walked about in her flat, doing whatever had to be done. It made no difference at all to the ache. This is it, she thought. It doesn't end. I want, I want, I want, I want, I want and I can't have. This is it, now. A human being is a pain-bearing machine.

Late on the third night she went to bed and lay awake listening to a battle that raged below, men and women fighting, doors banging, feet that ran, a drama that rose to crescendos, fell into lulls, tailing away finally till there was nothing but one man crying out there in the dark. His crying was long and terrible and tore her up. Oh, God help him, she thought. Whoever he is, whatever he's done, God help him. She could stand it no longer, got out of bed and put on her kimono and stuck her head out of the window, some half-baked idea of helping in her mind. But the man ran away when he heard her window open, a shadow along the wall. The yard was empty and peaceful. She would have to stop crying soon, she knew.

This couldn't go on. Her face was always wet. The cold night air stung her cheeks and she closed the window, closed the curtains, turned on the light and wandered about the room thinking about Raff, unable to sleep. It was incredible that he did not exist. She sat down at her table and he was there, very close and real in the silence after the crying man. He would walk in at any moment, invisible, touch her and say, What's the matter? What are you bawling about? Oh, stop crying! She saw his face in her mind so clearly that her heart felt like a tooth being pulled.

She'd been right all along: better to live alone, to stay apart from it all, better never to have a special friend but to care for everyone, distantly. Love brought sorrow in the end. Well, she already knew that. Life was just kicking it into her a little deeper. She stood up, hugging her ache. In the mirror she saw her strange face, older than it once had been. Time runs.

She went back to bed and fell asleep when the birds began to sing. The next day she thought she was better and took a trip to town, the first since before Christmas. But things conspired to set the ache going again. A cat. A pigeon. Someone's eyes on the tube. Anything that lived and could look her in the eyes set the ache off. People's eyes were like mines: everyone who had ever existed was buried somewhere deep down in every one of them. Sitting on the tube surrounded by mines, she broke into a sweat. How can I cope with this? she thought. She bought things here and there, some writing paper, a bag of apples and a Chinese cabbage, a magazine, a pair of cheap, dangly ear-rings, a bottle of red wine. In the late afternoon she went home and got drunk and danced about the room to the music on the radio, loud and brash and popular. Tonight will be the eleventh night since Raff died, she thought. She started to cry again but stopped quickly, danced with her glass of wine, laughing aloud when she felt like it and singing sometimes. Stay

217

drunk. 'Oh, he's all right,' she said aloud to her friendly self in the mirror, smiling. 'He's OK.' She was sure of it. He was OK. Somehow. She refilled her glass, went to the window and skygazed sentimentally, wishing she could get a message through to him. She was sure she could do it, she could do anything. Reach along the dark, inward-seeking ray. She wished there was some reason that might satisfy her as to why he'd lived at all, only to die so casually.

The sky grew dark and music came from windows. She finished the wine and felt an urge to be out in the cold so went down to the shops, trying to think of something to buy. As soon as the cold air hit her she knew how beauti-fully drunk she was, how strongly her heart beat, how full she was of wisdom and confidence. She met Sharon and Joe and Mandy trooping up from the tube station. 'Hello!' she said brightly, and they stood and talked, hunched against the bitter cold, clouds of breath between them. She didn't really know them all that well but it didn't matter at all because she could go anywhere now, talk to anyone, do anything.

They invited her up to their flat for tea and she found herself sitting in their bright, neat living room among all the plants, gazing down into a round basket full of a soft moving heap that was three kittens and a big tortoiseshell cat on an old Indian blanket. Sharon and Joe were arguing mildly in the kitchen. 'Look,' said Mandy, 'this one's got a funny eye.' She pulled up a thin spiky kitten with one anxious milky-blue eye and one slit. 'Mummy bathes it.' She was dark and solid, in blue gingham and a bow. The kitten's pink mouth opened in silent appeal and it struggled in her hands.

Judy's eyes filled with tears that she blinked back. 'Poor little thing!' she said gaily. 'Let's put him back.'

Joe came in and stood behind them. 'Want one?' he asked. 'They're ready to go.'

'Oh, no!' she said too quickly. 'I don't want a kitten.'

She knelt down and put her hand into the basket and the kittens rolled over her hand. She started to cry. 'I'm sorry,' she said, laughing about it, 'I'm sorry. It's the kittens. They set me off.'

'You're OK,' said Joe, 'don't worry. It's OK. You can do whatever you like in here.'

She put her face down to collect itself. How nice they are, she thought, I never really noticed before how nice they are. When she looked up Mandy was watching her closely. 'I'm all right now,' she said.

'Of course you are,' Joe said, smiling, sitting down and taking out his pipe. And if she took a kitten, she knew, it would purr in her ear at night, sit on her shoulder, grow, stalk about her room, gaze silently into her eyes, sit beside her in quiet communication for hours. Then it would go out one day and never come back and she'd always wonder what became of it, or it would get run over by a car. She'd see its stiff ears in a gutter and her heart would break.

Six or seven weeks passed. In early March the dullness of winter evolved into days of sharpened clarity, full of early frosts and brilliant skies.

Loretta, waking slowly from a half sleep at ten in the morning, heard Billy moving about in the next room. She lay in limbo listening until he came in and sat down on the bed beside her, a little threadbare about the gills but neatly dressed in his best jacket and clean jeans. 'How do I look?' he asked. He was going to see about a job but she knew he wouldn't get it. Other people got jobs, Billy didn't, not these days.

'OK,' she said. 'Yes, you look nice.'

He asked for money for his fare and she fished about in her bag that lay down beside the bed. 'Here,' she said. 'Try and bring some change.'

219

'OK. See you later.' He kissed her cheek and left, like a dutiful son kissing his mother. Loretta sighed, closed her eyes and heard his footsteps clattering down the stairs, taking them two at a time as he always did. The air in the room was cold, everything was cold, even his footsteps sounded cold against the steps. She'd stay wrapped up in bed, not sleeping, drifting in and out of thoughts, floating up and down, drowning and emerging again and again till she came to fully once more and thought about getting up. This was what she called sleep. It seemed silly to get out into the cold and shiver and think about what to wear, what to eat, how awful she looked, how the dust needed cleaning from the carpet, the dust that would be there again tomorrow.

Someone knocked at the front door. She lay listening. Sometimes, around mid-day, Judy would come knocking to get her up. But Judy was away and wouldn't be back till tonight, an interview up north. Whoever was there knocked again and as if on cue the bedroom door slowly opened itself. Anyone at all could be out there, your killer or the love of your life. Someone scuffled down the stairs. She lay on, warm and still like a pupa. It was very quiet. Finally, bored, she got up, put on her dressing gown and went into the kitchen, moved the washing up out of the bowl and had a wash, jerked her hair into life with her hands and thought about breakfast. She wasn't hungry. She got dressed in front of the fire, pulling over her head a jumper that was too short and had lost its shape. She would walk around all day trying to pull it down. This is all silly, she thought, putting on her make-up with the same habitual boredom with which she cleaned her teeth. She was sick of being skint. They couldn't go anywhere. They couldn't do anything. If anything wore out they couldn't replace it. They could eat. It was all just stupid.

First she went up to Walworth Road and got five pounds' worth of electricity stamps, reducing her total debts now to just under a hundred and thirty pounds and noting it diligently in her diary. She expected another debt soon, after court next week, a fine, couple of hundred maybe. She knew now that she wasn't going to prison. Not this time. To be safe she must never do it again. Loretta knew she'd do it again. She had to stay out of places with big bright displays. She'd break into a sweat and have to leave, run away from clean new jumpers in plastic bags, cream for the face, tins of peaches and plaited loaves and ear-rings like butterflies. She lived in horror of finding something in her bag that shouldn't be there. She got the tube to Balham where Rita and Keith lived now in a ground-floor flat with a big tangly garden they shared with a young Asian couple. But she didn't stay long. Rita was burbling on about gardening and Keith was dismantling a TV and spreading it out all over the middle of the floor. Rita took out her cards and sat down at the table and shuffled them, saying she was going to try and get in touch with Jimmy through them. 'The Fool!' Rita said, smiling. 'What do you bet we get the Fool?' But the first card she turned up was the Magician. 'Hah!' she cried loudly.

'Oh, stop it!' Loretta said, irritated. She thought the cards were witchy and sinister. 'What's that got to do with Jimmy? You didn't even know him.'

Rita talked of how Jimmy was lucky in a way, he wouldn't be here for Armageddon. She talked of doom and prophecy, holes in the ozone layer, murder on the streets, of Kali Yuga, the last age, the end of time and the world, until Loretta felt fear crawling up her gullet from some place in her stomach like a long tickling worm, and went home in a fog of confusion. She was sick of fear, fear of Armageddon, of war, of poverty, of stealing, of people with power. Fear was the element she moved in now.

She tried to tell Judy, who sat drying her hair by the fire in her flat, home less than an hour. She had no idea how the interview had gone, she said, no idea at all, she never could tell. She listened to Loretta speak in a quiet, matter-of-fact way about how funny she kept feeling lately – sort of – sort of like waiting all the time for something to happen, only not in a nice way, you know – something horrible . . .

'Like what?'

'I dunno,' she said. 'You know me, I'm not very good with words.' Then she said she felt all the time like someone was coming to get her.

'Who?' asked Judy.

'Dunno,' she said, and laughed, 'I don't know what I'm talking about.'

Later she said she was sick of everyone telling her she was paranoid. 'I don't think I'm that daft,' she said. 'Sometimes I think it's daft not to be scared. I don't think it is me, I think someone wants to lock me up and they'll probably get me in the end. And I think Rita's right. I think we're all going to die. I mean, why do we always think we're immune? It's *real*, isn't it? I mean, where's it all going to end? I'm glad I never had kids now, I tell you, I'm glad, I wouldn't want them around when it all — ' She laughed. 'There's no cavalry,' she said. 'The cavalry isn't coming.'

'Oh, don't!' Judy jumped up with her wet hair hanging limp and cold around her face. 'Please, Loretta. We're all just hanging on by our fingertips as it is.'

'But I'm scared,' she said in the same even tone. 'I'm really scared. Why shouldn't I talk about it?'

Emotion would have been better than the quiet fear seeping from her like a scent.

'Don't you go doing this to yourself, Loretta,' Judy said. 'Don't you go doing this to *me*.'

Loretta shrugged and went off to make the tea. Later Judy came across, and Littlejohn with a two-litre bottle of red wine. Littlejohn wore bright red and looked thin and mobile like a small monkey. His teeth were terrible.

Half-way down the bottle, he and Judy began to argue about the meaning of life. They sounded incredibly stupid to Loretta, like two fools each trying to think up a bigger story. Littlejohn thought there was no meaning, Judy thought there was. Then they changed sides without seeming to realise.

She went to bed and left them going round in circles, heard them leave and Billy come to bed, lay listening to the trains at Waterloo and the odd siren till some fight broke out below with much shouting and breaking of glass. 'Don't come near me!' a man screamed. 'Don't come near me! I'll cut your fucking head off! Once and for all, I'll cut your fucking head off!' Oh, shit, Loretta thought, here we go again. Billy slept on. Oh, I'm sick of this, she thought, I'm not putting up with this any more. Jesus Christ, I swear I'll do myself in if something doesn't change. But it finished and she dozed awhile until she heard Billy getting up and remembered that he was going to his mum and dad's today, then dozed again until he came in and kissed her goodbye. She lay listening to him running down the stairs. I'm always listening to Billy run down the stairs, she thought.

When she got up she felt strange. Something had changed. It was like a dizziness, as though she might be getting ill, so that she lay down immediately on the settee, afraid to move, a little panicked but anaesthetised. Had to take things easy. Under the table she saw what looked like a hydrogen bomb exploding all in purple, but it turned out to be a bunch of chrysanthemums in a photograph on the back of a magazine. She sat up, reached for the magazine and began leafing through it, came to a picture of a pretty woman in a lovely print dress, all soft blues and mauves and creams and purples. She could wear a dress like that. She knew. The positive impact of print, she read. This season's single most significant dress. Exquisitely coloured and impeccably cut with striking shoulder detail and soft flattering collar.

You could debit your Access/American Express/Diner's Club, etc., etc.

She stared at the picture for a while then got up, washed, dressed herself in a short red skirt and the jumper she was always pulling down, did her make-up, then noticed that the button of her skirt was hanging on by a thread. 'Bloody thing,' she mumbled and pottered about the place looking for cotton, short of breath as if with fear, unable to lose this feeling of unease, almost of premonition. She found a reel of blue cotton and sewed the red button on without taking off the skirt, watching the even, hypnotic movement of her thick able fingers with the long tough nails that never broke – such a detail she noted as if they were already gone, already just a part of memory, and realised with a shock what she was thinking of.

Over and over and over and over went the blue thread in the centre of the red button. I could do it, she thought. It was a story she was telling herself. Here's how she would do it: she'd get out what was left of the Valium, and all the sleeping pills she'd nicked from her mum's over the past few months, and she'd eat them down, one by one. After the first few it would be like looking over a cliff or staring into the barrel of a gun: you'd look at yourself and you'd wonder – Oh God, Loretta, what are you thinking of! – but there'd come a point where you knew you had gone too far. Then you would lie down and go to sleep. And oh, God, you would think, I didn't really want to die.

She'd thought about it before. People did it every day. Ordinary people, they walked past you in the street, sat beside you on the tube.

She wouldn't have to go to court next week. She wouldn't have to wait for them to put her in prison, turn the key on her, leave her there, shut away from the people she loved. She wouldn't have to wait around for them to blow her up or poison her or shoot her. She would never grow old and fat and wrinkled in a council flat with shit on the staircase and broken glass outside the window and nights full of screaming. She would just step away from it all, exciting, exhilarating, like playing truant from school and missing some ordeal you'd been dreading for weeks, damn the consequences. Let them carry on, that lot out there, writhing about like a box of maggots. She wouldn't be here any more, she would be . . .

She looked at the blue point at the centre of the red circle and froze. At different moments in her life she'd believed in different things. Sometimes she'd had faith in a great, open-armed, gentle God, sometimes in karma and rebirth, sometimes in nothing, sometimes in heaven and hell. At this moment she hung free, knowing nothing. A ball of fear came into her throat, stuck there and wouldn't go away. She tried to swallow it but it clung. Dear God, it wouldn't go away. It would never go away till she'd carried this thing through to an end. How strange and easy that all the answers lay no further away than this day she was moving through.

She jumped up, terrified, broke the thread, ran into the hall and grabbed her coat. Run away from these terrible feelings. What are you thinking of? Where is there to go? She slammed the door and ran down to the courtyard. What a day, bright blue, shiny, still cold but with a tinge of spring. She wasn't real. She was in a film, a camera followed her every move; every incident was soaked in significance, but the meanings were beyond her. She walked around the corner and met a man who used to live on their old staircase years ago. He was tiny and wizened and wore a shirt with the words President of the United States across the chest, held a long, thin, yellow leash on the end of which an incredibly beautiful cat sniffed at the slimy black gunge in a grid at the end of a drainpipe. 'Hello,' he said brightly.

'Hello,' said Loretta. The cat was magnificent –

smooth, tawny, like a miniature mountain lion. 'What a lovely cat!' she said.

'Yes,' said the President of the United States proudly. 'He's what we call a – marmalade cat.'

'Why is he on a lead?' she asked.

'This way,' he said, smiling and giving the leash a little tug, 'he doesn't get lost.'

Loretta moved on. She walked to Nina's with the fear screaming in her head all the way. Fear of dying, fear of living. She walked briskly down the dusty, thundering road on this lovely day, and no one looked at her. No one knew. Nina didn't know, even though she stood right next to her and looked into her eyes and spoke with her. But how could she know? Loretta moved through the film, delivering lines on cue, laughing on cue, smiling, sniffing her wrist when Nina dabbed perfume there, hugging Stephen as he leaned against her smelling sweet and laundered, admiring the beautiful dress which lay on exhibit across the bed. It was flame red with yellow tips, just like a tulip, and it belonged to her boyfriend's sister. Nina lay down on the bed beside it and caressed it as if it was a person. 'I covet!' she groaned. 'I covet! I covet!' Loretta laughed. Nina said she had to go to Wilfie's, 'Come on, you come with me, he got some money for me, we can *spend* it!' She was in very high spirits, took Loretta's arm like a child and led her out, leaving Stephen with her mother and sister, down in the lift with its vocal walls. Shit, the walls said, Fuck Bastard Nazis Gina loves Terry, Darren Bates has a great big hairy horn. Someone had drawn a picture of it.

They got on a bus and got off in Stockwell, bought raspberry lollies because it was such a nice day, sucked them till their mouths were red as they walked to Wilfie's house. A handsome boy of about fifteen dug over a bit of earth in the back yard and a little girl in a green coat roller-skated uncertainly up and down the path. A shed door stood open. Nina talked to Wilfie through the back

226

window and Loretta waited. Wilfie always acted as if Loretta didn't exist. A savoury smell drifted through the open window and her stomach craved food. The smell was the smell of cooking drifting over the schoolyard at eleven in the morning, the smell of breakfast drifting up the stairs on Sundays when she was a child.

A strong lanky young man appeared in the back door and performed an exaggerated double take when he saw Loretta, as if she were the most beautiful thing he'd ever seen. 'Goldie!' he exclaimed. 'Why haven't I seen you here before?'

'Because I haven't been here before,' she said. He pushed the shed door wider and went in. Loretta saw hutches and the patient grey faces of rabbits. He drew a rabbit out of a hutch and held it casually in his arms. 'How many rabbits have you got?' Loretta asked.

'Seventeen at the moment,' said Wilfie's brother and came out to show her the rabbit, a wondrously fat, matronly creature with a nose like pincers. Its eyes would not look directly at her.

'Poor thing,' she said. 'Poor thing.'

Then Nina took her arm again and they walked down the path and out into the street and down in the direction of the high street. Wilfie caught up with them after a moment but passed them by and walked on ahead without a glance. 'He's coming too,' Nina said. Loretta thought for a while then said she had to go and see someone up near Clapham Common, she might as well as she was up this way. Wilfie always made her feel a fool. 'Go on,' said Nina as they walked. 'Come with us.' She started to sing, not really caring about the answer. 'The tears of a clown', she sang, as they strolled down to the high street behind Wilfie's thick, intractable neck. She had a good voice. At the corner they parted. Nina jogged across the road after Wilfie; Loretta walked on absolutely aimless, walked for quite a long time until she found herself at a bus stop at the same time as a bus and got on it impulsively, showed her pass and sat down on the long seat near the door. They rode along leisurely, through unfamiliar streets.

After a few stops an old woman in a shabby cream-coloured mac got unsteadily on and sat down heavily next to Loretta, settling a big lumpy shopping bag across her knees and smiling apologetically. She started talking immediately, quietly, in a rather lost way. She was lucky to have caught it, she said. They don't wait for you, some of them. Her eyes were watery and pale, the skin under them drained, mottled. She held out a pink dry-cleaning ticket and asked Loretta to read out the price for her.

'One pound eighty.'

'Oh, good,' she said. 'That's not too bad, is it? It's for a short jacket. What would a coat be, do you think, a winter coat?'

Loretta had no idea, it was so long since she'd had anything dry-cleaned. 'Four pounds?' she guessed.

'Four pounds,' said the old woman sadly. 'Really? Things are dear!'

'Well, I don't know, really . . .' said Loretta.

Her eyes were bad, the old woman said, you see, she couldn't read the price. That's why she kept missing buses, she was afraid to get on in case it was the wrong one, and by the time you'd asked someone . . . She couldn't see much. There was nothing they could do about them, her eyes, they were hopeless. They'd told her she'd just have to put up with it. She'd had glasses but her eyes were really too bad for glasses, she said, they had to make the lenses too thick and she still couldn't see anything through them. Doctors? She never saw the doctor. She wouldn't give a doctor the time of day. 'Where are we?' She peered through the window. 'You can't see much today, it's so dark. You feel as if the sky's pressing down.'

Outside, the sun broke through high white clouds over little streets. Loretta had no idea where she was. She was

228

a stranger on a bus. This woman was talking to her. This old woman was familiar. She'd seen Mother Teresa on the TV, the old woman said. Mother Teresa was a marvellous woman. It was in New York, they were talking to all these tramps and giving them food and clothes. She was sorry for the tramps, some of them, some had had nice homes and jobs and everything but they'd been conned out of them. Everything was taken away from them . . .

Just come out for a bottle of Guinness. Stephen sleeping in his push-chair under the plastic, wet feet in slippers. Not at all the same old woman, but the same.

. . . but some of them, she said, were there because of drugs or drinking and she didn't feel sorry for them.

'*i* do,' Loretta said, 'I don't think they can help it.'

The old woman agreed at once because Loretta was just a stranger on a bus and it made no odds. 'Yes,' she said. 'It's a disease. It is. It's a disease and they can't help it. Poor things. It initiates terrible things. They can't touch one drop. Yes, and it's on again tonight, you can watch it. Look. They sent me a bill from the gas board, all in red, but it's paid five months now. I've got all the receipts. It's paid five months. They're telling me I owe them, but I'm just ignoring it because I don't owe them anything, they've made a mistake. I don't believe in letting debts pile up, I always pay straight away. Why should I have to get on the bus and go all the way down there to see them over their mistake? So I'm saying nothing. Why should I have to pay the fare? Maybe they'll cut me off. What do you think? They don't really care what they do to you even when it's their mistake. They've painted the pub, look, it looks nice, doesn't it? Oh, look at those lovely flowers!'

'Where are we?' Loretta asked.

'Coming up to the High Street.'

What High Street? she thought.

Then the old woman talked about Austria. Her voice

229

was so low and the bus so noisy that Loretta missed some of what she was saying and lost track of a story. The Austrians were the best people in the world. The best people in the world, the Austrians. During the war they took everyone in, they never closed a door on a refugee. That's Austrians for you. There's no one like an Austrian. The best people in the world. Not like this lot here. But they'll get the ones that are doing it and they'll be punished, very harshly. They'll get what's coming to them. No one can get away with that.

Loretta had no idea what she was talking about. The old woman started getting up cautiously on the wobbly bus, smiling bashfully at her unsteadiness as if it were a rather shameful defect. 'Goodbye, dear,' she said. The corners of her eyes were wet. The bus swayed as she reached for the silver bar and her body veered slightly. Loretta reached out and held her arm. The bus stopped. The old woman's cold claw covered Loretta's hand and squeezed once, very firmly, before she stepped down to the platform and was gone. Loretta turned as the bus moved off and saw her walking away along the crowded pavement, an anonymous old lady with crooked legs and a small body that leaned to one side.

On they went. Loretta wept a little, she didn't know why. No one was looking. The weeping reminded her of Jimmy. She remembered how awful he'd looked the day she'd met him in Littlejohn's, the day Dee shouted at him and he cried. She looked out of the window and sniffed, wiped her face discreetly, then took a little mirror out of her bag and checked to see if her make-up had run. Outside the sun shone down on trees in a big park. Suddenly she panicked. I'm going to die, she thought. I know it. I *am*. What am I going to do? I don't know where I am. I don't even know what's written on the front of the bus. She jumped up and stood on the platform, watching the street slip by. When the movement stopped she got off. There were shops, people. She was lost. This was mad. She stopped a woman and asked if there was a tube station anywhere nearby.

'Wimbledon Park's the nearest,' the woman said and pointed out the way. Wimbledon Park! Loretta thought. Fancy that. She searched anxiously for the station, suddenly wishing only that she could be at home and safe. She didn't know what she'd been looking for when she ran away, but it certainly wasn't Wimbledon. At the station, she stood for ages staring at the Underground map, trying to work out the best way home. There were so many . . . She was on the District Line. The District Line. The District Line was awful, she never had been able to work it out. She always got lost on the District Line.

She took a train to Earls Court, got off and wandered about for ages trying to find a train going east. Somehow she ended up changing trains three times. The Underground was crowded, very dear and familiar, like an old photograph of a good time. She watched people as if they were strange exotic animals, the way they walked, sat, guarded their eyes, tapped their feet to the barely audible tinny jinglings of Walkmans. Between trains she passed buskers here and there and dropped coins into their guitar cases. The Underground soothed her, rocking her home.

When she got out into the light again, all was madness and blaring horns. She ran home, closed the door softly and put on all the locks. Billy wasn't back, of course, he wouldn't be back for ages. She stood in the empty flat and listened to her heart beating, firm and loud and steady. She sat down. It was still there, fear in the throat. How silly. She'd just gone all the way to Wimbledon and back and it hadn't made any difference. It wouldn't have made any difference if she'd gone all the way to China. She looked at the clock and saw with disbelief that it was only ten past two. She'd been gone hours, she'd thought; hours even since she'd stood in the yard waiting for Nina and looking at the bright, round eye of the grey rabbit in Wilfie's brother's arms. Poor thing. Ten past two indeed. Time must be playing tricks with her.

In the quietness she heard the dim thunder of a tube train passing beneath the Buildings. Billy's old shoe lay in the middle of the floor. A pulse kicked in the heel of her hand and she watched it for a while in fascination, then stood and picked up the shoe and walked about the room holding it as if it were a baby. She stopped at the window and looked down. A flight of pigeons swooped through the yard. The silence was like something singing, but it was not out there, it was inside herself. She was like a bottle shaken, about to burst its bubbles. She put the shoe down neatly next to its mate, went into the bedroom and brought out all her mum's pills, took them out of the bottles and arranged them in different-coloured heaps on a low table at the end of the settee, near where she could rest her head, then just looked at them for a while. She felt nerves flicker in her stomach. It was like stepping out onto a stage, making a début. No, of course she wasn't really going to do it. She could never do it. It was impossible.

She went up onto the roof and stood by the railings. Looking down, she saw cars and cats and kids. Looking up, a lovely full cloudy blue sky. She saw St Paul's, Big Ben, skyscrapers, tower blocks, chimneys, advertisement hoardings, back streets, traffic, shops, the railway, and it was in her power to banish all London into the void. Somewhere inside her was a Black Hole sucking it all in, everything; till finally, when it had taken all the rest, it would take what was left. She'd be the last to go. Then she knew that she was really going to do it and felt her senses peak, elated with fear. And in the next second it was again impossible and she knew that she would turn and go, carefully wedging the rope in the door so it wouldn't bang if it got windy later, walk down to her flat, tidy up a bit and think about what to have for tea. Go on

232

living. Nothing could really happen because of this crumb of sense that was sure an end was impossible.

So she went back to her flat and filled two tall glasses with water and sat down on the settee and took the pills one by one, some of each. She hadn't thought it would take so long. Her dear, dependable fingers went on picking up pills, absolutely sure of themselves. She had to stop and wait sometimes because her stomach and throat objected. I'm doing it, I'm doing it, she thought, but I'm not really here, I'm just watching. She lost count. More? More? What now? I'll get some sleep. She lay down with her head on a cushion and closed her eyes. More?

More. More.

It came to an end, that place, those times.

Crazy, everyone said. Crazy the way things turn out. There must have been some strange star over the Buildings. Everything changed, changed beyond understanding.

Johnny never came back from Manchester; the last anyone heard he was staying at Raff's mum's. Billy was gone too. When Loretta died he went to his family for a while and left his flat in the care of Eric and Littlejohn. Willie stayed there sometimes, but these days he spent a lot of time at Dave Raffo's in Hammersmith. Joe and Sharon were gone too. They lived near Clapham Junction now and Mandy lived in Liverpool with Sharon's parents. Sharon had spent some time in a hospital up north getting unaddicted to heroin and addicted to Physeptone. When she was better, she said, when she was really better, they'd bring Mandy home.

She'd tried to do it alone at first, running at it like a bull at a gate like she did everything else. She told Joe it was a penance for Raff and Loretta, for not being nicer to them both when they were alive. She'd told Raff he was a creep and now he was dead. She never used to go and see Loretta, sometimes she'd pretended not to see her in the street so she wouldn't have to talk to her. And now she was dead. So she sent Mandy up to her parents for a long stay, determined that this was it. She wouldn't listen to Joe who wanted her to go to a hospital, even when he'd rambled on for a couple of hours in graphic description of what hell it would be. His words made her see herself in a picture in her mind, like in a film, vividly suffering: The Junkie Withdraws. Scene One. Action. She'd seen it so many times.

'What are you trying to do?' she asked. 'Put me off? You don't really want me to come off, do you? It makes you feel superior, that's why.'

'It's not fair,' he said. 'It involves me. What am I supposed to do? It means I get to suffer as well as you.'

'You bastard,' she said. 'You selfish, mean bastard.' He followed her about everywhere, talking all the time, so that they kept breaking out into snappish arguments. 'Go away,' she said over and over again. 'Just go away if you don't like it.'

'I can't!' he cried. 'How can I leave you on your own? This is blackmail!'

Then she started getting sick and he hung around awkwardly and kept making cups of tea with a slightly martyred air. The first day wasn't too bad, just like any awful Sunday. But then the throwing up started, the diarrhoea, the sweating and shivering; she took over the toilet and wouldn't come out. He heard her crying inside and threatened to break the door down, but she yelled through the door for him to leave her alone, leave her alone, for Christ's sake! He had to go round to Eric and Littlejohn's when he needed a shit. Finally she came out and went to bed and twisted about pathetically like a child with fleas. He brought her a bowl. She kept having to get up and run to the toilet and in between times she lay exhausted but unable to rest, all her nerves rubbing up against each other like displaced bones. She cried all the time, chewed her fingers and became sentimental over Mandy, her poor little girl, never been without her before, oh, my poor baby, my poor baby, looked at Joe with suspicion and fear, how he must hate her, how disgusted he must be to see her like this.

On the evening of the second day she heard him

235

mutter as he headed for the door. 'I've had enough,' it sounded like. She hung out of bed, dribbling into a bowl, eyes and nose running.

'Where are you going?' she said thickly, as sharply as she could.

'Coffee,' he said, taking money from a jacket hanging on the back of the door, 'I'm dying for some coffee. I'm going to get some.' She was sure he looked shifty. She thought his footsteps fading down the stairs had a kind of final quality. He isn't coming back, she told herself, he isn't coming back. This was what happened. This was what it had all been coming to. She got herself upright and put her feet on the floor. The cat slept peacefully with its one remaining kitten in the basket. It was five o'clock and the place was full of footsteps and voices. She rubbed her face and cried into her fist listlessly. What a bastard. What a terrible thing to do, leave her alone in this place. Like this. You wouldn't leave your worst enemy like this. Alone. She burned with fever, froze. The sheets were sweaty and hot. She hated him. She couldn't go anywhere so she lay back down and piled the blankets on top of herself and started mewling weakly, thinking of Mandy as if she were never going to see her again. Alone. That's what it would always come back to.

Half an hour late Joe came back and sat down gingerly on the edge of the bed.

'I can't get warm,' she said.

'What can I do?' he asked. 'What can I get you?'

She gave up the next day. Joe went and scored for her and it was over in a moment.

'You see, Sharon,' he said, when she was up again and sitting by the fire drinking some milky invalid pap, 'this is what happens . . . ' and he started lecturing her about what had just been happening to her body, getting a pencil and drawing diagrams on the backs of envelopes.

'God, you're boring at times,' she said. She didn't

think he knew what he was talking about and she didn't care anyway. 'Oh, not now, Joe,' she said dismissively. But he went on. She got up and lay down on the settee but he followed her and sat down, squashing her feet. He talked about medicine and health, quoting statistics, looking into her face and trying to draw her into a conversation. 'Oh, shut up, Joe,' she said. But he went on. 'Joe,' she said, 'shut up for a bit, please. I've just come through a very nasty experience. I'd like to rest.'

Joe stood up and bumbled about the room, fussing with things here and there, poking about in drawers and on shelves. She thought his face, when she caught sight of it, was ready to be irritated and she immediately wanted to irritate it. 'Can't you sit down and read a book or something?' she said in a nasty tone. 'You're like an old hen.'

'My God,' he said quietly, 'I can't even walk about in my own flat.'

'You miserable, moaning bastard,' she said, tossing over onto her side. 'That's why I'm like this – because of moaning bastards like you.'

'Blame someone else,' Joe said, tight-faced, sitting down and opening a book ostentatiously, 'that's right, blame someone else.'

There was silence for an hour. At nine o'clock she suddenly sat up and said she'd have to go to Liverpool and get Mandy. She looked round distractedly, as if wondering how to begin.

'At this time of night?' Joe said. 'What are you talking about?'

'Not now. Tomorrow.'

'Just like that?' He slung his book aside. 'You mean you're giving up? Just like that? Think about it. You bring her back now and you'll never do it. Come on, we'll try again . . .'

She felt all watery, edgy. 'I don't feel like talking,' she said abruptly and lay down again, 'I'm going to sleep

237

now for a bit.' But he went on talking again, about hospitals and doing it right, until she yelled at him to shut up.

'What!' he said. 'You started it. You suddenly sit up and start talking about bringing Mandy home and then you don't want to talk any more. Christ, talk about do as I do!' He stood up and walked about, a gnat humming away at the edge of consciousness, changing from a tone of annoyance to one of infuriating good sense. He said she couldn't keep sending the poor kid away every time she took a whim, he was fond of the kid and he wouldn't have it, she had to do it *once*, *now*, and get it over with. He was so full of good reasons that she hated him.

'I don't want to leave her up there too long,' she said, 'I know what my mum and dad'll do to her. You don't know what they're like. She'll come back all changed. She'll come back like some little replica of my mum and dad. You know. She won't be mine any more.'

'Hah!' he said, suddenly bitter. 'What do you want her to be, then? A little replica of you? Is that so marvellous, then? Doesn't look very marvellous to me from here.'

'Oh, fuck off,' she said.

He didn't speak for ten minutes or so. Then he said in the same bitter tone, 'You'll go and get her and bring her back here and everything'll drift back to just how it was.'

'Yes,' she said.

'You will. I know you will. Oh, yeah, I can see it all! I don't need a crystal ball. Nothing's going to change. Nothing's ever going to change. As long as I'm with you, nothing's going to change.'

'Tomorrow,' she said. 'Tomorrow, Joe.'

He laughed. 'Never,' he said. 'Never. You've blown it.'

She didn't speak.

He came and knelt beside the settee and talked into her face. He went on and on in a frantic voice about what to do, what they had to do. They couldn't just keep piddling along like this. You've got to get better. What's going to happen to us? He went on until she thought she was going mad.

'Tomorrow, tell me,' she said. 'I'm resting.'

'I wish *I* could rest,' Joe said sulkily. 'You don't think about what *I* put up with. I deserve a medal for— '

Sharon leaped from the settee, grabbed the milk bottle from the table and hit him on the head with it. Bonk! went the bottle and milk splurged down her arm and drenched her. The cats ran and hid under the settee. Joe shot from the chair and wrenched the bottle from her hand and she started to scream. She screamed that she'd kill him, she'd smash his stupid face in, she'd rip his stupid tongue right out of his stupid throat if he didn't shut his fucking mouth.

'Keep your voice down!' he rapped, pushing her away hard and waving his arms at her as if she was a bad smell. 'You don't speak to me like that!'

She ran into the bedroom, swept books from the shelves, ripped pages out, pulled spines off, kicked them against the wall. Joe stood in the doorway with tears in his eyes. She pulled a drawer out and scattered the clothes on the floor and started ripping one of his shirts. He ran, grabbed her, pinned her arms behind her and pushed her out of the room. He was much stronger than she was. He pushed her through the living room and out into the hall, then out of the front door. She ran across the landing, stumbling, as if she thought he was coming after her to throw her down the stairs. 'What I'm going to do,' he said, face set hard, 'first thing in the morning I'll go down and tell the welfare. I'll tell them what you're like. They won't *let* you bring her back then.' He grabbed a jacket from a hook and threw it at her. 'They'll take her off you!' he said. 'And it'll serve you fucking right!' then slammed the door and turned off the light in the hall.

'My shoes!' she screamed, flinging herself at the door and beating on it, kicking it with bare feet. 'My shoes!

239

My shoes, Joe, you bastard!' The door opened but he thrust her back with one great push, hurled out a pair of shoes and slammed the door again. She grabbed the shoes, sandals, the fool, on a night like this, the first things that came to hand. She put them on, hopping, screaming, threw herself at the door, cursing Joe and threatening terrible revenge, screamed over and over again and cried and wailed on the landing. Joe went to bed and lay in the dark staring at the ceiling and listening. He started to cry. She'd be all right. She'd go round to Littlejohn's or somewhere and in the morning she'd have calmed down.

Sharon ran down the stairs and stood in the courtyard. The crystal cold made her mind hard, she felt it set like toffee. She had a packet of white powder in one pocket and she found two pounds and some change in another, so she ran down to the main road and got on a bus, and then another one that went down Edgware Road. The jacket was too thin for a night in March, the sandals too skimpy, the spilt milk drying cold on her. It'll stink, she thought. Her legs were bare. When she looked down at them on the bus she was ashamed at how pale and hairy and thin they looked. She got off the second bus and stood under a street lamp at the side of the road, stuck her thumb out and gave up trying to make any sense of the night. The car lights were dazzling. She was going to Liverpool to get Mandy, that much she knew. Beyond, nothing existed.

She wanted to get onto the M1, but somehow missed it and ended up on an adventure of long, wide, thundering roads, bridges, urgent lights, strange people, soporific engines, bleak roundabouts, silent lanes where the distances between lights were like pits waiting for you to fall in. Any fool could see she was trouble, standing

240

there in the night with no luggage and those stupid sandals on her feet. Mostly she got lifts from single men in cars. She played hyperactive as soon as she got in, made a point of being mad and menacing, opened her mouth and streamed heedless, ugly nonsense, jiggled about, scratched, laughed, cried, sang, aggressively questioned the bemused drivers, who all wanted to know what she was running away from. 'Black magic,' she said. 'They put a curse on me. The Devil's following.' And she'd look back, as if to see him running after the car with great cloven-footed strides. Most of them couldn't wait to get rid of her.

Some time in the small hours she ended up on a long moonlit country road with white lines down the middle and fields on either side. A heavy frost glittered. There was no traffic. She walked for miles, sometimes crying because of the cold in her feet, sometimes singing loudly. There was a film she'd seen. These people were running away, battling against all odds, looking for a place called Sanctuary. That's what she was doing. She came to a ghostly roundabout where five roads met and orange lights gleamed. A shabby transit van was parked on a grass verge, the back doors open, and two guys a little older than herself stood nearby. One, small and fair, looked up at the stars through a set of heavy binoculars. 'Oh, wow!' he said. 'Oh, wow!' The other looked towards her as she approached.

'Are you going anywhere near the M6?' she asked. Tinny music came from a cassette player in the van. They stared at her. She saw pale faces in the gloom of the van, a heap of sleeping bags and clothes, a guitar. Some hot drink steamed in the lid of a flask.

'Where did you spring from?' the small fair one asked.

'London,' she said. 'Are you going anywhere near the M6?'

Somehow it seemed they never answered. 'Look at her feet,' she heard someone say.

'Where you going, chicken?' the fair one asked.

'Liverpool.'

'Liverpool! What you doing out here, chicken?'

She went into her mad act. She started to laugh and bop about to the music from the cassette player. The small fair one laughed and danced too, like a big clumsy schoolboy, and the others came out of the van. There were four of them and they were all drunk. She thought they might be a band or something, but there was only one guitar in the van. She chanted total gibberish at them, amazed at how it flowed like a great talent, possessed, speaking in tongues. 'Screwy,' someone said, 'screwy,' drilling into his brain with his finger. She said the Devil was chasing her.

'Come on now, chicken,' said the fair one, who was drunker than all the rest, 'I can't believe that.' He put his arms round her, dancing energetically, dragging her about till her sandals started coming off and tripping her up. A skinny boy with off-key eyes ran up and broke them apart as if they were fighting. Sharon started to cry. They put her in the van and laid her down on a sleeping bag and gave her coffee to drink, and the skinny boy with funny eyes took her sandals off and rubbed her feet. They talked and talked over her head: nothing made sense. She heard them laughing and arguing, getting in and out of the van, fooling about on the grass verge. Someone messed with the engine. She fell asleep.

Some stranger woke her up, lying on top of her with the whole weight of his body grinding into her belly. Stale beery breath and bony hips. It was dark and she couldn't see anything, but she smashed upwards and felt her fist connect with something soft and moist that went squish, probably a mouth. The weight groaned and rolled away and she saw the sky in the open door of the van, still dark, scrambled towards it, fell out onto the grass and looked back. The small fair one floundered like a beetle on its back. He hadn't even got his pants undone.

242

She ran, feeling drunk and sudden in the cold air. Half-way across the roundabout she realised she'd left her sandals behind, but it was too late to worry about that now, she had to keep running – not that she thought there was really much danger, just that it was what she had to do at this moment. She heard a shout. At the far side of the roundabout, she looked back. Figures hung about the van. The thin one with funny eyes broke away and speeded towards her, and she flew down a long dark road with trees on one side and a field on the other, her bare feet going slap, slap, burning with pain. 'Hey, no!' he yelled, coming after, but she couldn't stop and she wouldn't, even though she thought perhaps she should, she was running in a dream, faster than she'd ever run before, blood pounding. As she ran, she saw herself: the tragic waif, the strange, wild girl alone in the night, enigma, she would come to a river and stand on the bank looking down into the murky depths and her life would flash before her eyes, and at that moment the skinny one with funny eyes, the nice one who'd rubbed her feet, would come and save her life and talk kindly to her. But it didn't happen.

She lost him on a long curve of the road and rolled down into a ditch, scrambled under a fence and burrowed into the sudden thick dark under the trees like a mole turning away from the light. For a long time she lay in the darkness, listening to her heart and lungs labour back to normality, wondering why she wasn't at home in bed. She lay till the sky began to lighten through the high branches, then stood up and moved cautiously through the trees until she came out onto the road. It didn't look the way she remembered it. She started to walk back in the direction of the roundabout to look at the signs and see if any of them meant anything to her.

The world was blue and still, full of birds, and her feet were pink and bright and swollen and left traces of blood. It was so much further than she remembered that she

243

began to think she must have gone wrong, that this was some other road, some road that had never had a beginning and never had an end. She would die on this road.

The sun came up cold and white and a frost rimed hedges and fences with a sugary skim, twinkling under her feet. Every step was a step on ice. At last the roundabout appeared, bigger in the morning light. The van had gone but there was something dark hanging over one of the road signs near where it had stood. She walked straight across the middle of the roundabout, past all the signs, the names that meant nothing, and found it was an old brown sweater with great fraying holes in the elbows and some kind of hard resiny stains down the front. Her sandals stood neatly in the grass, side by side, remnants of a strange dream, proof that last night was all true, that she would not awaken in her bed in Kinnaird Buildings, she was here, lost, somewhere in the belly of England.

She put the sweater on under her jacket. It smelled worn and cosy. She couldn't get the sandals onto her big pink feet, so she left them there for someone to wonder about later, and walked on down the nearest road. It was so empty, so pale, that she walked straight along the white lines down the middle, placing each foot down carefully in front of the other and watching it protectively to make sure it got there OK. They looked so funny and alien to her, padding on naked, like pigs' feet. The fields looked very pretty, all in white. When she heard a car coming up behind she took no notice. It pulled in just ahead of her, neat and red and shiny. A window rolled down just as she came alongside, and she saw a man and woman, middle-aged and concerned. 'Are you all right?' the man called. 'Where are you trying to get to?'

She looked at them as if they'd just popped out of a cloud. 'I'm following the dotted line to Sanctuary,' she said.

The man got out of the car. 'Come on, love,' he said gently, 'that's where we're going. We'll take you there.'

Judy heard she'd got a job teaching up north. She made arrangements, found a place to stay with old friends, looked towards the change, made herself ready. After that the place became unreal, a show that continued to flicker around her, boards and rubble and corrugated iron and writing on walls, locked doors, courtyards, smells, stairwells, people who flickered in and out of the scenes like actors.

Billy came back. She would always remember how crowded and cosy his old flat was the night in September he arrived home, the sound of his key turning in its old lock startling everyone, almost scaring them, as if a ghost were turning it. He opened the door and stood there smiling at them, bright-eyed and slightly drunk. Everyone loved Billy. They made a fuss of him, cleared a space, hugged him, ruffled his hair, made him a cup of coffee. He said he was staying for a bit, anyway, he didn't really know. He said it was OK, they didn't have to move out. And they laughed and told stories and talked until the early hours. Survivors on a raft.

On Friday afternoon Billy was at Eddy and Dee's, and after that was always there, waiting among the changing faces.

And the play went on, peaceful enough, until a time came when she was walking about in an echoing flat, packing stuff into her old suitcase, homesick already for these old bricks. She'd wanted so badly to be away from it all, time and distance heals all things, move, change, seek your fortune. It was never here. And still she felt weird love for this place. She was leaving early tomorrow. Most of her things had gone on ahead and all that was left in her room was a box and a mattress and her case. Tonight she'd give the key to Billy. Someone might get six months out of it. She'd said all her goodbyes last night drinking in the George, she hated goodbyes, tomorrow she'd just slip away. She imagined it – nerves, strange platforms, running on automatic. These things she packed would see the light in another life. The last thing she stuck in her case was a souvenir, a little black pocket diary with awful, pathetic little entries: 'Council painted all our doors red.' 'Weather lovely. Cut Billy's hair. Water turned off.' 'Man beaten up outside. Auntie Bren's birthday. Went to Brixton.'

She remembered: the time she was babysitting at Eddy and Dee's, full of apprehension because Dee had just spent about an hour telling her how terrible the boys were, idiot delinquent wastrels, uncontrollable, hopeless, particularly Colin. Hulking great things in shin pads they were, with fags hanging out of their mouths. But they were OK. She liked them better than she liked Dee. Willie had come round with a carrier bag full of stuff that Billy was throwing out, did she want any? Some old make-up, Crazy Colour, cheap jewellery. She took the diary.

'I remember Loretta when I was little,' Colin said. 'She used to tell us stories. Remember that, Tom?'

'Yeah. One story. It went on and on.'

'Really silly stories, but they were really good. There was all these people in a taxi, and this taxi went all over the place, they were up in space . . . '

'Yeah, like a space taxi . . . '

'. . . and in the jungle, and sometimes they went backwards in time . . . '

'. . . really good, it was.'

'I liked Loretta,' Colin said.

She closed the case and sat back. Of Raff, there was nothing. Of Loretta, this. How casually the world would

246

wash over their traces. You'd find them on the files somewhere, of course, police, courts, that kind of thing. They'd meant more to her than all the famous faces in the world, but they'd left no mark. She didn't understand it yet. She didn't know why she was strong, why she survived this place and these people – unless it was just to stay alive and sane long enough to make some kind of sense of why Loretta was born to cry in the dock, Raff to grieve in his cell, her own self to feel like this. She hadn't known they'd come as close as this. Pointless to dream that you were through with the fray, when there it was – ancient, unstoppable ache, part of her now, growing mellow sometimes like good wine.

She went down to the café in the market. Willie walked by, saw her through the door and came in. They sat and talked like two old comrades. Willie looked smart and brushed. He was going away soon as a roadie with Dave Raffo's band. 'I've always wanted to get into all that, really,' he said, 'you know, music and everything. One way or the other. How about you? This isn't really what you want to do, is it? Teaching and all that?'

She laughed. 'It's OK,' she said, 'I can get into it. For a while. Who wants to look too far ahead?'

They sat quietly for a while, listening to the familiar, soothing sounds of the market and the tea urn and the clinking and clanking from the kitchen. It was good to be alive. 'We had good times, didn't we?' Willie said. 'One way or the other.'

'We did.' She smiled.

He had to go. He wanted to reach Hammersmith before the rush hour started. 'I've got your address,' he said. 'If I'm up that way with the band I'll give you a call.'

'Do,' she said.

'Sure thing.' He pushed his chair back and they wished each other luck, joining hands for a moment.

'Take care of yourself, Willie,' she said.

'And you.'

When he'd gone she studied the scene to keep it in her memory. The fat Italian man was reading the *Sun* behind the counter and a late fly grazed lazily on a greasy plate. She smelt coffee. And soft, underdone toast. And if one day Dave's band came playing up her way, she'd go to see them and she'd say to whoever she was with: 'See the one on the sax? I used to know his brother.'

She went home and finished packing, went into Billy's to give him the key and stayed watching TV for a while. Then she kissed him goodbye and tried for an early night but it was impossible to sleep, lying on a mattress in a strange denuded room, listening to the last gifts of Kinnaird Buildings. It gave her far voices droning on for ages, the muffled beat of music, the idiot baby voice of a woman endlessly calling a dog.

At eight she got up, took the tube to Euston and caught a train up north.

You can order other Virago titles through our website: *www.virago.co.uk* or by using the order form below

☐	Little Sister	Carol Birch	£8.99
☐	Come Back, Paddy Riley	Carol Birch	£8.99
☐	Turn Again Home	Carol Birch	£7.99
☐	The Naming of Eliza Quinn	Carol Birch	£6.99
☐	Scapegallows	Carol Birch	£7.99

The prices shown above are correct at time of going to press. However, the publishers reserve the right to increase prices on covers from those previously advertised, without further notice.

──────────────── 🍎 ────────────────

Please allow for postage and packing: **Free UK delivery.**
Europe: add 25% of retail price; Rest of World: 45% of retail price.

To order any of the above or any other Virago titles, please call our credit card orderline or fill in this coupon and send/fax it to:

Virago, PO Box 121, Kettering, Northants NN14 4ZQ
Fax: 01832 733076   Tel: 01832 737526
Email: aspenhouse@FSBDial.co.uk

☐ I enclose a UK bank cheque made payable to Virago for £
☐ Please charge £   to my Visa/Delta/Maestro

Expiry Date ☐☐☐☐   Maestro Issue No. ☐☐

NAME (BLOCK LETTERS please) . . . .

ADDRESS . . . .

. . . .

. . . .

Postcode . . . . Telephone . . . .

Signature . . . .

Please allow 28 days for delivery within the UK. Offer subject to price and availability.